# ANY OLD DIAMONDS

Any Old Diamonds

Published by KJC Books
Copyright © 2019 by KJ Charles

Edited by Veronica Vega
Cover art by Vic Grey
Cover design by Lexiconic Design
Print layout by eB Format

ISBN: 978-1-912688-08-1

This is a work of fiction. Names, characters, places, and incidents are either the product of the author's imagination or are used fictitiously. Any resemblance to actual persons living or dead, business establishments, events, or locales is entirely coincidental.

All rights reserved. Aside from brief quotations for media coverage and reviews, no part of this book may be reproduced or distributed in any form without the author's permission.

Green Grow The Rushes-O, British folk song

# Chapter One

*London, 1895*

How ought one dress to hire a thief?

Alec woke up with the question in his mind and couldn't let it go. He couldn't answer it either, no matter that his options were exceedingly limited. A lounge suit would presumably be best, for informality, but should he wear a colourful waistcoat, to indicate his divergence from sober respectability, or a plain one to avoid attracting attention?

He mused on that throughout breakfast and decided on his muted maroon silk waistcoat, but was immediately struck with uncertainty. Was a lounge suit right after all, considering they were meeting in, of all places, a box at the music hall? Ought he wear evening dress? The Grand Cirque was of the better class of music hall, and he would normally wear evening dress to take a private box, but what if the men he was to meet were clad as he imagined thieves to be, in rough fustian, perhaps with neckcloths pulled up over their mouths? No, that was ridiculous, and he'd been assured the criminals would look like gentlemen, but in *that* case...

Round and round it went in his head the whole day, a maddening litany. Alec knew perfectly well that he was fretting in order not to consider any of the larger questions, such as *What the devil are you doing?*

He didn't, couldn't think about that. He'd been driven to this extremity by the slow-building fury of years and the grief and anguish of the last six months. He wasn't going to back out now.

He spent the day completing a picture of Hyde Park in bloom for the *Illustrated London News*, because when he drew he didn't think so much. When evening finally came, he put on the grey lounge suit, tried all four of his waistcoats, discovered the maroon one had a spot on it, changed into evening dress, took it off again, and realised that after all this, he was going to be late.

"Alec, you dunderhead," he said aloud to the man in the speckled mirror. He hurried on the lounge suit, no time to play the fool now, hesitated for a painful second between a darker grey waistcoat and the bright green and gold one he hadn't worn for six long months of mourning, glanced at the cheap clock on the mantel, and grabbed the green. It suited him, at least. He only just remembered to snatch up the flimsy ticket on the way out.

It was a warm June, too warm to run, but he couldn't afford hansom cab fare so he hurried instead, while telling himself he needn't be on time to the minute. Punctuality was the politeness of princes, but did that apply when one was meeting criminals?

Holborn was its usual chaos. He picked his way through the crowds, past flower-stalls and shouting newspaper-boys proclaiming the last edition, and approached the Grand Cirque feeling unpleasantly sweaty for more reason than the thick heat. Christ, was he going to do this? Really? Was he going to keep an assignation and solicit a crime?

And if he turned around and walked away, what the devil would he do next?

That was the great unanswerable question, the one he'd stuck on during every sleepless night. If he didn't act, what *would* he do, today or tomorrow or for the rest of his life? If he missed this chance, would there be another, and would he have the nerve to take it, having refused the fence once already? He had a feeling he knew the answer to that one.

*It's now or never.*

He squared his shoulders, fished the ticket out of his pocket, and walked up to the doorman, feeling appallingly self-conscious and rather as if a policeman's heavy hand might descend on his shoulder at any moment. He hated that feeling, one with which he was all too familiar, albeit not for the current reasons. It would be so much nicer if he were risking arrest on the usual grounds, if the men he was going to meet were...well, quite different from what he expected them to be.

Music-hall misbehaviour à trois was a charming fantasy that distracted him up the several steep flights of stairs and shivered into nothing as he made his way to the indicated box.

He knocked. "Come in," a voice called, so he did.

The performance was already in full swing below, the noise of five men singing in close harmony and the groans of an unimpressed crowd blasting up. The smoky gaslight—no electrification here— cast a yellowish glow over the dark red walls and gilt decorations and left the box mostly in shadow. The box, and the two men waiting in it.

"Sit down," one of them said. "Mr. Pyne?"

Alec nodded. "Yes. That's me."

"Remind me whence you had our names."

He sounded very educated, with a university man's drawl. Alec blinked. "Er, I don't have your names. A chap named Holcomb told me you were the people I needed."

"We may be," the man said. "The question is whether we need you."

Alec's eyes were adjusting now and he was able to take a look at the pair. They both seemed a few years older than himself, thirty to thirty-five, perhaps. Well but casually dressed, Alec noted, and felt relieved he hadn't opted for his black tailcoat. The one who'd done the talking had a curling moustache, thick chestnut hair with a notable wave, and eyes that might prove to be blue in daylight. The other man had dark brown hair, darker eyes, and a substantial moustache and beard. Alec restrained the impulse to put his hand to his own naked face. More fellows were shaving now, particularly the fashionable sorts, but as far as many people were concerned, failure to grow a respectable moustache remained an indictment of one's virility.

The two men opposite him looked virile enough. The moustachioed speaker was strikingly big: broad, sturdy, and giving the impression he would tower over Alec when they stood. His bearded companion was of more usual proportions, lean and long-limbed in the way of hunting men. Both of them looked capable, confident, and not at all like the rapscallions of Alec's imagination. They looked more like soldiers. Or police officers.

"Uh," he said. "I don't know what Mr. Holcomb told you."

"Don't you?" Moustache said. "Pal of yours, is he?"

"An acquaintance. Not really even that. A friend of a friend said he might be the man to put me in touch with, uh, someone like you."

"I do hope Holcomb is sure of his friends." That was Beard, speaking at last. His voice was deeper than Alec had expected, not as aggressively upper-class as his partner's. "He told us you had a worthwhile proposition for the Lilywhite Boys. Why don't you tell us what that might be?"

"Uh," Alec said again, seized with urgent panic now he was on the verge of commitment. "Um. I don't wish to be rude but how do I know...?" He let that tail off in the hope that someone would interrupt him. They didn't.

"How do you know what?" enquired Moustache after a painful silence. He lifted a hand and counted on the fingers. "That we're the Lilywhite Boys and not, say, masquerading police officers, or friends of your pal playing a joke? That we'll keep your request private and not demand a large sum to forget about it? That we can do what you want, that you can trust us to make a deal, that you won't end up in chokey?"

"Well, yes," Alec said. "All of that."

"You don't."

"Oh."

"We can't really offer guarantees," Beard said. "Let alone contracts."

"You don't know who we are, and we don't know who you are," Moustache added. "For all we know, Mr. Alec Pyne, you might be a police officer yourself."

"I'm not."

"I dare say, but I'm not taking your word for it."

"Well, what do we do then?" Alec said, baffled.

Moustache smiled suddenly. He had a charming smile: the kind, Alec rather thought, that he'd often been told was charming and had learned to use accordingly. "We'll just have to rub along. Did Holcomb tell you an important fact about us?"

"He said if I played straight with you, you'd play straight with me," Alec said. "And then he added, 'They've got their own idea of straight, mind you.'"

Beard gave a crack of laughter. Moustache grinned. "Yes, that's about right. If you don't play straight with us, we'll resent it, and you'll regret it. Got that, Mr. Pyne?"

"Noted."

"Good. My name is Templeton Lane, and my colleague is Jerry Crozier." Beard—Crozier—lifted two fingers to his brow. "Now, why don't you tell us what it is you have for us, and we'll tell you if we're interested. And if we're not, or if our interest doesn't suit you, we'll all forget about this conversation and enjoy the show."

Alec took a deep breath. He thought of George, of Cara and Annabel, of Mother, and a small near-empty church, and the smell of squashed holly berries.

He said, "I want you to rob the Duke of Ilvar."

Crozier's eyebrows shot up. Lane's mouth curved. "Do you. How intriguing. Any particular reason?"

"He's rich."

"That's a good reason," Crozier said. "Is this a general suggestion for larceny, or have you anything more substantial to add?"

The close harmony singers stopped their warbling, to some applause. Alec hadn't really been aware of them but now the lower background noise made him feel self-conscious. He leaned in. Crozier's brows tilted, angling upward to the middle of his forehead as if silently repeating the question. Alec had never had that sort of eyebrow control, and envied those who did. Mind you, apparently it gave one wrinkles and one wouldn't want those; it was bad enough he'd turned twenty-eight and had already found suspiciously grey hairs among the blond at his temples.

Oh God, he was terrified.

"You look like a conspirator," Crozier said. "And one that's about to be sick, as well. Sit back, you're making me twitch."

Alec recoiled. Lane sighed. "Don't mind him. He's never got over the army." He flickered a glance over the side of the box, to the stage. "The dancing girls are about to come on. I assure you, nobody will be looking up here, or able to eavesdrop. You mentioned the Duke of Ilvar."

"A name to conjure with," Crozier said drily.

There was a roar of applause from below as the dancing troupe pranced on to the stage. Alec glanced over, made himself look back. "He's very rich. I suppose you know that."

"Immensely," Crozier said. "And much of his wealth is hung around the neck of his Duchess, who has one of the greatest collections of jewels outside royal hands as testament to his affection."

"Such affection," Lane added soulfully. "His devotion is legendary, and there has never been a breath of scandal against her name. Aside from notoriously cuckolding her first husband with the Duke, of course, but they married afterwards, so who am I to quibble."

Alec looked between them uncertainly. "Yes. Well. Ilvar is spending a king's ransom on a diamond parure—a matching set of jewellery—"

"We know what a parure is." Crozier spoke quite gently, without emphasis, but the words still jarred Alec, because these men, these well-spoken well-groomed men-about-town, were professional jewel thieves. It was hard to keep that in mind.

"Yes. Of course. Uh..."

"The diamond parure?"

"Earrings, a magnificent necklace, a bracelet. Matched stones of the finest quality. He commissioned it over a year ago to be a gift for her on the twentieth anniversary of their wedding. It cost eleven thousand pounds."

Lane whistled. Crozier's mobile brows twitched up.

"And that's what you want?"

"I'd think it would be what you want too," Alec said. "No?"

"Oh, unquestionably," Crozier said. "The difficulty would be getting it. Her collection is kept at the extremely remote Castle Speight which is heavily staffed at all times and equipped with the most up-to-date model of safe—a Chatwood, cursed hard to drill, with a Bramah lock, famously unpickable. Moreover, lacking the endearing carelessness of those born to the upper classes, the Duchess takes a great deal of care when travelling that her jewel case is constantly guarded. And the castle is never thrown open to visitors. It makes a fellow's job quite impossible."

Alec's mouth was hanging open. "How do you know all that?"

"Because we've considered the Ilvars and given them up as a bad job," Lane said. "They are perhaps the worst target in the British aristocracy. Or are we wrong?"

"I don't know about that. I—" Alec had planned this, rehearsed it, but the words stuck in his throat. "I, uh. I could get you into the house. Into Castle Speight."

There was a pause. The music blared, the dancers' feet thundered on the stage, the audience whooped, yet Alec's breath seemed far too audible in his own ears.

"Could you," Crozier said at last. "In what capacity?"

"There'll be a grand event there in August, for their wedding anniversary. A dinner. It'll be the first one they've held there in years, they don't usually entertain in that way. The Duchess will have all her most magnificent jewels and the parure will be presented. There'll be all sorts of guards, security, but—but you know how to, to—"

"Steal things?" Crozier said. "Yes, we do."

"Well, I'll be attending," Alec said. "And if you can come with me—"

"Noted. First question, Mr. Pyne: what terms do you have in mind for this?"

"Terms?"

"Do you simply want to see the Ilvars robbed on principle? Are you hoping to settle a grudge? Or are you looking for a cut of the loot?"

Alec felt his cheeks flush. "The latter. I, er, don't know what you usually..." He loathed negotiation at the best of times. "Fifty fifty?" It came out as a question despite his best intentions.

Crozier's brows angled again, one up, one down. Alec was becoming fascinated with that. "Ambitious of you, if we're doing the work and taking the risk."

"You couldn't get in there without me, though. And there's risk for me too."

"Which brings me to the next question," Lane said. "How will you be in a position to get us in?"

"I'll be able to." Alec didn't want to go into this. It was too hot in here, too smoky. He could feel the sweat beading on the back of his neck. "If I get you in as a guest, can you—"

"How long for?" Crozier interrupted.

Alec blinked. "How long do you need?"

"How long is a piece of string? We need time to assess the lie of the land. I don't intend to hold the room up at gunpoint, in a mask, like one of those dreadful Americans. We prefer to plan a little better than that."

"Specifically, we prefer to be a long way away from the scene of the crime when the police are called," Crozier added. "Ideally having ensured a solid alibi for our accomplices."

"Oh."

Lane winked at him. "We're called the Lilywhite Boys for a reason, old chap. Few arrests, no convictions."

"Well, that's...good," Alec managed.

"It is good," Crozier agreed, "and it's achievable given a bit of planning time. Again: do your powers stretch to that?"

Alec took a deep breath. "I could get you there a few days before the dinner. There will be a house party before the grand ball; I dare say I could add you to that. You, uh, you would need to present yourselves as gentlemen."

"Entirely achievable," Lane assured him. "And that raises the final and most crucial question: how is it that you, Mr. Pyne, are going to be present at the notoriously inhospitable Castle Speight on this touching family occasion?"

Alec's mouth was completely dry now. The performance had changed again while they were talking; he hadn't noticed it, except to become vaguely aware of a comedian's shrill Scottish-accented voice buzzing in his ear, waves of laughter.

He licked his lips. "I'm acquainted with him. The Duke of Ilvar. I can get you in. That's all you need to know for now."

Crozier and Lane exchanged glances, a flicker of a look. Crozier sat back. Lane steepled his hands, flexing them slowly. "Lord Alexander Greville de Keppel Pyne-ffoulkes, with a small f. Or even two small fs, when you think about it. Third child of the Duke by his first wife, deceased. By trade an illustrator for the picture papers as Alec Pyne. I can't blame you for shortening that mouthful."

"What—"

"We don't go into situations blind, Mr. Pyne, or should that be Lord Alexander. We knew who you were within twelve hours of you seeking this meeting. It is our habit to look ahead."

"Give me six hours to chop down a tree and I will spend the first four sharpening the axe," Crozier said in a tone of quotation. "We keep our axes sharp, Lord Alexander."

"Alec. Or Pyne. I don't go by the title."

"Why not?"

"I don't think that's any business of yours."

Lane leaned forward and tapped him on the knee. "Alec, old pal? If you want us to come to your father's house as your friend and rob him in his own home—to pose as your guest and clean out your stepmother's drawers—it *is* our business. No lies, no surprises. You work with us in full or you don't work with us at all."

"That is an option," Crozier added calmly. "We'd far rather you change your mind now than later. No hard feelings and all that. But if you go ahead, no finer feelings either. We would be very upset if you committed our time and then decided you couldn't go ahead with stealing from your own father."

Blood surged into Alec's cheeks. "It isn't like that!"

"We don't care," Crozier said, with terrible simplicity. "You're in or you're out. And if you're in, there will be no middle ground, no secrets, no sudden surges of decency in the third act. Either you're going to help us steal from your father and split the proceeds, or we'll shake hands now and watch the show."

"Actually, we're going to watch the show anyway," Lane said, and pointed to the stage, where a woman was coming on to wild applause. "Miss Christiana."

"About time. We're actually here for her," Crozier informed Alec. "You have a think."

On which they both turned to the performance. Alec sat, stunned. He'd imagined a lot of ways in which this conversation, this conspiracy might go; he hadn't pictured admitting his treacherous intent and then having that dreadful confession put to one side in favour of a music-hall act.

And a female impersonator to boot, he realised, as he heard the light tenor. The singer was painted for the stage but not to excess, and wore a wig with cascading dark ringlets and a high-necked dress suitable for a governess. The respectable appearance was doubtless deliberate, because she was singing "I'd Just Like to Know," a minor sensation of innuendo that required the performer to deliver the filthiest possible implications with total innocence.

The Lilywhite Boys hadn't been joking about being here for Miss Christiana, either, because they were both watching intently. Lane started laughing almost at once, a deep and infectious sound. Crozier's response was more restrained but his smile widened at the more outrageous lines, into a sharp-angled expression that was frankly wicked.

Miss Christiana would perform perhaps three or four songs, and then the Lilywhite Boys would turn back and demand a decision.

Alec had come here to set up a robbery, but he hadn't quite let himself think of it in the bare terms the thieves had used, the ones the newspapers would use if or when this went wrong. *Planned to steal from his own father, abusing his position as a son and the hospitality of Castle Speight...*

But his father had stolen from him, from all his children. He had stolen their birthright and the lives of luxury a duke's offspring might expect, and far, far more than that. Alec had no position as a son except on his father's humiliating terms, which made him feel hot and sick to consider. Castle Speight's hospitality was a joke, and not one that would draw the roars of laughter now echoing around the hall.

If the only way to get to the Duke of Ilvar was through the Duchess, and the only way to get to her was through her hoarded jewels, he'd bloody do it, whatever it took. And if that made him a villain, so be it. He wasn't going to abide by *Honour thy father*; he needn't trouble himself with *Thou shall not steal* either.

He'd be a criminal. That was what you were when you conspired to commit a crime, even if you didn't lift a finger yourself. A criminal like Crozier and Lane, both of whom seemed to be quite happy watching Miss Christiana sing, and laughing at the punchlines. They weren't racked with guilt, and nor should Alec be, because this would be revenge—for loss, for a lifetime of contempt, for the life Cara should have had and the one Annabel ought to have and the strain in George's eyes. Revenge because he'd finally accepted that he couldn't wait for fate or natural justice or God's will to punish the Duke and Duchess. It was down to him.

Miss Christiana had left the stage while he was lost in thought. The Lilywhite Boys were both watching him.

"You look as though you've decided," Crozier said. "Last chance: if you want to forget this conversation ever happened, it can be done without consequences. After this, we aren't open to changes of heart. If you say no now, you won't see us again. If you say yes, we'll be the best of friends." He smiled. It wasn't the most reassuring smile Alec had ever seen.

"I've decided. I want you to do it. To rob my father."

Lane and Crozier exchanged a swift look. Lane nodded. "In that case, thirty seventy. In our favour."

"Fine."

Crozier's brows flicked up. "Then we have a deal. Are you going to tell us why you're doing this?"

"Well, the money—" Crozier's eyes narrowed sceptically, as well they might. Alec scowled. "And because he's a terrible person and he deserves something terrible to happen to him."

"Well, that's us," Lane said. "We happen to people, don't we, Jerry?"

"Better than having people happen to us. When's the house party?"

"The grand dinner will be on the seventh of August, at Castle Speight," Alec said.

"So we have two months." Lane looked at Crozier, questioning. Crozier shot a glance at Alec, then lifted a single finger like a man bidding at an auction. Lane opened his hands. Crozier tilted a brow.

"All right, then," Lane said, for all the world as though that had been a conversation. "Jerry will be your new best pal and eventual guest. You won't be seeing me for some time after this, if all goes well. If you let Jerry down you'll see me when you least expect it, and not pleasantly, but I'm sure that's an unnecessary warning. Have fun, gentlemen."

He stood, proving to be as sizeable as Alec had feared. "Catch up tomorrow, Jerry. Pyne." He nodded at Alec, took up his hat and coat, and left.

Alec blinked after him then looked back at Crozier. "What did he mean by that, about seeing him?"

"That if you run to the police, now or later, you might be able to inform on me but Templeton will be at large and resentful. To illustrate that, a certain gentleman recently put pressure on our fence—receiver of stolen goods, you know—to pay him protection money. In the ensuing discussion, Templeton dropped one of the gentleman's henchmen out of a second-floor window. We look after one another."

"Out of a *window*? But—was he hurt?"

"He strained his shoulder a little. Oh, you mean the droppee? Yes. He was." Crozier's smile was satanic. "Don't play silly buggers with us. We play it better."

Alec swallowed. "I won't. I mean, I've made up my mind."

"Good. Right, then. If I'm coming to your family event as a friend, we should strike up that friendship. Where do you like to drink?"

"What?"

"If we're to be sufficient pals for me to attend your parents' wedding anniversary celebrations—"

"Father's," Alec said. "She is not my mother."

Crozier's eyes hooded but he didn't comment. "If we're to be sufficient pals for this, I shall need to strike up acquaintance with you, enough that you will have a plausible story should things go south. So where do you drink?"

Alec's mind went blank. Where he actually liked to drink was a quiet, unobtrusive public house called the Jack and Knave that catered for a very particular clientele. He had no intention of sharing that titbit, whatever the Lilywhite Boys said about secrets. "I go to the Stratton Club sometimes, the journalists' club. Or the Sketch. It's a sort of place for artists."

"I can't draw, and I prefer to avoid journalists for obvious reasons. Anywhere else?"

"Not often. I can't afford much in the way of night-life. I just go to the pub, really."

"Lord Alexander Greville de Keppel Pyne-ffoulkes just goes to the pub?"

"Alec. And yes, actually, I do."

"Well, that's no bloody good," Crozier said. "How about the Criterion Bar?"

Alec woke up the next morning with a sense of impending doom. He lay in his narrow bed for a brief moment, feeling the worry without being able to identify the cause, and then he remembered.

"Oh, shit," he said aloud.

He'd done it. He'd actually done it, he'd contacted the criminals and made the devil's bargain. He was part of a conspiracy to commit burglary. It was terrifying, and shameful, and yet he could feel that same golden thread of excitement running through the very real fear as he had the first time he'd followed a man down a dark alley with unlawful intent.

This wasn't the same thing, but perhaps it wasn't a mile away, because Alec didn't believe he was truly doing anything wrong in seeking male embraces, and he also felt a deep sense of justification at what he planned to do to the Duke and Duchess. The world would not agree, and his brother and sister would not like any of what was to come, but that couldn't be helped. The smouldering resentment he'd carried so long had caught into flame, and it would be his guiding light.

It, and the Lilywhite Boys. He was, he thought, probably glad that it was Crozier who would be his "new best pal". Lane had made him uncomfortable, even if Alec couldn't put his finger on why: it was something about the very charming smile he wore on his frank, open face while his eyes ran calculations. Crozier seemed a little more...Alec couldn't think of a better word than 'straightforward' even though that was wrong. Unambiguously dangerous, perhaps. Templeton Lane smiled and smiled and was a villain; Crozier didn't bother to smile.

Alec was to meet him in the Long Bar at the Criterion this evening. *I'll strike up a conversation,* Crozier had said. *Follow my lead. Feel free to be charmed.*

That seemed an extremely unlikely outcome, and Alec had no confidence he could sham it. He'd pointed that out as politely as he could, terrified he might ruin the entire scheme before it started by going bright red and stammering. If the Lilywhite Boys were depending on Alec seeming happy and relaxed in their company, they'd be in trouble. He'd said as much, but Crozier hadn't seemed concerned.

"Let them do their job," he told himself, and got out of bed to face the day, propelled by one positive realisation: he would have to go through this meeting and discover more about what was expected of him before he spoke to his siblings. He was not looking forward to the latter conversation at all.

Alec wore evening dress that night. It was, after all, the Criterion Bar. He checked his appearance in the mirror and was reasonably pleased with the results. The grey among the blond hair at his temples was only perceptible under close inspection; his nose was a little marked by the spectacles he used for close work but that couldn't be helped. He looked really rather well, considering; it helped that his evening dress was expensive and not greatly used, and that he had put on a little weight recently, filling out after the months around Cara's death when he'd barely been able to choke down a mouthful for rage, horror, and grief. He wouldn't stand out for good or ill, and that was all he asked.

He took an omnibus to Piccadilly, self-conscious in his smart clothing among labourers and clerks, and strolled into the Criterion Bar with all the insouciance he could muster. He hadn't been here for a couple of years and the tiled interior was more magnificent than he remembered, the mirrors bright under the electric lights. When he'd come here before he'd probably been drunk.

He ordered a whisky and soda and took a seat at a small table, sitting back and looking casually around in the manner of a gentleman awaiting a friend. It was something he'd done hundreds of times without thinking twice, but now he was absurdly aware of himself, as though he were somehow the object of everyone's gaze. He picked up his glass and sipped the drink in a manner that felt ludicrously wooden. If a stage actor handled a glass that clumsily Alec would have felt inclined to boo, yet he couldn't help it; his fingers felt stiff and sausagelike.

He must look like a bad narrative painting of a man waiting for a friend. He glanced around, wondering if he'd recognise anyone, imagined he saw pity or mockery in the few looks thrown his lonely way, knocked back the whisky and soda in the hope of a bit of Dutch courage, and rashly ordered another. He was actually startled when someone leaned over his table to address him.

"I say, sir, is this seat taken?"

Alec looked up and blinked.

It was Crozier. Or at least— No, it was Crozier, but he'd shaved. The beard had been trimmed into a sharp goatee, revealing a firm jawline, the moustache thinned to a neat line. It was a striking style that gave his narrow face distinction. *Mephistopheles*, Alec thought again. He wore evening dress as well cut as Alec's own, and his brown hair was sleeked back. He looked every inch the man about town with a bright red carnation in his buttonhole, and he was regarding Alec with an expression of courteous inquiry.

"Uh. Yes, certainly," Alec managed. "I mean, no, it's not."

"You aren't waiting for anyone?" Crozier suggested.

"No. Yes, actually, yes I am, I was, but he's late. If he's coming at all. So you might as well." Alec attempted a casual wave at the chair opposite and nearly knocked over his glass. The last time he'd been this tongue-tied about inviting a man to take a seat, he'd been panting in a back room within the hour, hot breath in his ear. He felt a momentary wish that his lawbreaking was going in that direction now.

Not that Crozier was quite so handsome as that previous man had been. He was a little more than medium height, though his sinewy build probably made him look taller than he was. Mid-brown hair, skin that was neither interestingly pale nor notably darkened by nature or sun. Not an unattractive face, of the sort Alec would sketch for the background of an army or clubland scene, and the dark brown eyes under his sharply defined brows were striking, but the goatee would be the main thing most people remembered. If he were a politician, the caricaturists would bless him for the goatee and curse him if he shaved. If the police asked for a description of 'the man who stole the jewels', the goatee was what they'd get.

He was looking at Crozier as he would a subject, and, he realised, Crozier was looking back.

"I do beg your pardon. Have we met before?"

"What?" Alec had a momentary panic—he couldn't have got it wrong, could he? This was surely the man from last night?—and then realised that Crozier must be playing his part of a stranger, in which case Alec had indeed been gaping at him in a way that merited the enquiry. "Uh, no, I don't think so. I'm sorry, was I staring?"

"Perhaps a little." Crozier's mouth curved, very slightly.

"I beg your pardon. I'm an artist," Alec explained, tongue taking over since his brain seemed not to be much use. "An illustrator for the papers. I'm always on the lookout for faces."

"How intriguing. Specific faces, or are you a snapper-up of unconsidered features for later use?" Crozier's brows slanted comically. "Good heavens, I trust you don't work for the *Illustrated Police News*. I'd hate to hear I had the looks for a murderer."

That was very nearly too close to the bone. Alec wasn't sure what to say for a second; Crozier went on with barely a break. "So do you acquire faces from among your acquaintance when you aren't drawing from life? It never occurred to me to wonder before, but now I think about those great crowd scenes and coming up with all the different people..."

"It is tempting to use friends," Alec admitted.

"Ah, but do you use enemies? Allot some tiresome bore's face to a pickpocket or a dubious bookmaker? I would."

"Also tempting, but I prefer not to have actions launched against me."

"Good point." Crozier was smiling properly now, the amusement reaching his eyes. "I'm fascinated. Do you specialise in any particular sort of illustration? Exotic scenes, courtroom incident?"

Alec found himself answering with a peculiar sense of familiarity. He was pretending to strike up an acquaintance with a charming stranger, yet it felt awfully like he was doing just that in reality. As though he were making light conversation, taking the other man's measure, wondering what sort of fellow he might be.

And, still, looking at him. Crozier's most distinctive feature was the pair of remarkably mobile eyebrows which gave visual punctuation to his speech, and their dancing movement was another thing you couldn't convey in a police sketch. They combined with his apparently habitual half smile to give Alec the impression that he was being laughed either at or with. He wasn't confident which.

"So are the illustrated papers your primary interest?" Crozier asked. "That is, do you illustrate books, say, or otherwise exhibit?"

"I'd love to illustrate more books," Alec said, instantly forgetting everything else. "Especially for children. This is a glorious time for illustration—the publishing techniques are improving hand over fist, and the public are coming to expect far higher standards. I'm being considered for a new edition of Shakespeare at the moment, as it happens. I don't know if I'll get the work, but it's nice to be in the running."

"I should say so. That calls for a drink." Crozier raised his hand with the sort of calm assurance Alec could never manage, and a waiter appeared within a few seconds. "Two glasses of champagne, thank you."

"That's, uh—"

"My pleasure," Crozier said. "Why books for children particularly?"

Answering that took several moments, in which the champagne came in two glittering glasses. Crozier raised his and inclined it to Alec's. They tapped the crystal together with a delicate *ting*.

"To art," Crozier said. "In all its forms."

"To art," Alec managed. The whisky and soda had gone to his head already; the champagne prickled against his lips.

They talked on: about Alec's current work on the *Graphic* and the *Illustrated*, and then about newspapers and the latest scandals. Crozier volunteered a couple of stories that made Alec choke on his champagne laughing, and grinned, and waved his hand for the waiter again.

"Dinner," Crozier said, several glasses later. It was past ten already, and Alec discovered abruptly that he was starving. "Join me? They do an adequate table here."

That was a gross understatement. Alec followed him, floating on a cloud of champagne and conversation, through to the restaurant. There Crozier recommended the rognons de veau and the sole, which was a relief since, between the small type, lack of spectacles, and the alcohol, Alec found the menu somewhat challenging to interpret. He gulped about half a bottle of Vichy water, and found himself more able to keep up his end of the rambling conversation. This soon veered into theatrical tastes.

"Are you a great lover of the music hall?" Alec asked.

"Not much." Crozier caught his blink, and shrugged. "My interest in Miss Christiana lies entirely in the fact that she's a friend's sweetheart so I was required to tell him she was wonderful in convincing detail. As an artist, you're doubtless familiar with the obligation."

"Oh." Alec assimilated *a friend's sweetheart* and *him.* "Yes, indeed, with exhibitions and so on."

"What I do enjoy, and I dare say I should be ashamed of this, is the melodrama," Crozier said, eyebrows sliding up to indicate his own absurdity. "I like nothing more than a thoroughly idiotic hero, a vapid heroine, a lost will, a stalwart comic man to find it, and a villain with a proper blood-chilling laugh. All of that accompanied by a suitably dramatic scene in which someone leaps off a cliff or a train is trundled across the stage to the heroine's peril."

Alec clapped his hands. "Yes! So long as the villain expires with suitable drama. Staggering, with a hand pressed to his brow, and a speech of repentance that explains all his machinations and tells the hero where the treasure is hidden."

"Oh, no, not repentance. I like the villain to be villainous to the end. He should curse the hero's goodness with his last breath and die seething in his own frustrated criminality. It's only fair."

"You wouldn't consider a change of heart on your deathbed?"

"No decent villain dies in bed," Crozier pointed out. "He expires in the toils of his own plot, on the steps of his grand house or run through by the hero's blade. And no, certainly not. If I were inclined to repentance, and I'm not, I'd want to start now. To do it on one's deathbed is to be sorry because one has been caught, and that surely doesn't count."

"You're not inclined to repentance?" Alec repeated. "What, ever?"

"Never." Crozier's eyes glimmered dark in the electric light and the glitter of glass and silverware and mirrors. "I'm not sorry."

"For what?"

"Anything." Crozier tilted his head, eyes hooding slightly, gaze roaming over Alec's face. "Except missed opportunities. I regret those, but that's a different matter, isn't it?"

"Mmm." Alec didn't want to think about his own missed opportunities now, the what-ifs and if-onlies. "I don't suppose you have many of those, do you?"

Crozier's smile widened a fraction. It looked a little bit dangerous, and it made Alec's toes curl delightfully. "Not many. They're such a waste. And so often what one wants is there for the taking, if one only makes the effort to reach for it."

Alec swallowed. He wondered, very much wondered, if he dared inch his foot forward and nudge Crozier's shoe with his own, to see how he reacted. He had an idea that he oughtn't, and for a moment couldn't quite remember why.

Oh, yes. It was because Crozier was a thief, and this—this dinner, this companionship, the smile in his eyes—was all a lie.

The thought struck harder than it should have. He didn't say anything, but something changed in Crozier's expression, his eyes losing their laughter, as if he'd read something on Alec's face that he didn't like. It occurred to Alec that his companion might in fact look rather ugly in some lights, or in some moods.

"In any case," Crozier said. "We've gone on rather late, haven't we?" He summoned the bill, again with that magical flick of his fingers, and they sat in a silence that was all the more notable because conversation had been so easy. Alec had a heavy feeling in his stomach that wasn't only the drink. He was unpleasantly aware that he'd be in a serious hole if he'd somehow failed a test and was asked to pay his share.

He wasn't. Crozier pulled out a well-stuffed wallet as the bill was produced, left what must have been a generous pourboire given the waiter's bow, and nodded to Alec. "Come on, old chap, let's see you home. I think you're ready to call it a night, aren't you?"

Alec very much was. The drink caught up with him as he stood, and he felt Crozier's steadying hand under his elbow, firm and warm. "Let's get you in a cab. I shall pop in and see how you're getting on tomorrow."

He steered Alec outside as he spoke, past the doorman. The cool night air felt like a bucket of water to the face, clearing his head as Crozier summoned a hansom cab and gave the man the address, then held the door open for Alec. "An absolute pleasure making your acquaintance. I'll see you later."

"Yes, see you tomorrow, old man," Alec managed, and clambered in. The door slammed, the cab lurched off, and he shut his eyes and concentrated on his breathing.

Dammit, dammit, dammit. How had he managed to forget what he was there for? What sort of bloody fool was he? Suppose he'd actually nudged Crozier's foot or made his interest clear? Christ, suppose Crozier had detected it anyway, and had been tempting him to reveal himself? The jewel thief, the unrepentant criminal would have had Alec in the palm of his hand from then on.

Or suppose Crozier had actually been flirting with him. Suppose he'd decided Alec was there for the taking, and he'd been the one to nudge Alec's foot, and they'd finished the night in one of Piccadilly's dark alleys, as could so very nearly have happened. Alec put his hands over his face and groaned aloud.

When he arrived home, the cabbie told him the fare had been paid already, at which point Alec realised that he'd never told Crozier his address, but the man had known it anyway.

He did not sleep well that night.

# Chapter Two

The next day, Alec went to the Turkish bath. It seemed like the only possible solution to a rotten bad head and a stomach filled with a sour stew of fear. He soaked and steamed and was impersonally pummelled by powerful hands, until both the worries and the alcohol had been temporarily driven away. He dozed afterwards for an hour, and woke feeling hungry, human, and newly determined.

He'd made his deal with the devil and there was no point fretting now. Last night had been about striking up a friendship with a charming and plausible man in public. Crozier was, it transpired, very good at being charming and plausible; Alec had been charmed. He surely didn't need to worry about that hint of possible flirtation: the way Crozier had spoken of the music-hall travesty singer didn't suggest a man who feared or hated effeminacy. He'd probably ended the night simply because he'd seen Alec was drunk enough to forget his role. There was no need to worry.

He told himself all that until he nearly believed it, then went back home to try to get some work done. He had the top floor room, with a skylight; it was a very decent space that allowed for a good-sized table and to hide his bed behind a folding screen. It wasn't a grand house or a fashionable location—Mincing Lane, on the wrong side of Eastcheap—but it was clean, and he could afford it on his earnings with no help from his brother, let alone his father.

Sometimes he felt proud of that achievement and his independence; sometimes he remembered that he was Lord Alexander Pyne-ffoulkes, slaving with inky fingers to keep the rent paid and his editors happy, and he felt like overturning the table and sending his pens and pots flying to the floor.

Not today. He had plenty of work to do, including providing a sample for a collection of fairy-tales. The publisher had given him a list of the stories to be included; when he saw "The Town Musicians of Bremen", with its dastardly gang of thieves, he laughed out loud. He sketched out a very nice composition—a dark rustic hovel with a low fire; a sinister robber recoiling in terror from the snapping dog and hissing cat as a cock crowed on the rafters—and was fiddling with the robber's eyebrows to achieve an impression of movement when there was a knock on the door.

"Mr Pyne, sir?" It was his landlady. "Visitor for you. A Mr. Jerry, he says."

"Oh. Please send him up. Thank you, Mrs. Barzowski, you're very kind."

Mrs. Barzowski knew he was a lord in disguise, and it had taken all the charm of which he was capable, plus dire warnings about speculative burglary, to persuade her not to spread the news throughout the house and to all her neighbours. She insisted on the *sir* and on bringing messages in person, and called him "Lord Alexander" in private as though to do so was a great privilege. She believed him to have been wrongly done out of an inheritance, which was true in its way, and that he would one day come into a title of his own, which wasn't. Alec had tried to disabuse her of that conviction, but it hadn't taken, so he accepted the advantages it brought and made sure his rent was always paid on time.

Crozier made it up the stairs a few minutes later. Alec heard him speaking to Mrs. Barzowski on the landing, smooth tone clear though the words were indistinguishable, and could imagine her bobbing in response. She doubtless thought him a gentleman, or perhaps a lawyer arriving with news of Alec's elevation to a non-existent coronet.

Crozier rapped on the door and entered, taking off his hat. He wore a light tan coat with a waistcoat in a darker brown, and a gold watch chain. He looked like a gentleman about town, significantly superior to Alec in his shirtsleeves.

"Spectacles?" Crozier asked.

Alec hastily removed them. "I use them for close work."

"Very reasonable. How's your head?"

"Better for a Turkish bath. I don't often drink much."

"So I gathered." Crozier's tone had his usual light hint of something between amusement and mockery. "Best to be careful in the near future, then. Still, we achieved what we intended. May I sit?"

Alec had one armchair, by the small grate. He indicated it and dragged over the chair he used for work. "Would you like tea?"

"Let's not trouble your landlady. That's a lot of stairs."

"It is. I need the light up here."

"It must be cold in winter."

Alec felt vaguely criticised. "Yes, and hot in summer. Do take your coat off if you're warm."

"I shall," Crozier said, suiting the action to the word. "Why does Lord Alexander Pyne-ffoulkes live in an attic?"

Alec opened his mouth. Nothing came out for a moment. He wanted to say "None of your business", knew he couldn't, but didn't have anything else to offer.

"Let me rephrase that," Crozier went on. "Do you understand what we did last night and what we'll be doing now?"

"Probably not."

"I shall pursue your acquaintance, so that you will have good reason to invite your new best friend to a family party. Hence, if I am caught or even suspected when your stepmother's jewels go missing, you will be seen as a dupe rather than an accomplice."

"Why does that matter to you?" Alec demanded.

"Because if you're arrested I'm quite sure you'll give me up to the police. Therefore I don't want you arrested. My presence in your life has to be plausible, and so does your attendance at a celebration of the Duke and Duchess of Ilvar's marriage. Understand? You can't just walk into your estranged father's house with a stranger and have the jewels go missing."

"I understand that very well. I was going to talk to my siblings tomorrow."

"You're going to talk to me first." Crozier spoke quite pleasantly but Alec felt a prickle on his skin. "I want to know all about the Pyne-ffoulkes family, all about your charming father and delightful stepmother, and very much all about why you live in an attic working for your bread while your sister Lady Caroline lies in something near a pauper's grave."

Alec couldn't breathe. He sat, mouth open, staring at this damned intrusive impertinent bastard with pure hate boiling up inside him, and Crozier shook his head. "Can you illustrate a book, or a story, without a brief? I need the brief. I need to know what not to say; I need to know how to tell your story and who is going to raise questions and how we answer them before they're asked. I can't help you if I don't know the situation."

"Of course your main interest lies in helping me," Alec said bitterly.

Crozier gave him a look. "My interest lies in helping myself to the Duchess's diamond parure and getting away clean. Is that not what you asked for?"

"Yes, well, that's very sensible." Alec knew he was being absurd, but shame and resentment were overwhelming all common sense. "I'm sure you'd be quite ready to give over your family history for profit. Forgive me if I'm not."

"As if you've anything to tell me that's worse than my history," Crozier said. "Do you imagine I'll be shocked by anything you have to say? Do you think I care?"

Alec snorted. "At least you're honest."

"That's precisely what I'm not. Consider me the antithesis of a Romish priest. I take confession, I keep your silence, but instead of absolution I give you vengeance. That's what you're after, isn't it? Some way to get through the armoury of wealth and title, to hit the Duke where it hurts."

That was savagely accurate. Alec rose, needing to move, needing not to see Crozier's face or anyone's. He went to the skylight, staring out over the rooftops, took a few deep breaths.

"My father met Mrs. Clayton when I was six. Clayton was my father's estate manager at Castle Speight. He came from a good family that had had a crash. His wife had no birth, a little money, not much beauty, or so I'm told. Apparently she had something, though, because my father was obsessed with her from their first meeting and their affair became public extremely quickly. My mother was unwell. She had had a terrible time when Annabel, my younger sister, was born, and never really recovered. So my father—it wasn't surprising for him to take a mistress, but he didn't even try to be discreet. And then, you see, Mother died, and my father told Clayton to petition for divorce so he could marry Mrs. Clayton. Ordered him to. Mother hadn't been dead six months. Father was still wearing mourning."

Crozier didn't say anything. The glass of the skylight was grimy. Alec rubbed at it with his thumb but the muck was on the outside; he couldn't reach it to clean it off.

"Clayton wouldn't do it," he went on. "The local story is, he told my father in the street, 'You've made her your whore but you'll never make her your wife.' Everyone knew he was being cuckolded by his employer, and I suppose preventing them from marrying was his revenge. He didn't keep his grievances private, though: he spoke quite wildly about my father ruining his marriage and destroying his happiness. They say he was drinking too much. And then he was found dead, in the grounds, some little way from his cottage, with his gun by his side."

"Considerate of him to do it outside."

"Oh, no, it wasn't suicide," Alec said sardonically. "The coroner said so, because of the missing ring."

"What's that?" Crozier enquired, perking up.

"A very fine antique emerald ring he always wore. It was a family heirloom, to be passed to his son or returned to the next heir, his brother, if he died without issue. The ring was about all the Claytons had left from their crash, and it wasn't on his body when it was discovered. That allowed the coroner to float a theory of a poacher shooting him, whether by accident or on purpose, and robbing the corpse. So the verdict was death by misadventure."

"What a remarkable conclusion."

Alec snorted. "My father is the richest, most powerful man in three counties. Of course the inquest wasn't going to accuse him of driving his mistress's husband to self-murder. They'd have found for divine intervention if they could."

"The march of justice," Crozier murmured. "Go on."

"Well, my father married Mrs. Clayton five months later. They should both still have been in blacks, but they held a full wedding, not even privately, but with all possible pomp and ceremony."

"Attended by the great and the good, I suppose?"

"Fewer than you'd think, actually," Alec said. "It was less than a year after Mother's death, and a lot of people wanted nothing to do with the business. The Duke of Ilvar, and nobody from the Royal Family attended his wedding. The Duchess was furious. I remember her shouting."

"Mmm. And how was she as a mother, afterwards?"

Alec laughed. There was nothing to do but laugh. "Oh, she loathed us. There was George—Earl of Hartington, you know—Cara, me, and Annabel, and she didn't want four children. She was twenty-five when she married Father, and George was fifteen. A stepson only ten years younger? No, she hated us, and she made sure we all knew it. George because he was outspoken about the insult to Mother's memory; Cara because she was sickly. The Duchess can't bear sickliness, you know, it revolts her. I'm not worth her notice, and Annabel—one might have thought she'd want Annabel. She was so young; she could easily have come to love a new mother who cared for her at all. But the Duchess wanted her own children."

"I don't recall they have any?"

"No. She was expecting a couple of times. I used to lie awake at night wondering what would happen if she had a son, with George and me ahead of him in the line of inheritance. What she might do. Just childish fears, you know," he added hastily. "In any case, it never came about."

"I don't suppose that made her fonder of her stepchildren," Crozier said. "It all sounds very unpleasant. I understand the Ilvars are not popular outside the home either."

"In Society? No, not at all. My father isn't the sort of man who's liked, if you know what I mean. He's invited for his title, not himself. And of course he's entitled to pride because of his position, but once he started demanding, not just courtesy but humble deference to the mistress he married—well, the sort of people who like dukes don't much like that. And she's every bit as proud of her place as he is. She ranks above everyone but the Royal Family now, so she never tried to win friends, or good opinion. I don't know if she thought she'd gain them by right or if she just doesn't care."

"One could almost respect that, you know. Like a medieval queen."

"She is medieval. She runs Castle Speight 'sacked if seen', so if any servant who isn't meant to be there dares to intrude on her view, they are dismissed at once. If she catches a housemaid doing her job or sees a footman in the wrong place or a groom not in the stables, that's their lot. God help anyone who is meant to be there but doesn't bow with sufficient deference, come to that. The locals call it Castle Spite."

"They must have quite the changing roster of staff. Interesting. So she wasn't much of a stepmother to you. Your father didn't seek to improve relations?"

Alec rested his head on his arm. He hadn't spoken about this in years. Family wasn't a subject he discussed with anyone but his siblings, who already knew. "No, not at all. He took her side in the arguments—there were a lot of arguments—and he always made it clear that if it came to a choice between his wife or his children, he'd choose his wife. Eight years ago it did, and he did."

"Leaving you where?"

"In an attic," Alec said. "George has a small income as Hartington—well, a very good one for a young man, which is what it's meant to be, but he's had Cara and Annabel, our sisters, to support since the break, and a family of his own now, and a wife who didn't expect to penny-pinch when she married an earl. He's had to shoulder all the family obligations because Father won't. He's never even met his grandchildren, do you know that? George has two sons, one of whom will be the Duke of Ilvar eventually, and Father doesn't give a damn. He won't acknowledge any of us unless we bow the knee to him and grovel to his wife."

"And you won't."

"We oughtn't have to. I don't say the Duchess should have loved us, but the fact is, Annabel was four years old when they married, and I was eight, and we didn't deserve to be punished because we wept for our mother. George oughtn't have to be de facto head of the family, with all the burdens and none of the benefits. Cara—" He broke off, glaring through the glass at nothing.

"No," Crozier said. "Some might say that nobody at all has a right to the kind of obscene wealth possessed by your family, but I quite see that if you're born to it, it would be exasperating not to have it."

"I'm well aware George's income could support all the families in this street, if he lived like the families in this street," Alec said testily. "But he's a duke's heir. He's got to keep up appearances, to keep them up for his wife and children. You said yesterday, one ought to reach for what one wants and not miss opportunities. Well, George and his wife and his children and Annabel have the opportunity to be part of the highest society. And if George gets a job as a clerk, say, or Annabel becomes a governess, they and their children will suffer for it. You must know that."

"They'd prefer aristocratic poverty to joining the middle classes?"

"Yes," Alec said. "They would. Because George *will* be a duke one day, when Father dies and if he and his children have become an object of pity and contempt to their peers, well, that's not fair on them. And Annabel is the Duke of Ilvar's daughter. It's not unreasonable that her intended's family should want her to bring something to the marriage, but Father won't give her a penny for a wedding portion. And if she could marry and George didn't have to worry about her any more, that would take a strain off him too. She and his wife don't get on awfully well—nobody's fault, but it would be better for everyone if they didn't share a house. If I could give her a sum to marry on—"

"Is that it?" Crozier asked. "Are you funding Lady Annabel's dowry with the Duchess's jewels?"

"Henry, with whom she has an understanding, is a gentleman," Alec said. "Which means he needs to marry money rather than making it himself." That came out slightly more sarcastically than he'd intended, and he heard the ghost of a chuckle from behind him. "I don't mean to be rude. He's pleasant enough, but not the most energetic fellow, or terribly bright. He's a drone, not a worker bee."

"And as a worker bee yourself, you disapprove."

"Not really. I'd have liked an idle life of luxury as much as anyone."

"Would you?" Crozier said. "This room seems to me a hive, as it were, of industry. It suggests a man who puts importance on his work."

It didn't lack markers of his profession, Alec was aware: he had pictures pinned haphazardly to the walls, pots of drawing materials, piles of images for reference. It was a working space more than anything and he did feel a certain satisfaction in his Bohemian existence, at least when the commissions came thick and fast. Not to mention that artists and journalists tended to have better conversation than sons of gentlemen, to be rather less demanding in matters of dress, and considerably more open in their pleasures.

"I have a knack for drawing," he said. "And as it happens I like it, and the society it's brought me into, well enough. Naturally I'd rather have more money; I dare say we all would."

"I dare say." Crozier sounded rather dry.

"If Father had given me an income to live on, I don't suppose I'd ever have taken up drawing seriously, and I'd have missed out on a lot of things. But he didn't cut me off to teach me to live a useful life. It wasn't a lesson; he just doesn't care. So even if I don't feel I've been wronged as George and Annabel have, it's still not right." He took a deep breath. "And then there was Cara."

"Yes," Crozier said. "Tell me about Lady Cara."

"He wouldn't pay for her." Alec stared out of the skylight. There was a cat on the roof opposite, a brindled one, basking in the sun. He fixed his eyes on it, because sometimes, if one fixed one's eyes on a thing, one didn't cry. "She was never strong, always short of breath. The Duchess called her sickly. She ought to have been in the country, with clean air, but instead she lived with George. He did try to send her to the seaside when he could, but with all the expenses—he couldn't afford to keep up two households, and I needed to be in London to get work, and she didn't want to go to a sanatorium on her own. And then last autumn the fog was so dreadful that I wrote to Father. I begged him to invite Cara to Castle Speight. I told him she was unwell, that she needed to be out of London, and please would he help. And his secretary wrote back and said His Grace could not countenance my request unless Cara wrote to make a personal apology for her intolerable insolence. His *secretary*."

Crozier was silent. The brindled cat blurred in Alec's vision. He blinked the tears away. "She caught a cold. It would have been a mere chill for anyone else, George's boys constantly have them, but it came at the same time as that bad week's fog in early December, and she died. Her weak chest, you see. It was very sudden. We'd been worried, but we didn't expect her to die."

"I'm sorry," Crozier said softly.

"So am I. And Father refused to pay for the funeral. He said the expense was not convenient."

There was a slight pause. "That's quite a statement from one of the richest men in England."

"Yes. He said he had an obligation to his Duchess which took priority. That was the diamond parure. As if he couldn't have afforded to pay for the funeral too, as if his own daughter's funeral shouldn't have been more to him than another set of jewels. George had to pay, and we didn't have flowers. Cara loved flowers but in December—hothouse lilies are awfully expensive— There was holly. One of the vases was knocked over and berries rolled everywhere, on the floor. People trod on them." He remembered the red drops splashed like blood against the stone and the sharp smell.

"Yes," Crozier said, as though he were agreeing with something, instead of listening to Alec ramble about holly. "I see. It's the insult of indifference."

Alec swung round at that. Crozier was only a couple of feet away. Alec hadn't heard him move. "That's exactly what it is. He has no right to be indifferent. No right to treat us as though we don't exist. No right not to come to Cara's funeral, not to care."

"I'm surprised he wasn't concerned with public opinion."

"We didn't want people to know. George says it would make things worse if everyone was talking about us as hard done by, and he's probably right. And in any case, I don't think Father would care what people say. He's so entrenched in his outrage at people's failure to pay suitable homage to the Duchess that he doesn't see anything else. It's the only matter of right or wrong in his world. And Cara would rather have died than apologise. She *did*."

Crozier's brows angled down. "An extreme stance even in a family dispute."

Alec had no intention of going into her reasons. "Well. Is that what you wanted? Enough of my family misery to be getting on with?"

"It's a start." Crozier seemed unconcerned by the belligerence of his tone. "The obvious question: Given the situation you've described, how do you propose to claim your place at the anniversary dinner?"

Alec put his chin up. "I'm going to apologise. I'm going to reconcile with my father and bow to the Duchess. He'll want that: it will prove he was right all along."

"And what have your brother and sister to say to that?"

Alec's stomach clenched. "I haven't spoken to them yet."

"What are you going to say?" Crozier pressed.

"Well, I'm not going to tell them I've hired thieves," Alec snapped. "I don't know. That I'm tired of the fighting, that I'm giving in to Father in order to wring money out of him for Annabel. What else can I say?"

"That you need the money yourself. It's very heroic to sacrifice yourself for your sister, but firstly she might refuse the offer, and secondly, if you announce that you'll do anything to get money for her and then the jewels go missing, your siblings would be fools not to link the two things. Whereas if you admit to a minor villainy now, they will believe they know what you're up to, and there won't be an outstanding mystery to which the theft will, in due course, be a solution."

"Oh. I see, I think. So I should say I want his money, and I don't care about what he's done?"

"Not that you don't care, but that you can no longer keep to those principles. Let's say you have accrued gambling debts. You've fallen back into expensive society—that's me—and need to hold your own. You're tired of scribbling for pennies. You'd prefer to have lilies at your funeral."

Alec couldn't help wincing. Crozier held his gaze, giving a deliberate shrug. "Forget your sensibilities. You'll need to ask your father for money, lots of it, well before we do the job. Another safeguard: why would you steal from the goose when it's started laying you golden eggs again?"

"Yes. Right. Christ." Alec made a face. "George and Annabel will despise me."

"I'd say it's considerably more likely that once one of you has thrown in the towel, the others will follow. Try not to despise them if they do."

"I don't think they will," Alec said with some understatement.

"In that case, yes, this is likely to be unpleasant for you with the people you most care about. Are you prepared for that?"

"Am I prepared to have people say cruel things to me?" Alec asked, almost incredulously. "Yes, probably I am. I went to school with everyone quite sure my father had married his mistress after driving her husband to suicide and covering it up. I grew up in the Duchess's power. I think I can tolerate my brother and sister's poor opinion for a couple of months. I don't much want to, but I can."

"Good, because you'll have to. If your father is to believe in your submission, you can hardly be on good terms with the offspring who defy him, can you?"

Alec hadn't quite thought of that. "I suppose not."

"Three months," Crozier said. "Two to prepare, the job, and then at least another month of good behaviour before you arrange to be cast into the outer darkness once more and can rebuild bridges with your siblings. This is what we call playing the long game, and it has a price. Don't imagine any of this comes free and easy."

Alec tried an eyebrow lift. "You look free and easy enough."

Crozier's lips curved responsively. "I already told you. I'm never sorry."

He was two feet away, very close in a room which seemed suddenly rather smaller than usual. He wasn't sorry, and he didn't care about things, and he was going to guide Alec down the primrose path to villainy, and Alec wished to God he hadn't drunk so much last night because it always made him randy the next day. The last thing he needed right now was, for example, Crozier taking two steps forward, grabbing his hands, pressing him against the wall or down over the drawing table...

The second last thing he needed right now was to be sporting a hard one, and he was well on the way. He put a hand casually behind his back, in order to dig two fingernails into the sensitive ball of his thumb. "Well. I'd better get on and speak to my siblings, then."

"Before your father? Would you do that if you had no ulterior motive? What if he's not interested in your submission?"

Alec resisted the obvious, tempting, unsayable reply. *Keep your mind on the job, damn it.* "Uh... I don't know what I'd naturally do. Probably not this at all. I'd rather speak to George first."

"Or is it that you'd rather put off contacting your father a little longer?"

Alec glared at him. "I dare say you're very acute, but it doesn't make you any more likeable."

Crozier laughed aloud. "I'm sure it doesn't. Look, from what you tell me, it will be harder than I suspect you realise to do as your father wishes. You'll have to say a number of unpalatable things. Yes?"

"Yes."

"Tell them to me."

Alec didn't want to tell him anything. It stuck like brambles, all of it. He shut his eyes, which didn't help, and opened them to find Crozier a silent step closer.

"You're crossing the Rubicon," the thief said softly. "If you were doing this because you meant it, you'd be renouncing a great deal of what has guided your life to this date. As you aren't, you're taking a significant step down a path that you don't want to walk. But this is nevertheless the way to your goal, so tell me, what will you need to say?"

"That I apologise for my insolence to the Duchess." Alec's throat felt thick; he had to force the words out. "That I regret my failure to give due respect to my father and my father's wife. That I pray to be accepted back into their good graces, that I promise proper filial piety from now on and will—will do as I'm told."

Crozier nodded slowly. "Yes, that's rather a lot to swallow." He paused for a fraction of a second. "Do you not like to do as you're told?"

"It depends what I'm being told to do," Alec said. "Just as it depends what there is to swallow."

Crozier's eyes snapped wide, and Alec felt a fierce pulse of satisfaction—*wrong-footed you there, you bastard*—alongside the appalled realisation that yes, he had said that. There was silence for a few seconds. Alec's blood was pounding; he could hear Crozier's breath and his own. The air felt thick.

And then Crozier smiled, and Alec thought, *Oh shit.*

It wasn't a nice smile, or a complicit one of shared understanding, or even the sort of smile that was a precursor to being bent over a table. It was a smile that could only be called predatorial. His brows were slanted in a truly satanic way, and Alec's ribcage was suddenly rather too tight for comfort.

"That's very true," Crozier said slowly. "If it's a matter of humiliating necessity, say, to which you're driven by sheer desperation...that wouldn't be good, would it?"

"Not at all." Alec's mouth was dry. He swallowed involuntarily, saw Crozier's eyes dip to track the movement of his throat.

"Desperation is a terrible thing," Crozier said. "It's amazing what a man can find himself doing once he's on his knees."

Alec tried very hard not to whimper. He wasn't sure if he'd succeeded. Crozier's smile tilted, a crooked curve. "You know, in my line of work it's useful to have a few characters. Identities, you might say, entire personalities that you can slip on or off like a garment. It's far easier than struggling to reconcile difficult realities or remembering a mass of loose facts."

"I don't understand."

"It's simple enough. Don't write your letter as Alec Pyne, degrading himself in his own eyes with lies he'd rather not tell. Write as, shall we say, 'Lord Alexander', the weakling nobleman who comes on in Act One. A man of no real strength, easily swayed by bad company, who'll do absolutely anything he's told to."

Alec blinked. "A character from the melodrama, you mean?"

"Precisely. The effete young cipher, the hapless plaything of stronger men's will. Create the part and play it. And then, you see, you'll have Lord Alexander ready and waiting whenever you need to go to your knees. For any reason."

"That's your professional advice, is it?" Alec managed.

Crozier took one more step forward, so he was far too close, mouth almost at Alec's ear, breath warm. "I'd be delighted to help you create the character."

Oh God. Alec had to lock his knees to stand straight. This was all appallingly wrong and a terrible idea and…

…it might work. The Lord Alexander that Crozier had sketched out would write the vile, humiliating letter that he needed to write. He'd do anything a strong ruthless villain like Crozier wanted. Anything at all.

"Or," Crozier said softly. "Perhaps I could let you think about it, and you could have my words at the back of your mind as you write your letter and create your character, and try it out on paper and in person. All that time you could be speculating about how far Lord Alexander can be pushed, and what he can be made to swallow. Do you think that might help your inspiration?"

"Possibly," Alec said. His voice was a trifle high.

"Give it some thought." Crozier stepped back. "I, meanwhile, am going to do a little digging. Meet me at the Cafe Royal, two days' time, eight o'clock. Have your approach to your father made and sent by then, Lord Alexander. Don't fail me."

He took up his hat and turned on his heel. Alec stared at the door long after it had closed.

*In over his head* didn't even begin to describe it. That conversation ought to have been a humiliating agony—Cara, the plain awfulness of what he intended to do—and instead it had become the thing it had, and now it felt almost like a game. A wicked game with stakes he didn't want to consider, but still a game, and he wanted to play. He wanted to win this round, to meet in two days' time with the letter written, to prove to Crozier that he could manage his hand. As it were.

Oh God.

Alec walked over to the door and threw the bolt. He leaned on it, bracing himself with his right hand, unbuttoned himself with the left, paused.

Crozier had clearly wanted to leave him in this squirming state of shameful arousal. He'd seemed to feel that would fuel Alec's ability to create his character. And he might even be right, because if three-quarters of Alec's mind was on his painfully tight cock, perhaps he could manage his more distasteful duties without thinking too much.

He released himself, buttoned his trousers again, and went to the table, but hesitated over a pen. He took up a pencil instead, twisting it in his fingers, thinking about Lord Alexander. A weak-willed aristocrat, a spineless clothes horse, easily bent to another's commands...he let the pencil drift over the page, creating something not his own face but not so far off as to be unrecognisable. A character that would instantly strike an experienced viewer of the melodrama as a third rank villain, never to be trusted, though liable to repent in the final act. A weak mouth, a petulant curve to the slightly open lips, a sulky, evasive look to the eyes...

He could do this. He could create a version of himself that resembled his truth as much as the sketch did his face and write the letter without staining his own soul, because it wasn't him. Lord Alexander would submit to the Duke of Ilvar's will, and grovel far more than Alec could stomach, and Alec would stand back and laugh as he did it.

And as to Crozier, and what the devil he'd been playing at talking Alec into this state of desire and humiliation and pretence...he'd just have to find out on Friday night at their assignation. He only knew that if Crozier had been acting in character, he'd been sufficiently immersed in his role to have sprung a very substantial bit of stiff. Crozier had been as caught in that moment as Alec, and if he was being toyed with, at least it was by a skilled player.

He let his mind dwell on that thought as he reached for the pen.

# Chapter Three

Alec sat in the Earl of Hartington's drawing-room, knees pressed together, carefully holding his teacup. The clock ticked. He felt unwell.

"What..." George's lips moved as though he were trying out phrases, or his brain wasn't quite connecting to his mouth. "What do you mean you've written to Father?"

Alec felt a stab of guilt. George looked so worn. His cuffs had clearly been turned, his furniture was faded, his wife was swelling with her third child and obviously not enjoying the process any more than the first two because she looked pallid and drawn. Alec had made a vow not to add to George's burdens and had prided himself on achieving financial independence, about which his brother had been vocally disapproving and privately relieved. He didn't want to make things worse now. He wished Melissa and Annabel weren't here.

"Written to say what?" Annabel demanded. She was looking well in a dress that wasn't too obviously last season's and was decidedly fresher than Melissa's voluminous garment, reused from her previous interesting condition. "What do you mean, Alec?"

Alec exhaled. "I wrote to ask him for a rapprochement. To get back into his good books. That's all."

"You *wrote*? To him? After Cara? After everything, you actually *wrote*—" Annabel's voice was rising rapidly up the scale.

"You cannot be serious," George said. "Does the gross insult he offered our sister mean nothing? Do you propose to call that woman mother? Have you run mad?"

"No, I haven't. The fact is, I need rather more money than I can earn. That's all there is to it."

"You said you were doing well. You said you didn't need my help."

"I'm doing perfectly well," Alec returned without thinking. He'd made that assurance so often. "That is, I have been, but I have encountered some unexpected expenses and, well, I'm simply tired of scrimping and saving and struggling to keep my head above water."

"Don't you think we all are?" Annabel struck in. "Haven't we been for years? Do you think I enjoy appearing at the minimum possible of parties in a dress that's been refurbished for the fifth time—"

"Then maybe you should follow your brother's example if George can't keep you to your liking," Melissa said furiously. "Considering he supports you as well as his own children, all of whom go without for your adornment—"

"I wasn't complaining!" Annabel cried, going scarlet. George shut his eyes.

Alec said, loudly, "But that's the point, isn't it? That we're not keeping our heads above water. We're not managing."

"But you were," George said. "You *told* me you were."

"Well, I'm not," Alec snapped. "Or not enough. I've got some bills I can't pay and—"

"Then give them to me." George sounded exhausted. "You know very well I never wanted to turn you into a tradesman."

"Hartington," Melissa said, shooting Alec a look of startling viciousness. "May I remind you your son is to start at Eton next year, and your second son will also require an education."

"I will support my family. All of it." George spoke with determination that was as heartfelt as it was threadbare.

"How?" Melissa almost shouted. "You're already stretching every penny until it snaps! Will we turn off the cook next, or should you like me to black the grates myself to save the housemaid's wages?"

"Alec has never asked me for a penny before now and if he needs help this once—"

"It's not a case of *this once* and Melissa is quite right," Alec said. "There's no reason you should be responsible for my gambling debts."

There was a tiny silence, then George, Melissa, and Annabel all said, "Your *what?*" in a discordant chorus of fury. Alec's nausea rose; he could hardly have felt more guilty if he had indeed run up bills at baccarat. *Be Lord Alexander*, he told himself. *Play the part.*

"How can you gamble when you know damned well you can't pay?" George thundered over the two women. "What sort of irresponsible, stupid, dishonourable way to behave—?"

"Do you have *any idea* how hard George works?" Melissa was demanding. "Do you have any idea how much he already has to do for your family as well as his own?"

"How could you?" Annabel cried. "Haven't we been made enough of a disgrace already? Alec, how *could* you?"

Alec let his shoulders rise into a defensive hunch and adopted a petulant tone to match. "I'm Lord Alexander Pyne-ffoulkes. As George says, I oughtn't be a tradesman."

"You said you enjoyed it!" George protested.

"You promised you wouldn't ask George to pay your bills," Melissa added over him.

"Well, I'm not, and I don't see why you're all shouting at me as though I am. I don't have any intention of hanging off George's sleeve. I simply want to live according to my station, and I'm tired of this endless fighting with Father. Where did it get Cara?"

George's mouth dropped open. Annabel said, "Alec!"

"Well, it's true." The words came with surprising ease now, almost as though part of him believed them. "If Cara had given up fighting with Father she might be alive today, because she'd have been living by the sea instead of coughing her lungs up in London. She's dead, and we couldn't even send her off with flowers, and for what? It's not as though she persuaded anyone outside this room to take her part, or as though Father suffered in the slightest by her stand. It's all a stupid waste of time. I've only got one life and one chance to enjoy it and I'm going to take it."

"How can you?" Annabel whispered. "You know what he did."

"I know I'm a duke's son and I've spent eight years scraping a living where my peers are enjoying their youth," Alec said. "I know I'm twenty-eight and I don't have any prospect of more than a single room and drudging at the draughting table for the next thirty years and I'm embarrassed by my wardrobe when I mix with gentlemen. And I know that we'll never get the victory Cara wanted. Well, I don't propose to keep fighting a war I can't win for no gain at all. I'm sorry if you don't like it, but I don't much like living this way either."

Annabel had gone white. George was going red. Melissa looked between them, and at Alec, and he prayed with everything in him, *Don't agree with me, please, please don't agree...*

"You can't mean it," Annabel said. "You made a promise. Have you—have you been waiting for Cara to die so you can go back on your word?"

It was a dagger-stab, and Alec flinched. *Play the part*, he told himself fiercely. "Well, I do mean it, and I don't see that a promise is binding when the person one made it to is dead, and the fact it, it wasn't a fair promise in the first place. We only had Cara's word for the whole thing."

Annabel gasped shrilly. George rose. "Leave," he said, and the harried household manager sounded like a peer of the realm then.

"Get out of my house, Alec. I hope you will think again but don't come back until you do. Cara—your promise— Get out. Get out of my sight."

"There's no need to be like that," Alec said, through lips that hurt, and that was when George started shouting.

Alec was still stiff with misery the next day, filled with it so that every thought he had floated on a dark churning sea of unhappiness. He dressed for the evening with automatic movements and felt like an observer of the whole proceeding, as if he were watching himself on the stage. The Second Villain, weak and vile, cast out by his family.

He hadn't even heard back from his father. He'd cast every relationship that mattered into hazard, bet it all on a single card that wouldn't be turned over for God knew how long. If Father had his secretary write back to signal his lack of interest in his second son...

He did not want to go out with Crozier now. He wanted nothing less than to pretend friendship with the vicious devil who was escorting him down a path he should have rejected out of hand the moment it was proposed. But he was the one who'd started this, he'd thrown away the love and respect of his siblings by his own choice, and he might as well carry it through. So he dressed with no enthusiasm at all, and dragged himself wearily to the Cafe Royal.

Crozier was waiting at a table. He rose to greet Alec with a smile that turned to a look of concern in which Alec didn't believe for a minute. "I say, old fellow, are you all right?"

"Not marvellous," Alec said, sitting. "I've done that business of which we spoke when we last met. Wrote my letter. Spoke to my brother and sister."

"Have you had a reply to the letter?"

"No. It was entirely as you'd have wished," he added bitterly. "I crawled on my belly with all the unctuous phrasing at my disposal."

Crozier's brows rose. "You look like you need a drink. Waiter!" He lifted a finger. "We're in urgent need of a bottle of champagne here. Lord Alexander requires a hair of the dog that bit him before his respected father does the same. Talking of whom, is the Duke of Ilvar expected in tonight? Find out, will you?"

The waiter bowed and removed himself. Alec blinked. Crozier had suddenly become the epitome of the affable, confident, very nearly vulgar man about town, the character shift total and somewhat unnerving. "Are you serious? Is my father coming here?"

"I doubt it. I just want your presence noted. So, an unpleasant conversation with your siblings. What did you tell them?"

"That I'd decided to give in because I had gambling debts and I was tired of fighting."

Crozier nodded. "Well done."

"Is that all you have to say?" Alec demanded. He wasn't even sure what he thought Crozier should say; he simply wanted to hit back at someone in this miserable mess he'd created. "I've alienated my brother and sister, and for what?"

"In the larger sense, don't ask me," Crozier said. "From my point of view, you've taken a temporary loss to play for a very substantial gain."

"If it happens."

"Granted, but this is how you'll make it happen. It's a long game. I told you that."

The waiter reappeared with a bottle, which he uncorked with a loud pop, adding a bow to Alec and a murmured regret that His Grace of Ilvar was not in fact expected. Crozier thanked him, and slipped him a generous tip once the glasses were filled.

"Your health."

Alec made himself raise his own glass. "I've no desire to get drunk again."

"Very wise. But I'd rather you didn't look like a man on the way to his own execution. Can you cheer up, do you think?"

"I doubt it, since I've alienated the people I most care for," Alec said, low and savage. "You told me you weren't sorry for anything you've done. I'd like to know how you manage that."

"Practice helps. So does enjoying the fruits of your actions, which you won't do for a while. So, also, does reminding yourself that shame is merely society's weapon, used to keep us obedient."

"Sorry?" Alec said. "I wasn't expecting political philosophy."

"It's not complicated. I'm sure you've done things of which you'd be utterly ashamed if they were made public, while feeling perfectly content with the actions themselves. Therefore, shame isn't about what you do, just what gets found out."

"Rubbish," Alec said. "Of course we ought to be ashamed of things we do. I *am*."

"And will you withdraw your letter and tell Hartington and Lady Annabel you've changed your mind? Go back on yourself with nothing achieved?"

Alec snorted. "You sound like Macbeth. 'I am in blood stepped in so far that, should I wade no more, returning were as tedious as go o'er.' Nobody would ever repent based on that argument."

"People repent when they fail," Crozier said. "'But screw your courage to the sticking-place and we'll not fail.'"

"You know your Shakespeare. So you must know that attitude didn't go well for Macbeth."

"He was infirm of purpose. Are you?"

"I'm disgusted with myself." Alec tossed back his champagne in a gulp. Crozier reached across with the bottle to top up his glass. "If you're interested in how I feel, that's how. I feel dirtied and degraded in my own eyes—"

"I told you to create a part and act it."

"I did. But it's no good saying that my grovelling to Father was false if my brother's anger and my sister's disgust are real."

"But they aren't," Crozier said. "Or, at least, they aren't based in reality. They've formed a mistaken impression of you, admittedly because you've deliberately given them that wrong impression, but it's still wrong."

"And they still won't want to speak to me."

"How fortunate that you'll be preoccupied." Crozier's brows angled invitingly. "You've a lot of ground to make up with the Duke in a short time. I've got things in hand but you, my friend, will need a smile on your face. Tell me, what would put one there? You didn't seem a particular aficionado of the music hall. The opera? The theatre? Sporting events? No? Then what?"

As though Alec gave a damn for fashionable entertainments. "I don't care. Whatever you want."

Crozier picked up his glass and took a deliberate sip. "You're not listening. I want you looking significantly less doom-laden, so we're going to talk about things you enjoy. What are those?"

"Oh, I don't know. I like the theatre but I haven't seen anything recently, so I can hardly make conversation about that."

"Then I shall procure tickets for something. Melodrama or the nobler heights of Shakespeare?"

"Whatever you choose."

Crozier exhaled audibly. Alec hunched a shoulder. "You want to exhibit me in public as part of your 'long game'. Forgive me if I don't find that an enjoyable prospect."

Crozier's facial expression didn't change, but his eyes did. They hardened, or chilled, so that he looked quite suddenly like a man who broke the law for a living, and Alec felt a pulse of sudden alarm. He knew damned well he was behaving like a sulky boy over a fate he had brought on himself, and it seemed as though Crozier's patience with that had come to an end.

Crozier leaned forward over the table, wearing a pleasant smile that didn't touch his eyes. Alec knew an impulse to blurt an apology, if it would only head off whatever was coming.

"Lord Alexander," Crozier murmured in a confiding tone. "Apparently I need to make myself clear. The purpose of this excursion is to establish that you're charmed and delighted by your new best friend, so you will be charmed and delighted or I will fucking make you. I suggest you fix your thoughts on eleven thousand pounds' worth of shiny stones, and the chance to stick it to the Duke in a way he won't forget." He smiled with a clubman's practised warmth. "And if you still want to wallow in self-disgust and degradation, I will happily take you into a back alley and give you something to be really ashamed of. Anything to cheer you up."

Alec felt his mouth drop open. Crozier lifted his glass and tilted it as though making a toast. "I don't care how you approach your role, Lord Alexander. Willing or not, you're going to do what I want, so you might as well take it with grace. As it were."

Alec could feel, physically feel, the blood rushing to his cheeks. "That's—that's—"

"Entirely up to you," Crozier completed for him. "Notwithstanding, you seem to be struggling with all sorts of moral complexities and remorse and self-doubt, none of which I find troublesome. I could take charge of this, Lord Alexander."

"Take charge," Alec repeated.

"Make the decisions. Tell you what to say, and write, and do. I will make sure you come out of this job clean; you have my word as a dishonest man on that. Do as I tell you, and it will all be taken care of. Might it not be easier, and more pleasant, simply to do as you're told?"

Alec's toes curled in his shoes. His heart was pounding with a mixture of humiliation, anger, and desperation. *I'll fucking make you* still rang in his ears. "And how far does doing as I'm told extend?"

"Smile," Crozier said. "The waiter is coming. We're having a pleasant chat. Smile, *now.*"

Alec forced his mouth into the required shape. "I'm not hungry."

"But you're going to eat. Ah, marvellous," he added to the waiter with an instant smile. "Tell me, is Monsieur Francois offering his sweetbreads tonight? For both of us then, and a half bottle of Pouligny-Montrachet, I think. One hates to rush a good wine, but Lord Alexander has an engagement. Thank you."

"Do I have an engagement?" Alec asked when the waiter had gone.

Crozier divided the last of the champagne between their glasses. "Do you want one?"

"I don't know what you're asking." Alec felt a little flown by drink, very tired, exceedingly on edge. "I don't understand any of this. I don't know what to do. I had the most awful row with George and Annabel and I'm terrified my father won't write back and it will all have been in vain. I don't know what you want from me, and I'm tired of trying to make decisions when I'm not even sure I should be doing this at all."

"Then let me make them. It seems to me you've enough to do being Alec Pyne, illustrator. Why don't you put Lord Alexander under my direction?"

Alec could have wept. It was a momentary impulse, but so strong he had to shut his eyes briefly to regain control. He moistened his lips. Crozier's eyes flicked to his mouth as he did it, and he saw one brow tilt. "As long as—as long as you understand the difference."

"Well, I think I do," Crozier said. "Do you? It seems to me that Alec is a courageous, talented, dedicated artist making a success of himself on his own terms, with admirable determination for one brought up to be an idle waste of air."

"Oh." Alec felt himself going pink with shock and, undeniably, a twinge of pride.

"Whereas," Crozier continued, "and do correct me if I'm wrong, Lord Alexander might *be* that very idle waste of air. Lacking in all determination, all too ready to bend to the whim of a stronger will. Positively wanting to be given orders—or even not to be given a choice?—in a way that Alec's pride couldn't possibly condone."

"You make me sound like Dr. Jekyll and Mr. Hyde."

"Dr. Jekyll's hidden urges were monstrous ones, if I recall. Selfish cruelties and callousness. I think your secret vices are an entirely different matter."

"What about you?" Alec demanded. "Do you have a Mr. Hyde, or am I talking to him now?"

Crozier threw his head back and laughed. "Ha! No, the good doctor's potion wouldn't do much for me. I fear there's no virtuous do-gooder lurking within."

"You don't have a secret life as a vicar?"

"No, I'm straightforwardly disgraceful." Crozier grinned at him. "And you're changing the subject."

"So would you, if you were me."

"My friend, if I were you, I'd have gone out and taken what I wanted years ago. Or, rather, given it. May I make a proposal?"

"What?" Alex said, with some trepidation.

"We'll eat. Discuss work and theatre and light subjects. And then we'll go somewhere private and you will tell me, quite honestly, what, let us say, Lord Alexander wants, without shame or prevarication or fear of being overheard. The truth. Have you ever told anyone the truth?"

"More often than you, I'd bet!"

Crozier grinned crookedly. "On this specific subject. No, I didn't think so, somehow."

"Perhaps that's because I don't want to."

"Don't you?"

Alec shifted in his chair. He wanted to keep fighting, and he wanted to surrender. He felt an urge to toss Crozier's presumption back in his face, and a stronger one to give in, to confess the shameful desires and longings and see what happened. He wondered if he'd feel this urge to confess after participating in a robbery. *Only if the policeman is particularly handsome*, he told himself, and took up his glass to stifle a nervous laugh.

The sweetbreads arrived. Alec had forgotten Crozier had ordered for him, and the thought gave him an internal squirm that was somewhere between uncomfortable and enticing. He'd never have chosen sweetbreads, left to himself. They were delicious.

"So, the Shakespeare book," Crozier said. "Have you heard anything from the publisher yet?"

Alec made some reply, was drawn to explain the commissioning process for illustrators and the likely competitors for the role, and to his own astonishment became caught up in the conversation. It felt unreal to be discussing work, and a glass of Pouligny-Montrachet on top of the champagne added to that, but he rarely had the chance to talk shop except at the Sketch, and there he was always in competition with louder, more confident men who knew they belonged. Crozier wanted to listen to him, or was astonishingly good at pretending to, and Alec was startled to discover that his plate was clear.

Crozier summoned the waiter with a crook of his finger. Alec said, "Surely I—"

"Not at all. My pleasure. Shall we go?"

Alec followed him out. Neither had brought an overcoat; the evenings were getting warm, the air thick. Alec almost wished it was colder. He felt overheated and sweaty.

They walked in what any observer might have taken for companionable silence. Alec wondered if he'd find himself pushed down an alleyway. The tension throbbed in his wrists; he flexed his hands, trying to loosen fingers that felt clumsy.

If they went down an alleyway. If Crozier told him to go to his knees. If he could just forget, let go—

He hadn't thought about his family situation in an hour. He realised that with a small shock and felt a dull throb of misery at the reminder, but Crozier was knocking on a discreet door of a very ordinary-looking house, and greeted the slab-faced man who admitted them with a murmured word. Alec followed him in, trying to look around without showing that he was doing so. The house seemed to be a hotel, with a certain amount of noise and tobacco smoke issuing from down the hall. Crozier led the way upstairs to a small room, and ushered Alec in.

He'd expected a bedroom. He'd honestly expected that, rather than a sitting room with a small card table, a chaise longue, a couple of armchairs by the empty fireplace.

Crozier gestured to one of the chairs, and locked the door, an act that didn't make Alec feel any more secure. "There's brandy in the decanter, although it's bloody awful here."

"I've had enough, I think."

"You aren't missing anything." He seated himself in the opposite chair, steepling his fingers. "Well, then. We said you'd tell me what it is you want."

"No, you said that. I don't recall agreeing."

Crozier's lips curled. "And yet you're here."

That was undeniable. Alec stared at his own hands, ink-stained, the index finger dented by use of a pen. The faint noise of male carousing rose from downstairs.

"Tell me about Lord Alexander," Crozier said softly. "You've drunk Dr. Jekyll's potion. Alec Pyne goes in like the weatherman to his house, Lord Alexander comes out. What does he want?"

"Oh, not to be responsible," Alec said. His voice was rather thin. "To have someone—someone like you—tell him what to do. Not to have to struggle for job after job, always hoping and worrying. Not to feel guilty he can't support himself and his sisters while his brother feels guilty for not supporting him. Not to be constantly aware of—of things that are wrong. Not to care they're wrong."

"No. That's you," Crozier said. "Lord Alexander *doesn't* care. Lord Alexander is the weaknesses you fight, the moments of indulgence, the truth you'd prefer wasn't true. What does he want?"

Alec wanted to say that was nonsense. But it had been so easy to argue against his siblings, to reject Cara's insistence, and the promise they'd made her, and the lifetime of miserable helpless anger. He'd felt the power of the words as he'd spoken them, because they *were* true to his feelings in a horrible shameful way that he'd been trying to run from.

He tried to run from so much.

"And what does it mean if I tell you? That all of it is real? That it's what I am deep down?"

"That it's part of you," Crozier said. "Why should it not be? Dr. Jekyll came up with his potion to separate out his worse impulses from his better precisely because he had worse impulses. Everyone does. His tragedy came about because he tried to eliminate them."

"Whereas you think I should embrace them."

"I think you should acknowledge they exist, and then spend less time making yourself miserable about the fact that you're imperfect. Really, if you think *you're* flawed, you ought to spend a day with Templeton."

"But I don't want those impulses to exist," Alec said through his teeth. "That's the point."

"But they do. *That's* the point. You can try to eliminate every trace of them like Dr Jekyll and tear yourself apart, though preferably not in such a Gothic manner. Or you can accept that your soul is as tarnished and mouse-nibbled as everyone else's and consider what to do about it. You aren't really going to give up your work and grovel to your father for income, are you? No matter how much easier and more pleasant it might make your life?"

"No."

"Because?"

"Because it would be utterly shameful of me."

"Why? Where does the shame lie? Who would it harm?"

"Me," Alec said. "I'd be revolted by myself. It wouldn't be more pleasant, it would be weak, and wrong. Utterly wrong."

"Weak," Crozier repeated, dwelling on the word. "Very well. In that intriguing conversation a couple of days ago, you told me that whether you like taking orders depends on the order. Do you remember that?"

"Yes."

"Is that another of Lord Alexander's foibles, to enjoy submission? Is that weak too?"

Crozier's eyes were intent. Alec swallowed. He didn't like this probing. It felt as though a scalpel were gently separating congested layers of thoughts that had become matted and tangled together, and it hurt to have them picked apart. He'd thought Crozier was simply going to fuck him. "I. Uh."

"You aware that there is an entire industry of houses and whores that cater to such desires, because so many people share them?"

"Are you talking about flagellation and that sort of thing? Because I don't want that. At all," Alec added, to avoid doubt.

"Don't want to want it, or actually don't want it?"

"The latter. I've no idea why anyone would enjoy being whipped."

"No accounting for taste," Crozier said. "So what is your taste, Lord Alexander? What particular orders do you want to take? What is it you'd like to be made to do?"

Alec shut his eyes. He heard the soft sound of Crozier rising from his chair, sensed movement, felt a hand close gently on his chin.

"I asked you a question," Crozier said. "Answer me. Do you want to be told what to do—in the right circumstances?"

Alec's breathing rasped in his own ears. He wanted to say something, something clever or defiant, to push Crozier's hand away and tell him he was entirely wrong. It would be so much easier if he was wrong.

"I think Lord Alexander is looking to surrender himself," Crozier said softly. "That can go bad easily." Alec wasn't aware he'd reacted to that, but he felt Crozier's fingers tighten slightly all the same. "And, I suspect, did. What are you thinking of?"

"There was a man." Alec didn't open his eyes. The room was warm; Crozier's fingers were firm but not tight. He'd never told anyone this; there was nobody he could tell for the shame of it. Nobody except this stranger-friend, this openly dishonest man who demanded the truth, and now the words came with surprising ease. "I wanted—oh, just to have him do it. Up against a wall. I didn't need him to care for what I wanted; I just wanted him to have his way, you see. And I said that, and when he was done he, uh, he pulled me round and spat in my face. So when you ask what I want—"

"I see," Crozier said. "Christ. Good Lord, there are some cunts in this world."

Alec's eyes snapped open. Crozier released his face and propped his backside on the arm of the chair. "Do you know this fellow's name?"

Alec shook his head. "He was just a man. Someone I met in a public house. I suppose I—"

"Don't finish that sentence," Crozier warned him. "Unless you were going to say 'shouldn't have kicked him in the balls till he passed out', and even then I'd disagree. Well. That sounds a very discouraging experience."

Alec attempted a smile. "You might say so."

"Extraordinary. Here I am, entirely consumed by thoughts of pushing you up against a wall myself, biting your lovely neck and hearing you gasp as I have my way with that delectable arse, and you tell me about this mannerless tosspot. I'm offended."

Alec stared up, speechless. Crozier brushed a strand of hair over his ear, a touch so gentle that Alec shivered. "If you want to be used, Lord Alexander, you have no idea how I should enjoy using you. And I don't spoil my tools."

Oh God. Alec's throat was closing, and the blood was rushing away from his head. Crozier's smile crooked at his silence. "I did say *if.*" He was so close Alec could feel his heat. They hadn't kissed; they hadn't even touched. "Explain it to me. The heart of it, the thing you need. Not to be hurt, I grasp that, and not to be treated with contempt. So what is it that's making your breath short and your eyes so deliciously dark at this moment? What is it you want?"

"I don't know. I can't say."

"Lord Alexander?" Crozier took his chin again, fingers a little harder this time. "I want you to explain. I don't care how little you want to. You *will* tell me."

Alec swallowed. The room felt unbearably hot and close. "Not to—not to have a choice, I suppose."

Crozier gave a slow nod. "To say no and be overruled, powerless in a ravisher's hands? Is that your pleasure?"

"No. No, that's not—I don't—"

"Spit it out," Crozier said softly. "And don't shut your eyes. Look at me."

Alec clenched his hands, making himself get the words out. "It's not that I want to be forced to anything. I just want someone else in charge. That's all."

"Ah." It was a breath. "Not someone cruel, or careless. Just someone to take the burden of choice and responsibility and decision from you."

"Yes. Yes, that's it." It sounded extraordinarily simple, put that way, or extraordinarily foolish. "I dare say that's contemptible."

"You say wrong," Crozier told him. "A pliable, obedient young nobleman doing my bidding is the best idea I've heard in months. If you *wanted* to pant and beg and spend at my command, of course."

"Oh God."

Crozier's fingers released Alec's chin, skimmed down his throat. "You understand that I'm not a good man, don't you?"

"Yes."

"And yet you'd put yourself in my hands anyway." It wasn't exactly a question; it wasn't quite a statement either.

"Yes," Alec said anyway. It was what he wanted and Crozier had stripped it bare for them both.

"Entirely in my hands. Which is quite appropriate, since these hands steal jewels." He ran his fingers up Alec's neck, stroking the skin against the grain of stubble. "Such a pretty thing. Are you hard?"

Alec nodded. Crozier's fingers tightened a fraction. "I like words, Lord Alexander. If I ask you a question, I expect an answer. Are you hard?"

"Yes."

"Because?"

"You. You're making me hard."

Crozier rose, without letting go of Alec's neck, manoeuvring himself round so he leaned over the back of the chair. "Unbutton yourself."

Alec reached for his waistband. His fingers were shaking. Crozier said, "Slowly. No. Slower."

One button. A second, a third. Alec had kept his evening dress for longer than a man of wealth would; he was glad that it wasn't fashionably and tightly cut. He loosened his drawers, couldn't help inhaling as his fingers bumped his own prick.

"Take it out," Crozier said from over him. His hand encompassed Alec's throat, pushing back slightly, just enough to be not quite comfortable. "And take hold of it. Don't move."

Alec swallowed, his throat working against Crozier's fingers, his prick swollen against his own, throbbing for attention. Crozier gave a soft hiss. "Beautiful. You'll do what I tell you."

"Yes."

"Let's see you play with it. Slowly, now. Slide your fingers, up and down. Move your fingers round, I want to watch you." Alec adjusted his grip, dreamlike. "You're going to bring yourself off, very slowly, while I watch. I want to see you, and I want to hear you."

Alec groaned low, the sound vibrating in his throat and against Crozier's palm. He felt movement as Crozier leaned close.

"Rubbing yourself off in full evening dress, on the orders of a man whose face you can't see. There's a position to be in, Lord Alexander. Spread your legs wider. And slow down. I'm going to take my time."

"Are you—" Alec began, and clamped his lips shut.

"I said I want to hear you. Do you want to know if I'm bringing myself off while I watch you?"

"Well. Yes."

"No." Crozier sounded amused. "Tempting though it is. No, I think, when I next spend, it will be with you splayed before me and crying my name."

"Oh God."

"If you prefer, but Jerry will do."

Alec almost laughed, breath hiccupping. Crozier's hand was moving now, an undulating pressure on his throat, pulsing in time with the strokes of his own hand. "Yes, I'm looking forward to making use of you. Pressing you up against a wall or pushing you down onto a bed. Both, possibly. You don't like to talk when you fuck, do you?"

Alec shook his head, a tiny movement.

"I'll wager you moan, though. I'm quite sure you moan and whimper and writhe while a man has his way with you. Christ, I want to use your body till I'm sated and you're sobbing. Faster, now. I want you to spend knowing I'm going to fuck you, and how hard, and to think about spreading your legs when I tell you to—"

"Jesus!" Alec said, and then he was coming, prick pulsing in his fingers, Crozier's hand pushing brutally hard against his throat so that his head was held back as his hips jerked helplessly. Imprisoned, and coming for his gaoler. He gasped and spasmed, shuddering in relief, and Crozier's grip relaxed.

"Christ," he said, sounding almost a little shaky. "Well."

Alec licked his lips. He'd managed not to spend on his black trousers, thank heavens, but his hand was sticky. Crozier's arm came over the chair, holding out a handkerchief.

"Thanks," Alec managed.

"My pleasure. In every possible sense. Did I gauge that correctly?"

Alec nodded, concentrating on cleaning himself up, not sure he could look round. "Yes. Very much."

"Good. Excellent," Crozier said. "In that case, I will see you in, shall we say two days?"

Alec jerked round in the chair. Crozier was still leaning on the high back. He wore his usual mildly amused expression, except that his pupils were wide, his lips reddened and slightly parted. "But— Aren't you going to—"

Crozier extended one arm and touched his finger to Alec's lips, as a nursemaid would a child who needed silencing. "Who gives the orders here, Lord Alexander?"

It sent a shudder through him. "You," he said, against the pressure of the finger.

"If I want to fuck you, I'll tell you so. Or I'll just do it. Push you up against the wall without a word, shove your trousers down and have you in silence, without troubling to discuss the matter. I wonder if you'd come harder that way."

"I don't know," Alec whispered, feeling the pressure against his lips. *Please do that. Please.*

Crozier held his gaze for a moment longer, then stepped away. "We may find out, sooner or later. So we both know where we stand, I'm not going to seek permission, but I will take refusal." Alec nodded, but apparently that wasn't enough, because Crozier's eyes narrowed. "I'm not sure you're listening, Lord Alexander. If something is not to your liking you *will* say so. I don't take pleasure in inflicting unwanted suffering. Unlike wanted suffering, which I can do all day. Got it?"

"Yes. I'll say."

"Good. After all, I can be *so* much worse if I can push to the edges of your pleasures."

Alec gave him a look. "Is that intended to be an inducement?"

Crozier grinned evilly. "You tell me. Very well. I shall seek theatre tickets."

"You'll what?"

"Theatre. We discussed it at dinner, remember? I'm tempted to suggest the touring production of *Jekyll and Hyde*. It's well done, and seems somehow appropriate. I'd be happy to see that again."

"I've heard it's very good." Apparently they really weren't fucking any more. Alec got up, straightening his clothing, legs a little uncertain under him. "I'd like to see it."

"You'll receive instructions. If you haven't heard from your father by then, we will consult on next steps."

"Right. Yes."

"You look blank."

"I'm finding it quite hard to keep track," Alec said, with some understatement. "You know, being Second Villain to a jewel thief, and trying to manage my family situation, and having you do, er, what you just did, and then back to jewel theft. It's a bit confusing."

"I see no reason the duties of Second Villain shouldn't include being First Villain's helpless sexual plaything. It would make the melodramas a great deal more entertaining. Follow my lead, do as directed, and leave the rest to me."

Alec could almost feel the weight slipping from his shoulders. It was an appalling temptation. Crozier was a bad man; he'd made a point of that himself. Bad, highly competent, very evidently someone who liked to be in charge of every possible element. And all Alec had to do was give up and let him take over.

"Good Lord, you look exhausted," Crozier said. "Let's get you a growler."

"I don't have the funds. And you can't keep paying for me."

"Oh, the Duke of Ilvar will be paying eventually. Don't worry about that. In fact, don't worry at all about any of it." He ran a finger gently down Alec's face, slid it under his jaw. "Everything is entirely under control."

# Chapter Four

Alec did his best the next day. He tried to work. He tried not to listen for every knock at the door in case it was the postman bearing a letter from his father. He tried not to think of what would happen if his father rejected his overtures and he'd alienated his siblings in vain, and he tried particularly hard not to think about Crozier's promises to take care of it.

*Everything is entirely under control.* It was so tempting to believe him.

Alec had been seven when his mother died, quite old enough to be aware of the world fracturing around him. He'd been left in no doubt of the relative importance his father placed on his second wife and his offspring; he'd also been very thoroughly taught at school that the sins of the father were visited upon the children. Alec had been a pariah for years, the other boys gleefully repeating the things their parents said about the Duke of Ilvar and his new Duchess. If only they'd known.

Growing to manhood and carving out his own career hadn't brought any more certainty. It should have—and, Alec had sometimes thought in rebellious moments, it would have, if he'd cut himself off from his brother and sisters. If he was permitted to be plain Alec Pyne who earned his own living and mixed with journalists and artists and was of no interest to anyone... But he wasn't, because he was Lord Alexander and his behaviour reflected on his brother and sisters, clinging onto gentility by their fingertips.

Cara had once suggested Annabel might train as a copyist, a perfectly respectable occupation for a woman. Alec still winced at the memory of that argument, and George and Melissa's fury. They were the heirs to Ilvar; sooner or later Father would die, and George would be duke, and assuming Father hadn't ploughed every bit of his capital into jewels for the Duchess by then, they'd be able to take their place in society. But not, as George had pointed out, if his sister were a type-writer and his brother a newspaper drudge. They had to hold to their stations in life or they would be nothing. What sort of man would marry Lady Annabel Pyne-ffoulkes, with no portion to speak of, if he had to pluck her from an office?

Alec's descent to the industrious classes didn't reflect nearly so badly on the family as Annabel's would, but George had still been disappointed that Alec was working at all, and that, since he was working, he wasn't doing so in a bank or a stockbrokers' firm. That would have been a respectable occupation, where he could actually bring in enough money to make a difference or, even better, strike a bargain with a banker's daughter who would pay to become Lady Alexander. If only Alec had had the capacity.

It had added up to a wearyingly familiar sense of isolation even before his estrangement from his siblings. Cara had known him, but she was dead; George tried his best, but he'd never understand. Work had brought friendships as far as they went with people constantly scrabbling for the same jobs, but little else. It had come out very quickly that he was titled—one could hardly mix with people who worked on the papers and expect to keep that sort of secret—and his colleagues had generally lost interest in him when he'd refused to spill secrets of Society that he mostly didn't have. And his private life was, frankly, a blank. He'd had plenty of encounters, thanks to boyish good looks—he had a feeling that wouldn't be the case much longer, given his blond hair had started to grey and his wide blue eyes were acquiring crow's feet—but nothing that had lasted. Men didn't tend to seek him out twice; he was silent and passive to a fault in the bedroom and the kind of men who liked that in a partner had not so far proved to be men he wanted anything to do with.

The fact was, he reflected as he sketched the next day, sunlight streaming through the skylight and hot on his hand, he was lonely. He was neither fish nor fowl socially, he disappointed his family whatever he did, and though he had plenty of acquaintances, he had very few real friends. He'd never had those, because how could you make friends when you couldn't tell people the truth?

He'd told the truth—one truth—to Jerry Crozier and he wasn't quite sure why, except that he'd already put himself in the man's power so he could scarcely make matters worse. That, and there was something about Crozier's shameless confidence, the casual authority, that Alec wanted in his own soul. Wanted to have, wanted to be had by: he wasn't sure which.

He wished to God he could talk to someone about this, but there was nobody, and he wasn't sure what he'd say anyway. *This fellow told me to stroke myself off while he watched. No, that was all. No, he didn't touch me, except for his hand on my throat. Not like that, I could breathe, just holding me still. Yes, best fuck of my life. No, I can't name him. He'd be angry if I spoke about him in any way, and he frightens me a little bit.*

It was an uncomfortable thought. Crozier could be a charming companion and an intelligent listener, and he'd teased out precisely what Alec wanted so carefully and given—no, *offered*—it to him. And yet he was frightening; he took what he wanted and wasn't sorry, and when Alec had tried his patience too much, the look in his eyes had been genuinely alarming.

Alec had put himself in this dangerous man's hands anyway, and been promised that everything was under control, and the dreadful thing was, he believed it.

He didn't get a great deal done that day. The next day brought a rejection on the Shakespeare job, which was a blow, an acknowledgement of his submitted artwork for the fairytale book, and a stiff note from George requesting he reconsider his foolish actions and offering fifty pounds to meet his immediate obligations. Alec doubted Melissa would be happy if she heard about that, sent his brother an appreciative thought, and penned a brief, sulky note of refusal. There was no letter from his father.

What would, what *could* Crozier do if the Duke chose not to reply?

He'd find out soon, he decided, because the second post brought a ticket for *The Strange Case of Dr. Jekyll and Mr. Hyde* plus a scribbled note on Army and Navy Club notepaper:

*Evening dress not required.*
*Call me Jerry.*

The former was a relief, since he'd sent his one shirt for laundry; he wasn't entirely sure what to make of the latter. Jerry. It seemed uncomfortably intimate, but intimacy was the impression they were trying to give in public, and if one could toss oneself off at a man's command, one could surely use his first name.

He put on his better suit and the green waistcoat, spent too long prodding at his hair, and went out with a jangling combination of nerves and excitement, and a little pot of petroleum jelly in his pocket because one never knew.

Jerry was lounging outside the theatre when Alec arrived, chatting with the doorman. He straightened as Alec approached. He looked rather more clubbable today, in a smart check, like an ordinary sort of man about town. "And here he is. Good evening, Lord Alexander."

"Jerry, old fellow." Alec found he was smiling. "I hope I'm not late?"

"Not at all. Thanks for your advice, Drummond." He tipped the doorman, raised his hat in jovial manner, and led the way in.

"What did you want of the doorman?" Alec enquired.

"It never hurts to make friends in low places. Particularly when they can obtain one boxes at short notice, and let one know about the comings and goings of all sorts of interesting people."

And doubtless let other people know about Alec's comings and goings with Jerry. He nodded and followed his companion through the crowd to the stalls.

The play was marvellous. Alec had loved the book, and though the stage version lacked its subtlety, the atmosphere of terror was superbly done, and Mr. Mansfield's twisting physique truly horrifying as he shifted from the philanthropic, kindly Dr. Jekyll to the monster of selfishness Hyde. Alec shuddered along with the mystery, gasped at the cruel attack on the harmless old man, found himself praying that Dr. Jekyll would somehow overcome his worse self even while he knew the end was inevitable.

And all the while he was aware of Jerry Crozier next to him, very close, not touching. He didn't think Jerry's attention was on the play.

They went along to the Coal Hole on the Strand afterwards for a bite to eat. It was noisy, the kind of loud masculine noise Alec didn't much like, with red-faced men braying and shouting and a pall of smoke hanging over everything, but the food was good.

"What news?" Jerry enquired once they'd addressed a generous portion of steak and kidney pudding. He had to speak loudly even with Alex close up to him on the shared table, calf pushed up against calf.

"Nothing. Or, negative news. I didn't get the Shakespeare commission."

"Ah, that's a shame. Sorry to hear it."

"Well. And there's been no response to my letter either."

"There, I can offer some assistance," Jerry said. "Your father and his wife will be at Lady Sefton's soirée on Saturday. If I obtain invitations for us both, is he likely to cut you dead?"

"If you *what?* How will you do that?"

"Don't worry about it. Answer the question."

"I…don't know," Alec said. "I don't even know if he'll recognise me. I haven't seen him in eight years."

"It could be worse. At least you haven't had any recent blistering rows. Well, we won't take any chances."

"What are you going to do?" Alec asked uneasily.

"Leave it to me. And make sure you look your best. Do you have all the needful—gloves and so on? I want you looking smart as a new pin. No poverty in evidence."

Alec thought of his last pair of gloves, unfortunately yellowing. "Um. I can probably—"

"No probably. We'll deal with that."

"Why? That is, he'll surely assume I've got back in touch for the money, so why pretend I haven't?"

Jerry clicked his tongue. "Because we don't want to embarrass him. If you look shabby-genteel, it would be a reproach to his paternal care. There will be plenty of people watching to see how you behave: it must be with the greatest filial respect. Nothing for which the highest stickler could reproach you or your father, or indeed your stepmother."

"Yes. Of course."

His reluctance must have been clear. Jerry gave him a sideways look. "You know you'll have to do her equal courtesy, if not more."

"Yes."

"And you're monosyllabic again. Is that really harder to swallow than the other?"

Alec's chest felt tight. He didn't much want to discuss this here, so he simply nodded.

Jerry sighed. "Will this be a problem?"

"No. I'll do it. I don't much relish it, that's all."

Jerry contemplated him, then tossed a few coins on the table. "Come on."

"Where?"

"Outside."

Alec followed, once again. Out of the Coal Hole, down Carting Lane's steep slope, through the shadows of tall buildings on each side, towards the smell of the river, salty at the high tide but still stinking of fish and rotten wood, and down towards Victoria Embankment Gardens. Alec's pulse was hammering. It was far too risky here; one did sometimes see men sneaking in and out of the bushes, but the chance of a patrolling constable was far too high and it was twilight now, not pitch dark.

Yet Jerry strolled on, unconcerned, and Alec paced him, heart in his throat, feeling himself hardening almost in response to the tension, waiting to be pushed into the bushes.

Jerry didn't break his stride. They went through the gardens, onto the Embankment, and to Alec's bewilderment, came to a stop to look out over the softly heaving river.

"Er," Alec said.

"Fresh air, for a given value of fresh," Jerry said. "And a chance to speak in slightly more peace. Why do you loathe your stepmother so much, when it's your father who had the responsibility to you? Or are we blaming her for his failings?"

"I blame them both. She's a horrible woman—proud, unkind, resentful—and he's done everything in his power to encourage her. He's selfish and weak, and all the crueller because he's weak, and she encourages that. They make each other worse."

"And yet she's harder to swallow?"

"Well, I'm meant to honour my father," Alec said. "The Bible says so. Maybe it's easier for me to hate her."

He fixed his eyes on the water, black in the dimming light. He could feel Jerry's gaze.

"Maybe," Jerry said at last. "All the same, I want you making your obeisance to her as though she were the Queen of England. If she's proud, you feed her pride. If she's uncertain of her position underneath the facade, you show absolute certainty. Whatever she wants to hear from you. Got it? You and I need to be invited to Castle Speight, and if you get this right we will be, and once Temp and I have a foot in the door, my degenerate scion of a noble race, your troubles will be over. What game are we playing?"

"The long game," Alec said, half annoyed, half amused at being instructed. "I do recall. I'll do it. Er, how do you propose to get Mr. Lane in?"

"As my valet. He makes rather a good one. Has a way with servants."

"Gosh. And, I really do have to ask, how on earth can we go to Lady Sefton's soirée when I for one am not invited?"

"Oh yes you are," Jerry said. "Our names will be on the guest list, and nobody will question that. I should mention that mine is Vane."

"Sorry?"

"Gerald Vane. A *very* distant relation of the Marquess of Cirencester's family, with no claim at all on their notice," he added, with a self-deprecating smile that Alec would bet he'd practised in a mirror, it was so perfectly pitched.

"Isn't that a bit risky? What if there's a Vane there?"

"There's dozens of Vanes. The family runs to multiple sons and has done for generations. There's no reason at all you should doubt my claim to the name, by the way, since I was introduced to you as such by a gentleman in a club who now escapes your memory."

"In case anyone asks later on?"

"You're getting the hang of this. I'll collect you at your lodgings at eight on Saturday. Make sure you've eaten. I don't want attacks of nerves or incautious drinking. Then just follow my lead."

"What? I mean, are you not going to tell me what to do?"

"With all due respect, you're no Mr. Mansfield," Jerry said. "And moreover, we—Templeton and I—take a Wellingtonish approach to plans: we react and adapt. I don't want you expecting any particular thing to happen; I want you to have a very pleasant evening, and to react to whatever may occur as you would normally. Just remember that you want to return to your father's good graces, and if your terribly exciting and dashing new friend provides a way to do that, naturally you will seize the opportunity."

"I don't know if my father likes dashing and exciting people," Alec suggested cautiously.

Jerry clicked his tongue. "Give me some credit."

"Leave it to you?"

"Everything in my hands. It worked before."

The words tingled through Alec. "This is rather different, though."

"Yes and no," Jerry said. "You find yourself unsure of what you want, how to get it, and whether you even ought to try. Well, I know what you want, I can supply it, and I have no doubts as to your capacity. I think you have *remarkable* potential." He drawled the adjective as if giving it a long, slow stroke. "And I'm going to prove it to you."

Alec swallowed. "Are you?"

"Do you know what I most enjoy about my work?" Jerry said, unexpectedly.

"The money?"

"Ha. No. That, as they say, is how one keeps score. No, I like the unseen power, the knowledge that we have and others don't. I will walk through Lady Sefton's marble halls on Saturday, and spread my nets to snare the Duke of Ilvar, and nobody but you and I will know what we're doing there. I'll move them like chess pieces, the ladies and gentlemen of wealth, and they won't even know they're pawns."

Alec believed it. Jerry's words had a quivering tension that made his toes curl and sent shivers of alarm and excitement up his spine. "That's a disturbing tack to take."

"You think so?"

"Well. Yes?"

"You don't see the appeal in knowing something they don't know?"

"Not really."

Jerry turned to face him, and jerked his head. "With me." He strode off without explanation. Alec followed, through the haloes of gaslight that pierced the gathering darkness, towards the dark underbelly of Waterloo Bridge. A friend had been relieved of his watch, wallet and tiepin there quite recently. He thought he could see shapes moving in the gloom.

"Ought not we go round, or up the stairs?" he suggested.

"No."

"But—"

"Lord Alexander." Jerry's tone was quite calm. Alec swallowed, and followed, into the cold, dank depths under the great bridge. The shadows were deepest between the huge supports and there were figures in those shadows, just visible, and sounds of panting, the slap of flesh. It stank of river-mud and damp stone and human dirt.

Jerry took his arm and pulled him into the dark. Alec went with him, almost stumbling, and was turned and shoved towards a wall he could barely see. He put his hands up automatically and found them pressed against slimy-rough brickwork, his face to the wall, Jerry's foot between his own feet, kicking them wider. Then there was a push of a body against his back, and Jerry's breath on his neck as he leaned heavily in, and Alec braced his forearms against the wall and tried to remember how his lungs worked.

"Lord Alexander." Barely a whisper to his ear; Jerry's hand sliding round his hips and cupping his groin. Alec moaned in his throat, trying to keep silent because this was insanely dangerous, pushing forward into Jerry's possessive hand. Jerry was massaging him, a firm, deliberate pressure through his clothing, and he was hard himself, a stiff stand pushed against Alec's arse. Alec had no idea what he was going to do, and if Jerry kept this up he'd spend in his drawers from the terrified excitement.

Jerry squeezed his bulge. Alec couldn't help a breathy whimper, and then his buttons were being undone, warm strong fingers intruding between his legs, and Jerry had his prick in hand. He wrapped his fingers around Alec, still for a long second, and his hand moved. Alec bit his lip savagely to keep silent as that commanding hand worked him with short, sharp strokes, the urgency and the terrible recklessness of this combining in a rush of excitement. He came absurdly fast, pulsing violently against the wall, with the stink of the river in his nose.

He sagged. Jerry's arm tightened, pulling him upright, mouth to his ear. "Remember this. When you greet Lady Sefton on Saturday, when you play the gentleman and introduce me to the Duke, remember that I had you like a cheap tart under Waterloo Bridge. I promise you, Lord Alexander, you're going to love that. Now tidy up."

He tugged at Alec's waistband. Wordless, Alec tucked himself away. He did up his buttons before he turned, despite the darkness; Jerry took his arm and they headed out of the deepest shadows of the bridge. Two, three steps towards the relative brightness of the gaslit night, and then a bulky figure stepped into their way.

"Oi." A deep voice. "What's this?"

Jerry gave a weary sigh. "My good man, kindly move aside."

"Suppose I don't." The man came forward. His silhouette didn't suggest a policeman, thank God, but that was all the good that could be said, and Alec could feel a stir of interest from the huddled figures around them, as well as some rapid footsteps hurrying away—probably other indulgers thanking their lucky stars. "What's a couple of swells doing down here? I reckon I ought to call the peelers. What about that, eh?"

"Pair of mollies," a high voice came from the dark, adding an epithet, and there was a giggle. Alec's stomach tensed with apprehension. False complaints of indecency were a highly profitable line, and most men would pay up to avoid the humiliating consequences even if they were innocent. It would be a great deal worse if this alley extortioner knew they were guilty.

Jerry had both hands up, placating. "Now, look, fellow, let's be reasonable, eh? There's no need for unpleasantness."

"I'll tell you what there's need for." The man took another intimidating step forward. Alec shrank away, and hated himself for it, even as the thug poked a finger into Jerry's shoulder, looming over him.

"Please, my good man," Jerry said, sounding rather less confident now. "Really, there's no need for trouble. I'm sure we can come to an amicable—"

Alec didn't see it coming. Jerry was still speaking as his right arm stabbed up in an uppercut at brutally close range, driving under the man's ribcage as if trying to punch him in the heart. An immediate left hook to the stomach drove the air from the thug's belly; Jerry put a savage knee into his groin, and then as the man folded forward, Jerry caught his hair and brought up his knee again, this time into his victim's face. There was a crunch, and the big man went down to all fours making an airless, gargling sound.

And now they could run. Alec shot a glance at Jerry to make sure he was coming, but he wasn't. He'd moved back a little, and as Alec stared he took one light step forward, and kicked.

It was not the kind of kick Alec had seen in brawls, short jerky stabs of the foot. It was, in fact, very reminiscent of the kick with which Preston North End's centre forward had started the FA Cup Final when Alec had illustrated it for a boy's paper. There was a terrible, meaty thwack as Jerry's foot connected with the man's head; he went arching over backwards, hit the ground heavily, and didn't move again.

"Scream for the peelers and I'll come back and fucking do you," Jerry said loudly, apparently for the benefit of the watchers, because the man on the ground didn't look as though he was in any state to hear anything. "Goodnight, all."

He strode off. Alec stared after him for a second, and then almost sprinted to catch up, feeling his shoulder blades tense with the consciousness of the people behind him. There was absolute silence from the shadows.

Jerry led the way along the Embankment heading towards Temple station, but turned up Surrey Street, through a flow of people, until they were on the brightly lit Strand once more.

"Uh, Jerry? Ought we not to, to…"

"What?"

"Send help? I think he might need a doctor," Alec said, with some understatement.

"Any fuckster who tries to blackmail me may think himself lucky not to need a mortuary." Jerry spoke with a certainty far more alarming than any threat. "You know what that fellow was up to. He's learned a valuable lesson about attempting extortion."

"He might die!"

"Yes. That was the lesson."

Alec stared. Jerry shrugged.

"But—"

"But what? Are you suggesting I should have paid him? Appealed to his better nature? Let him take my wallet and call the peelers anyway?"

"We were under Waterloo Bridge," Alec said, from the side of his mouth, voice low. "If one does that kind of thing—"

"Then what? One can expect to be beaten and blackmailed, and one deserves it? Do you suggest we ought to have paid up as some form of molly tax?"

"Well…" Yes, Alec realised, that was indeed what he thought, or at least, what seemed inevitable. Of course one would be threatened, blackmailed, punished. That was how the world worked. "No, I'm not saying that, but if one breaks the law—"

"Extortion is illegal," Jerry pointed out. "Blackmail is a consequence of gross indecency, getting one's head kicked in is a consequence of blackmail, and so the world spins. Why should your actions merit punishment and his escape it?"

Alec wasn't sure how to answer that. "Well, what about your actions? Isn't arrest the consequence of what you do?"

"Indeed, so I take steps to avoid it. If someone wants me to take the consequences, they'll have to make me. That's how it works. No Fate, no great hand of divine justice. Can you not think of any upright gentleman who's got away scot free with crimes that others would hang for?"

Alec stopped dead. Jerry took half a pace onward, then turned with a frown. "Alec?"

"Nothing," Alec said. "Sorry. I'm sure you're right, and in any case I'm not going to go back down there to help that man, so I'm probably being stupid. I think I should go home. I'm a little tired."

Jerry raised a hand for a cab, and one duly moved off from a rank a little way down the street. Alec wanted to know what it was about his manner that made his hand so much more visible than Alec's used the same way. "I will collect you on Saturday. Keep what I told you in mind, won't you? And—" He removed something from a pocket and pressed it into Alec's palm as part of a handshake. "Get yourself ready, Lord Alexander. We're going to make your father proud."

Alec looked at the paper when he was alone in the cab. He wasn't even surprised to see a ten-pound note.

He shut his eyes and leaned back against the hard seat.

That was the second time Jerry had—he wasn't even sure what verb to use. *Brought him off* didn't begin to describe it. Jerry had fucked him, no matter how little physical contact had been involved, and Alec was uncomfortably aware he hadn't done a damn thing in return. He was quite used to men whose only concern was their own cockstand, and if Jerry had, for example, first brought himself off and then ordered Alec to do it for him under the arches, that would have been entirely comprehensible in a way this wasn't. Or if he was one of those who only liked to watch—but Alec could still feel the hard pressure against his arse from earlier. He didn't at all understand this.

Maybe Jerry simply liked men to be putty in his hands. The way he'd spoken about the power he'd hold over wealthy people oblivious to the serpent in their midst; the way he'd spoken of the Duke.

Alec thought about Jerry Crozier's cold lust for control, and the few seconds it had taken him to leave a deadly threat unconscious and bleeding, and the fact that he'd unleashed this man on his own father. He was still thinking about that when the cab drew up on Mincing Lane, and when he got out, he was smiling.

# Chapter Five

Saturday.

Alec hadn't heard anything from Jerry in the intervening period, which had been mostly a relief, nor from his father, which was not. He'd harboured a tiny hope that the Duke or his secretary might send some acceptance that would make it unnecessary for Alec to arrive at a house to which he wasn't invited, greet a host who hadn't invited him, and play a role he hadn't been told about to achieve an end he didn't understand.

It was the stuff of nightmares, and Alec had no idea why he wasn't paralysed by terror. Perhaps it was so much a nightmare he couldn't believe he was doing it, and thus he could drift on as though it were all a fantasy. Perhaps it was Jerry, who seemed to walk in another world altogether, one in which theft and violence and gross indecency were casual diversions, and who'd put Alec so firmly under his thumb. Panicky helplessness merged with the sense of surrender to Jerry's will until he wasn't sure what was fear and what arousal.

He read the newspaper avidly but saw no reports of a death or even a serious assault under Waterloo Bridge. He also bought new gloves, had his clothes pressed, his shoes polished, and his hair cut, and at eight o'clock on Saturday he was ready and waiting in his room when Mrs. Barzowski announced his guest in tones of barely-suppressed excitement.

Jerry strolled in. He looked superb, impeccable from sleek hair to shoes, with a rosebud of vivid pink in his buttonhole.

"Elegant," he said, looking Alec up and down appreciatively. "Very grand indeed. Finery suits you."

"It suits everyone."

"Not at all. Templeton in evening dress looks like a gorilla that fell into a tailor's shop."

Alec choked. Jerry grinned, strolling closer. "So. Ready?"

"I hope so."

"What's my name?"

"Vane. Gerald Vane."

"Excellent. Shall we go?"

"No. Wait. Sorry, but what if I get this wrong?" Alec blurted. "I'm truly not sure what you want of me."

"I want you to go to a party—you can do that, yes? To make pleasant small talk. And, when an opportunity arises, to greet your father and stepmother with respect and courtesy, and introduce me as your friend. That's all. Well, almost."

"What else?"

Jerry smiled again, slower. "I told you to remember something. Do you?"

"Yes, but right now—"

"What was it?"

Alec made a frustrated noise. Jerry came another step closer. "Bear in mind," he said softly, "you are Lord Alexander this evening. My Second Villain. What do I want you to remember?"

Alec met his eyes. "You had me against a wall under Waterloo Bridge."

"Like a cheap tart. Shall I do it again?"

"Not under Waterloo Bridge."

Jerry stroked a finger across Alec's jaw, trailed it down his neck, onto his shoulder, walking around him as he did it. Alec stood, still and straight, feeling Jerry come close behind him, the finger stroking up his throat again, under his jaw. "How about at Lady Sefton's soirée?"

"You can't!"

"I could," Jerry murmured. "I'm very tempted by the possibility. It would be absurdly risky, needless to say, but you are so deliciously obedient, I feel almost obliged to abuse that. I think I could take any liberties I like with this lovely unresisting flesh. I *know* I could. Are you aware your breathing changes when you're getting hard?"

"No," Alec said, voice somewhat high.

"You may take my word. I can hear you wanting me." His other hand was sliding up and down Alec's arm. "Do you know what I want?"

"I don't have the faintest idea."

Jerry laughed, a breath of air against his neck. "I want to make you spend, again and again, until you're whimpering. I want you aching for what will happen when I next put my hands on you. I want you so trained to my touch that your breathing hitches when I walk into the room. I want to wind up your anticipation until you're quivering for my orders, begging for them."

"You want a plaything," Alec whispered.

Jerry's hands paused. "If you choose to put it like that. Do you want to be one? No thought, no will"—his thumb slid over Alec's lips, pushed in—"just responding?"

"God. Yes. Please."

"Then there we are. A match made in heaven. Oh, I will make you beg to be played with, Lord Alexander."

"What about you?" Alec said. "We've done this twice and you haven't—"

"Please," Jerry murmured into his neck. "Do I strike you as a philanthropist?"

Alec almost laughed. "I can't say you do, no."

"I will take my pleasure as it suits me, when it suits me. *If* it suits me, and not until." He puffed a breath into the nape of Alec's neck, making him shiver. "Now. You and I will attend this milling crowd of fools, and if your thoughts are three-quarters on what we'll be doing afterwards, that is no bad thing. You won't be afraid, because I am in control, and you won't fear your own performance because I am in control of that too. Understand?"

Alec grimaced, unseen. "If you say so."

"I beg your pardon?"

"Yes. Yes, all right."

Jerry's hand tightened. "I'm in control, of everything. Understand?"

"You're in control," Alec repeated, and this time he felt a tiny loosening in his tight nerves. Of course Jerry knew what he was about. Of course he had a plan. He let himself relax into the feeling. "Carry on."

"That is my very good partner in crime." Jerry moved away as he spoke. "Take a moment, because the line of your suit is not helped by the stand you're sporting. And then we will go, and we will enjoy this. Trust me."

Alec stared forward. There were a number of things he wanted to ask: *Why don't you ever look in my face when we do this? Do you want me, really, or is this all to keep me up to the mark? What exactly are we doing?*

Did it matter? This wasn't the sort of affair that gave a chap a false sense of hope, the kind that even briefly made one think that there might be some kind of companionship and affection. Alec knew and hated that hopeful feeling because it so inevitably led to painful disappointment. No matter how hard he tried to expect nothing at all, he always found himself yearning for more, imagining that this time might be different, and simultaneously waiting on horrible tenterhooks for the withdrawal, boredom, excuses that he knew would come.

He couldn't fool himself now. One would be a madman to hope for anything from Jerry Crozier. One couldn't feel deceived when one knew from the start that the chap was up to his 'long game'; one couldn't be disappointed in an affair if one truly had no expectations of one's partner. There was nothing here but the fucking. And if Jerry really wanted what Alec had to offer in that regard, if he wanted to take the reins that Alec wanted to surrender—well, it wouldn't be safe, or sane, but it would meet a need he'd never been able to fulfil with more normal, less criminal men.

He was riding a tiger. He might as well enjoy it.

"You look lost in thought," Jerry said. "Pleasant thought, too. Hold on to that, and let's go."

Lady Sefton's town house in Belgravia was bright with electric light, spilling out into the evening. Alec and Jerry abandoned the cab two streets away and walked there, resplendent in black. They'd travelled in silence from Eastcheap. Alec didn't have anything to say except "Are you sure this will work and we won't be thrown into the street?", and he already knew the answer he'd get. Whether he believed it was up to him.

There was a thin stream of men in black and women in bright colours making their way up the impressive outer stairs. Jerry joined them with a casual, confident stride that Alec concentrated on matching. Up the stairs, and to the open door where a butler stood, flanked by a dozen footmen to take overcoats—Jerry had told him not to wear one, or a hat—and a man in evening dress waited by a lectern. It was a visitor's book, Alec realised, which was to say a courteous way of ensuring Lady Sefton knew who was coming in.

Jerry gave a nod. "Mr. Gerald Vane and Lord Alexander Pyne-ffoulkes. Thank you." He didn't pause, simply strolling in. Alec hurried after him, unable to believe the man at the lectern wouldn't hold up a hand or call them back.

He didn't. Alec caught Jerry up and they followed the sound of a string quartet drifting along the ground floor. A wind instrument playing something else was audible upstairs. He should have known this would be a musical evening: the Seftons were famous for their patronage of the arts. Alec was preparing, with no great enthusiasm, to make intelligent remarks about music when a hand landed on his arm.

The thought *Police!* erupted in his head with stunning force. He whipped round in a panic and saw a familiar, grinning, puzzled face.

"I say, Pyne-ffoulkes, isn't it? Did I startle you? Romley, you recall, from school. It is you, isn't it?"

"It is indeed," Alec responded, trying to force his heart back down his throat. Jerry had vanished from the corner of his vision. "I do beg your pardon, I was in a brown study."

"I'm not surprised," Romley said. "Do you know, there's no card room, and all this tootling is enough to drive a man to drink. *And* there's an opera singer later."

"Oh, there's not."

"At least the champagne's cold. Come and take a glass, I haven't seen you in an age. What have you been up to?"

Jerry had made him practise how he would deal with this. Deflection first. "Yes, it's been an awfully long time. But what brings you here, if it isn't your love of music?"

Romley snorted. "My fiancée, what else?"

"Oh, congratulations," Alec said. "Who's the lady, and does she realise the challenge that faces her?"

He didn't actually remember a thing of Romley beyond his face and a vague impression he'd been good at rugger, but that kind of remark was obligatory, and got the obligatory laugh. Romley swept two glasses of champagne from a passing waiter, and proceeded to drink his own and two more while Alec sipped at his. He asked Alec twice what he'd been up to and why he hadn't seen him around; Alec headed that off with mentions of his bereavement, which would naturally exclude him from parties for six months, and then a vague reference to keeping his nose to the grindstone.

"But ain't your father a duke?" Romley demanded. He wasn't slurring, but his face was going distinctly pink. "My old fellow's a banker himself, insists a man should make his own living. Sitting on his moneybags and doling out a measly allowance."

"It's the new way," Alec said. "Modern times. Work's the thing for improving moral character and all that. I dare say there's something in it."

Romley snorted. "Nonsense. Let the fellows who want to get ahead work, and then hand on their earnings to the fellows who don't, that's what I say."

Alec made a noncommittal noise that Romley could interpret as polite agreement and led the conversation off down a path of school reminiscence, a feat that proved surprisingly easy. He was, he realised, enjoying this rather more than he'd thought possible. He dreaded the few social events George or Annabel pressed him to attend, but when one treated the intrusive questions as a game, seeing how easily they could be turned away, their sting seemed less and their meaning more distant.

Romley introduced him to a couple more gentlemen. Alec found his role settling on his shoulders easily. He resisted any temptation to voice opinions that could be construed as critical of his father, smiled pleasantly, asked men about themselves and told them they were interesting ("never fails", Jerry had said with an eye roll). He wasn't sure if this was what Jerry had wanted, but he'd been told to make himself pleasant and in the absence of other instruction, he did it.

Perhaps ninety minutes into the evening, he heard the raised voices.

They weren't that raised. He was in the hall and the speakers were in the main drawing-room. The hubbub of conversation through the house was quite drowning out the musicians' efforts. But he still picked out the raised voices because he'd heard them so often before.

He excused himself from his little group, and headed towards the sound of the Duke and Duchess of Ilvar at war.

The drawing room was brightly lit and busy but less noisy, which was hardly surprising because naturally people were listening in. Alec made his way through the crowd of guests trying to pretend they weren't watching, and couldn't help but cringe as he saw what was going on. Lady Sefton, his unknowing hostess, resplendent in blue with a sapphire necklace, was facing the Duchess of Ilvar, and one didn't have to be an aficionado of female fashions to know that Her Grace was overdressed. She wore a magnificent red silk gown that would have suited a ballroom if not a Court presentation, and a three-string necklace of glittering diamonds and rubies. Her red gloves were elbow length and adorned with rings, but no bracelet, and she had a hand raised in a demonstrative fashion, one pointing finger a little too close to Lady Sefton's face for courtesy. Alec couldn't hear what she was saying but the hectoring note was all too clear. Beside her Ilvar stood, bottom lip pushed out in the way he had when he was angry. It made him look like a petulant, bearded child.

They were older. Of course they were; it was eight years since he'd last seen them. The Duchess was now in her mid-forties, and statuesque in a way that suggested a dowager in the making. She would probably be a magnificent and intimidating older woman. The Duke, meanwhile, had become an old man rather than a middle-aged one to Alec's eye: grey-bearded, bald-headed. He stood with her, both of them bristling with affronted pride. It was a very familiar pose.

Lady Sefton looked equally affronted. She was speaking at the same time as the Duchess—never a good sign—in a low, rapid voice. Alec hesitated, not sure what he was meant to do, and felt a tap on his shoulder.

"I say." It was Jerry, looking as though he'd been hurrying. "Isn't that your stepmother with our hostess?"

"It is. I don't know what's up."

"I rather think I do. I'm going to have to interrupt the ladies. Could you introduce me, old man, so I don't seem quite so much of a bounder?"

"What, now?" Alec asked, putting very real alarm into his voice at the prospect of getting involved in what looked like an almighty scene. It seemed the kind of thing one would say if innocent, and he was sure he detected a tiny glint in Jerry's eye.

"Precisely now. Or I can brave the lionesses' den alone, but I do really need a hearing, and at once."

"I'll take your word," Alec said, sounding as dubious as he felt, and heard a couple of faint chuckles from around them.

They walked forward. The Duchess was saying, "I insist that you take action at once as to this disgraceful matter," while Lady Sefton contradicted her in a low, icy undervoice. The Duke was red with insult, and he did not look pleased as he noticed intruders into the little space around the angry ladies.

"I'm sorry to interrupt," Alec said. This entirely failed to interrupt anything; he was ignored except by his father, who swelled visibly. Alec made himself raise his voice and took a step closer to the warring women. "Excuse me, Lady Sefton, Your Grace, Father? I think my friend may be able to help."

"I beg your pardon?" Lady Sefton said, turning.

She was about to say, *Who are you and what are you doing here?*, he was sure. He hurried on. "Her Grace the Duchess of Ilvar, Mr. Gerald Vane. Jerry has something important to say, madam." He bowed as he spoke.

The Duchess said, through stiff lips, "What could this person possibly have to say to me?"

"It's about this, Your Grace," Jerry said, and pulled a glittering handful of light, red and white, from his pocket.

The Duke's breath caught. Lady Sefton said, "Ha!"

The Duchess's eyes widened, and she snatched at the jewels he held. "My bracelet! Where did you find this? How do you have it? Explain yourself at once!"

Jerry bowed. "Yes, ma'am. I picked this up in the gentlemen's hat-room."

"I beg your pardon, sir?" the Duke said, menacingly.

"I see," Lady Sefton said, with immense satisfaction. "I suppose you dropped it, ma'am, and it was kicked by an unwary foot. I must regret that you chose to assign blame to unknown evildoers or my staff rather than your inattention. I do feel, if you will attend a simple evening event with jewels fit for a ballroom, it must be your responsibility to care for them."

The Duchess reddened. She hated to be proved wrong, always had, would never forgive anyone who embarrassed her, and Alec could have sworn aloud. If Jerry had only told him what he'd meant to do—

But Jerry was speaking. "I'm extremely sorry to contradict you, Lady Sefton, but I'm afraid you're not in possession of all the facts. The clasp has been cut."

"What?" The Duke held out an imperative hand for the jewel.

"Nonsense," snapped Lady Sefton. "Let me see at once."

The Duchess handed the bracelet to the Duke with a triumphant glare. He was longsighted, like Alec, and wasn't wearing spectacles; he held it at arm's length and squinted.

Lady Sefton plucked the bracelet from his outstretched hand and gave it a cursory look. "Nonsense. I can see evidence of no such thing. It has simply snapped."

"I beg your pardon," Jerry said diffidently, "but I don't think it can have snapped. I looked at it when I picked it up. The clasp is cleanly cut; the gold chain that ought to have secured it is broken as well, with no partially open link. I don't see how that could have happened without a violent pull that the Duchess would have noticed."

"Naturally I should," the Duchess agreed. "Quite right."

"Are you suggesting, Mr., er, Vane, that someone cut the clasp deliberately?" Lady Sefton demanded. "Do you imply a robbery took place? And if so, perhaps you would explain why they did not, in fact, steal this most valuable item?"

The Duchess drew herself up, inhaling sharply. Jerry replied to Lady Sefton with entire calm. "I do think your ladyship's hospitality may have been abused, yes. As to why someone left the bracelet behind, I don't know, but it was underneath an open window in the hat-room. Perhaps it was dropped in the course of escape? If you have a detective present, perhaps he ought to look, and enquire if anyone else has lost a jewel. That's all I can suggest."

Lady Sefton's eyes narrowed. "You might have said this at once, sir."

Jerry's brows angled steeply in a silent expression of astonishment, but he bowed. "I beg your pardon. I do apologise I wasn't more immediately persuasive."

Lady Sefton opened her mouth at that, closed it, and swept away in silence. The Duchess gave a single nod of intense satisfaction. "Really, what is the world coming to? The insolence of accusing me of carelessness, with a thief loose on the premises."

"Quite, my dear." The Duke gave Jerry a very slight inclination of the head. "Your assistance is appreciated, Mr.—" He waved a hand.

"Vane," Jerry said with the self-deprecating smile he'd used before. "I'm proud to have been of any small service to Her Grace."

The Duke took that as his due. "The Cirencester family?"

"A very distant offshoot, sir."

"Very well." The Duke gave them both a nod of acknowledgement and dismissal, took his lady's arm, and led her away.

Alec let out a long, shallow breath. Jerry took his elbow. "That was more excitement than one expects a musical soirée to offer. I fear I've landed myself in our hostess's bad books, though. Shall we go? Nightcap?"

They strolled out. Alec felt a nervous fizz along his spine, as though he were about to hear a cry of "Stop, thief!", but they sauntered down the stairs without incident, stopping to exchange goodbyes with a couple of Alec's acquaintances, and strolled casually away, Jerry chatting idly about the merits of the string quartet. He led the way to a nearby public house—apparently they were indeed having a drink—and took a table.

Alec didn't dare say a thing until he had a glass in his hand. He sipped rather than downing the lot, against all instincts, and said, "Well."

"Well, indeed." The room was noisy enough that Jerry had to lean forward a little; they wouldn't be heard. "Very satisfactory, I thought."

"I don't have the faintest idea what happened. Except that my father scarcely looked at me."

"Oh, tut," Jerry said. "What happened materially was that I cut the bracelet off her wrist. Easy in a crush with a small cutter, especially when women wear them over gloves. More importantly, you and I helped the Duchess put one over on Lady Sefton. They loathe one another. Her Grace had the chance to upbraid Lady Sefton for having a house riddled with thieves, and she will enjoy that even more when the other women start shrieking."

"Other women?" Alec said faintly.

"Temp was working too, did you not spot him? We'll make a profit on the night. In addition to which, I got Her Grace out of a rather tight hole."

"What hole?"

Jerry's eyes were sparkling like the Duchess's jewels. "The bracelet was glass. I'll swear to it."

"No!"

"I think so. Very good glass, must have cost a few bob to make, but nevertheless, glass. And she would not have wanted that made public, after her loud outrage at losing the thing; she'd have looked ludicrous. I wonder whether she's hoarding the real things, or selling them."

"Hoarding," Alec said with certainty. "She insisted on having all Mother's jewellery instead of letting it go to Cara and Annabel. She wouldn't even give them a few pieces as mementoes, when Father was larding her with her own. Cara used to call her the Dragon, because she slept on her heap of treasure."

Jerry nodded, apparently unsurprised. "Jewel mania. Or greed, perhaps, but jewel mania arises with remarkable ease. Some people will do anything to possess a glittering rock, or a bit of solidified oyster mucus. I've seen diamond merchants weep over stones, and thieves run their head into nooses in the lust to possess. Never stand between Templeton and an opal: he becomes emotional."

"Do you have jewel mania?" Alec asked curiously. "Is that why you do it?"

"Good Lord, no. Or, at least, I haven't succumbed yet, but I am not prone to obsession. I don't set my heart on things."

"Really? Never?"

Jerry smiled, rather sardonically. "I like to control my situation. One can't do that if one is consumed by the lust to possess a bag of emeralds, or another man's wife. If you can't walk away, you're in trouble."

"But you can't walk away from everything."

"Watch me," Jerry said. "Now. We've brought ourselves to their graces' attention very nicely. Tomorrow you'll write a brief note to the Duchess as politeness dictates, expressing your hope the experience wasn't too distressing, and with no ulterior motive visible. After which, we'll wait and see. I'm pleased with the night's work."

"It seems like rather a lot of work for very little, to be honest," Alec said. "I'm sure you know what you're doing, but my father barely glanced at me."

Jerry was lifting a glass to his lips. He paused at the words, holding it in mid-air, then put it down. "Were you hoping he would? Alec, do you want to achieve something other than what I'm here for?"

Alec tried, very hard, not to react. He wasn't sure if he'd succeeded. "How do you mean?"

Jerry's brows tweaked in the middle, lifting towards his nose. "Bluntly, then, if what you want is your father's attention, there are easier and more legitimate ways to go about that."

"That's not what I want. What would I do with his attention? He doesn't care about me, or any of us, and that won't change. I just meant that I thought we were bringing me to his notice this evening, and I didn't feel he noticed me."

"He had nothing to be displeased with. He will have expected to be outraged by you, and he wasn't. That's a significant achievement on which we'll build."

"Outraged?" Alec said blankly. "Why would he think that?"

"Because he's wronged you, and we resent people we wrong. They say *Hell hath no fury like a woman scorned*, but it's not true. Hell hath no fury like the one who did the scorning, especially when they're made to face up to their actions. Our challenge here is to persuade the Duke that you won't embarrass him with reproaches, or force him to be conscious of his sins. He needs to know that you won't be a problem."

Alec took a sip of whisky and soda, contemplated the glass for a moment, then drained it. The spirit seared down his throat. He coughed.

"Steady."

"I don't want to be steady. I want—" *Not to be negligible. To be more than an absence. To have someone look at him and see him and think something other than, Don't embarrass me by your existence or offend me with your injuries.*

He *didn't* embarrass people. He didn't complain about his father's miserliness with love and money, or bemoan the jobs he didn't get, or fuss when lovers gave him the cold shoulder. He never made a fuss. He tried to be as unobtrusive and inoffensive as he could, and even then he was found inconvenient simply for existing with a title and no unearned income. Meanwhile, Jerry was a walking insult to civilised rules, yet he sauntered into great houses and got waiters' attention, and Alec was quite sure he never felt guilty about taking space any more than taking jewellery.

The hell with it. The absolute hell with it all.

Jerry was watching him. Alec put his chin up. "So, was our conversation before we left my rooms all talk, or do you mean to act on it?"

Jerry grinned, a smile with more teeth than was quite safe. "Why don't you come with me and find out?"

They went to a hotel Jerry knew, walking in silence. There were plenty of hotels in London where one could take a room and invite a friend up with no questions asked; still, Alec found his heart thudding unpleasantly as he waited, for fear of a spiteful maître d' or chambermaid. Jerry showed no such concern.

They went upstairs. The boy opened the door, lit the gas, drew the curtains, took his tip, bowed himself out. Jerry fastened the door.

Neither of them had said a word since the cafe.

Jerry looked at him. Alec looked back. Jerry's lips curved a little. "Lord Alexander."

It was a name, a declaration, a question in its way. Alec said, "Yes," to all of it.

Jerry took him by the shoulder and pushed. "Against the wall."

Alec half-stumbled over to the wall, hands out against the patterned paper, feeling its tiny corrugations under his palms. Jerry's fingers slid into his hair, then raked down his neck. Alec could feel breath on his skin.

A hand came round his waist, a thumb hooking into his waistband, then sliding out, over the front of his trousers, massaging there. Alec's breath caught, and he heard Jerry chuckle softly. He leaned forward, bracing his forehead against the wall, and simply stood as a knee nudged his thighs apart and hands roamed his body. Fingers pulling across his face, pushing between his lips; fingers between his legs, cupping and squeezing him to hardness through the cloth; breath on the back of his neck from a man he couldn't see. He was trembling with the tension.

Jerry leaned in, putting a lot of weight on Alec's shoulders, making him gasp. "I want to fuck," he said softly. "And since you're here, I'm going to fuck you."

"Oh God."

A hand at his buttons, unfastening the trousers, shoving them and the drawers down. Alec stood, bare and undignified, waiting for a moment as cloth rustled behind him. He jerked as a warm hand cupped his bare buttock, feeling his muscle tense, and Jerry's fingers slid along the curve that made.

He didn't seem to be in any hurry. Fingers trailing up and down Alec's thigh, over his arse, tucking up his coat- and shirt-tails, cupping his hip. Alec pressed his mouth against his forearm to stop himself asking for anything. He wished he could see Jerry's face, and was glad he couldn't. This way, the hands on him might have been a lover's touch.

Jerry let out a breath, almost like a sigh. "Lord Alexander." His finger was probing, slicked with something, warm and intrusive. "Look at you. My lord the duke's son, quivering for it. What a sight." His teeth grazed Alec's neck gently, as much bite as kiss.

Alec swallowed hard. His prick was heavy, the blood throbbing in an uncomfortable demand for attention that Jerry wasn't giving. The slick finger pushed in, crooked upward. Alec yelped into his forearm. "God. Jerry."

"Uh-uh," Jerry murmured. "You don't like to talk, so I don't want to hear a peep out of you. Not a word. Not a sound. Just silence while I do what I want."

Alec inhaled hard, feeling the hairs on his skin prickle. Jerry's finger slid out, and then, finally, there was that blunt pressure, and Alec tried to widen his stance, pushing ineffectually at the cloth trapping his ankles. Jerry was breathing hard, his cock well slicked but still impossibly too large for the space allowed. Alec bit down on his forearm against the burn, breathed out to release his muscles, felt his body give way to the intrusion. Jerry's teeth were on his neck again. Alec tilted his head to offer more access, felt Jerry's lips move, and the slow, steady pressure continued.

So slow. Jerry was taking his time, each thrust barely worthy of the name, pushing into Alec in fractions of an inch. He had one hand braced against the wall; he got the other round Alec's chest, gripping tight, holding him up even as he invaded Alec's body, each stroke a little further, until Alec was splayed helplessly against the wall.

"Christ," Jerry rasped in his ear. "You titled tart." He began to move more as he spoke, slowly at first, sliding steadily out and in. Alec's shoulders were heaving. He clamped his lips together, felt Jerry's teeth on his neck, his ear. "That's right. Keep your mouth shut and take it like a gentleman. *God.* When I rob your father's home I'll pile jewels round your neck, and have you wearing nothing but diamonds."

Alec couldn't help a noise at that. Jerry almost snarled, arm tightening. "I said, be quiet while I fuck you." He moved harder on the words, hips speeding up, and then it was all Alec could do to lock his knees and stand against the onslaught, Jerry taking him with savage command, the upward friction making his toes curl and his prick throb. He wanted to beg for relief but this was Jerry's turn, Jerry's pleasure. The thought almost brought him off by itself. He gasped into his arm as he was bumped against the wall by each thrust, and then Jerry's hand slid down to grip his straining erection and Alec sobbed aloud at the prospect of relief. Fingers slid over his length, fast, sharp movements to match his thrusts, and Alec came, spread and impaled like a butterfly on the wall. Jerry made a breathless noise, and then he was slamming into Alec without regard, brutally hard, and panting as he spent.

They stood, locked together, chests heaving. Alec's cheek felt hot against the wallpaper. He was suddenly very aware of the intruding presence in his body, and of Jerry's face in the crook of his neck.

"Christ," Jerry said at last. "Hold on, now." He pulled out gently. Alec couldn't help a wince. "Sorry. Just a moment, stay there." He moved away. Alec leaned against the comforting wall—it felt like an old friend after all this—trying to calm his breath. Jerry returned after a moment, and Alec squeaked at the feel of a cool, wet cloth.

Jerry made a hissing noise between his teeth, like an ostler calming a horse. "Steady. God, you're a pleasure. Was that as you wished?"

"You must have noticed," Alec mumbled into his arm.

Jerry's other hand settled on his hip for a moment, a touch that felt almost comforting. "I saw you liked it. I want to know how to make you love it."

Alec lifted his head at that. Jerry blew lightly on his ear, startling a shiver out of him. "I can't think of a better hold to have over a man than knowing his desires, every little odd turn of them. If I have your desires I have you in the palm of my hand, which is exactly where I want you." He licked Alec's neck, a deliberate scrape. "So, if there's anything I can do to that end, I hope you'll tell me for next time."

*Next time.* No wonder people skipped happily down primrose paths to damnation. Alec could see everything that was terrifying about this, but all he felt was a quiver of anticipatory excitement and, undeniably, warmth. Jerry might be a manipulative criminal, but he was a manipulative criminal who cared what Alec wanted. Perhaps that was merely to serve his own desires; it didn't matter at all.

He tried to turn and realised that, absurdly, his trousers were still around his ankles. He bent to hoist them up and turned then to see Jerry watching him. The thief looked sweaty and dishevelled, eyes bright, face flushed. He looked wild, in fact, as though his usual iron control had slipped, and Alec felt a twinge of satisfaction.

"That was wonderful," he said. "Um…"

Jerry stroked a finger gently under his chin. "Spit it out. How do I bring you to your knees?"

"You didn't need to bring me off," Alec blurted. "Not right away. If you didn't want to."

"Ah-ha. I could take my pleasure and leave you whimpering for yours? What an extremely good idea. Oh, damnation. 'Had we but world enough, and time', I should be delighted to experiment, but not tonight; I must go. Soon."

Alec had known they'd be leaving—it was one thing to take a room, quite another to both emerge in the morning in full evening dress. It was still a tiny disappointment. "Of course. Uh, what next?"

"Write that note to your stepmother and wait. I'll be in touch soon enough. Keep a clean nose, too."

"Sorry?"

"You've attracted your father's attention. It would be wise to imagine his eyes on you when you're not with me."

Alec blinked. "You think he'd have me *watched?*"

"If I were him I'd ask questions. It's merely a precaution. And don't worry. The long game is going well."

# Chapter Six

Alec wrote to the Duchess as instructed, a strictly courteous note as he would to a woman who had exhibited tender feelings to be distressed. He worked. He went to the Sketch for a drink, but confined himself to one and declined to discuss anything but publishing gossip; he didn't go to the Gilded Lily or the Jack and Knave. He didn't try to see George or Annabel.

George sent him a clipping from a newspaper.

*Lovers of family harmony were pleased to observe that the noble Lord I. seems to be 'on terms' with his son Lord A. once more. The two were observed in friendly conversation at the home of Lady S., at the soirée made notorious by the presence of a daring sneak thief.*

It was accompanied by a single line: *I hope you're happy.* Alec didn't reply.

And then, on Wednesday, the letter came.

*Dear Lord Alexander*

*His Grace the Duke of Ilvar expects your attendance at Pyne House on Friday at 11 am.*

*Yours sincerely*

*F. Merrow, Secretary*

Alec felt an urgent wish that he had some way to get in touch with Jerry, to demand, *What do I do now?* That was ridiculous; he knew very well what to do. He wrote a polite response to Merrow assuring him of his receipt of the invitation, went to check that he'd have impeccably clean clothing, and then lay on his bed, looking up at the ceiling, rehearsing the part of Lord Alexander. He felt really pretty well prepared when a note arrived from Jerry on Thursday, suggesting a drink at the Criterion Bar that evening.

"My father wrote to me," he informed his companion once they had their drinks, a pair of gin fizzes to acknowledge the hot weather.

"Did he, by God." Jerry's mouth curled with satisfaction. "And?"

"I have an appointment tomorrow."

"Good man. And have you a plan?"

"I'm going to be Lord Alexander. I'll ask to make amends and to be on terms again. After that, it will depend on what he wants."

"And if he asks you if you need money?"

"I'll say yes."

Jerry nodded. "Good. There have been several items in the gossip columns about your rapprochement, I don't know if you've seen?"

"My brother sent me one. I— Hold on. Did you do that?"

"They're always keen for material. And a narrative of Ilvar reuniting with his children to set against the stain of his neglect would be welcome, I'd think, if he's looking for public approval around the time of the anniversary. Not that you should suggest as much."

"Good heavens, no." He was right, though. The Duke could buy his wife a private railway line for her convenience, and jewels as other husbands bought flowers, but he'd never been able to purchase public approval or liking. Even time hadn't managed that.

There were music-hall brides who had claimed their places in the aristocracy more effectively than Her Grace—not, perhaps, the appalling Lady Euston, but certainly the Countess of Moreton, who had been a trapeze artist and killed a man, yet was universally popular. Then again, Lady Moreton had charm, humility, and a delightful sense of humour. The Duchess had none of those, and her unpopularity had rendered both herself and her husband as close to pariahs as was likely for very rich people in this age of Mammon.

Jerry's brows tipped. "What are you thinking?"

"Nothing," Alec said automatically, and then, "Well. Only that it struck me, in other circumstances, if a man stood by his wife in the teeth of all opposition, and was unshakably loyal for twenty years at great personal cost, we'd praise it as the height of marital love."

"Touching," Jerry said, with absolutely no sincerity. "I'll send a bouquet. Now, are you going to ingratiate yourself with them so I can rob them?"

Alec almost laughed. "You really don't let me forget what we're doing, do you? Not for a second."

"Forgetting what you're doing can be fatal. Can you do this, Alec? Have this conversation, hold yourself back and present Lord Alexander? Keep your secrets and win our entry?"

"I can do it. I've practised—you know, what Lord Alexander will say. I won't feel terribly proud of myself, and my brother and sister— well, they're already disgusted so it can't get much worse. But I'll do it."

"I'll be proud of you," Jerry said softly. "There's something strikingly piquant about you. It's the contrast, I think. You have such determination, more than you realise. A remarkable quiet sort of strength." Alec's lips parted. Jerry smiled, wolfish. "And soon enough I'm going to reduce you to utter helplessness. It's a delightful prospect."

Alec swallowed. "That's— I'm not sure if that's encouraging or not."

"Oh, I think you know which. Go forth and conquer, Lord Alexander. I will see you—let us say on Saturday, for a full report. Keep me in mind."

Alec did keep him in mind. It was ridiculous that he could be flattered by such a reprehensible, dangerous, obvious liar as Jerry. But he held on to *determination, remarkable, strength* as though they were truths, and to the thought of Saturday as if it were a lovers' meeting. As though words and the prospect of a fuck were talismans to protect him through a meeting with his father, the first in eight years.

"I have been most dissatisfied with your conduct," the Duke of Ilvar informed him. They were in the study. Alec hadn't been asked to sit down; he felt like a child in front of his headmaster. "I cannot be expected to acknowledge as my family individuals who display ingratitude, obduracy, and disrespect towards my wife."

"No, sir."

"Your behaviour, and that of your siblings, has caused me great distress for twenty years, and had inflicted untold harm on the Duchess. The contumely she has endured would have broken a lesser woman. If it were not for her remarkable strength of character— You do not see the dignity with which she sustains her place. You do not understand her suffering, or care for her troubles. It has all been hers and mine to bear."

The Duke's lower lip was jutting in that petulant way as he rehearsed his laundry list of injuries. Alec curled his toes in his shoes until they cramped and tried not to think of squashed holly berries, the stinking fog, Cara's harsh coughs. *I can't listen to this. I can't nod and smile. I can't—*

*Jerry had you like a cheap tart under Waterloo Bridge. This is nothing.*

"I'm very sorry, sir," he said, and heard a wheedling note in his own voice. "If we had been older we might have understood the Duchess's difficult position better. If I may say, sir, a friend of mine recently—and with the greatest respect—cited Your Graces as an exemplar of marital love, loyalty, and fidelity under the greatest pressure."

"Yes," the Duke said. "That is unacknowledged. In this age of divorces and disloyalty, my Duchess has proved herself a hundred times over, yet the malice and envy with which she is greeted are unceasing. And it is worsened by your obstinacy. My wife is blamed because I will not tolerate the impertinent rudeness of my offspring! Was ever a man expected to endure the insults of his children as I am? And it is your behaviour that has done this, Hartington: yours and Caroline's and Alexander's and Annabel's, because you resented that I, left a widower in the prime of life after a highly unsatisfactory marriage, considered my own happiness. All of you should be ashamed. All of you owe me and, far more, the Duchess a humble apology."

"I, uh, I'm Alexander, sir. Not Hartington. And Caroline is dead."

The Duke of Ilvar batted impatiently at the air, brushing that away. "A slip of the tongue."

"I beg your pardon," Alec said numbly. "And you are right, sir. I have done a great deal of thinking recently, and realised I have a great deal to regret about what happened in our family. We ought to be celebrating your anniversary. I am sorry we have not been on terms, sir, and I regret the part I played in it, and my—my youthful folly. It is a hard thing for a child to understand adult behaviour, but as a man now, I do understand, and I beg your forgiveness, and I will beg it of the Duchess if I may be granted an audience."

Was that overdoing it? He caught a shrewd look in his father's eyes and thought it might be for a panicked moment, then the Duke said, "And I dare say you'd rather be my pensioner again. Wouldn't you?"

Alec straightened his shoulders. "Well, if you must have it, yes, sir. I was very young when the falling-out took place. If I had been older, I would have considered matters better. And I wouldn't have cut myself off from my position based on an argument I scarcely remember and didn't fully understand. But the fact is—well, I won't deny I've found the last years a struggle to make ends meet, and I've an itch to return to my proper place, but that's not all. I don't want this poison between us any more, sir. When I encountered you at Lady Sefton's—" He swallowed as noticeably as he could. "It struck me how much time has been lost over nothing. That I would have wanted to greet my father and stepmother as a son should. Whereas the only reason I dared approach you was that my pal Vane had found the Duchess's bracelet."

"A very sensible man, that," Ilvar said. "One of Cirencester's relations, he said?"

"Distant, yes. He asked me to convey his respect, and hopes that Her Grace was not too distressed by that unfortunate incident."

"Most kind. Naturally she was displeased. Really, what is the world coming to when one can be garrotted and robbed in a private home in such a way?"

"Oh, outrageous, yes. I don't mean to impose too far on your time, sir. But if it is possible, now or later, for me to make my apologies to Her Grace, I will wait on your word to do so."

The Duke eyed him. "You wish for a reconciliation."

"Yes, sir."

"And your brother and sisters?"

*Sister. Singular. Cara is dead, can you try to remember that?* "I…can't speak for them, sir. We've rather fallen out."

"Have you indeed? Let me be clear, Har— Alexander. *If* I am to acknowledge you once more, and *if* my wife chooses to forgive your years of insolence, which I do not say she will, we will expect you to respond to our magnanimity with gratitude and to conduct yourself accordingly. We will not forgive twice."

"No, sir. I understand. I'm very sorry, sir, for everything. I hope to do better."

The Duke nodded. "Very well, you may go. If I want you, I shall send for you."

Alec met Jerry the next evening. He'd dressed as perfectly as he could and practised a smile in the mirror until his face hurt, and he walked calmly in and didn't kick any tables over, but all the same he could see the assessing look behind Jerry's society smile.

"Hello, old fellow. All well?"

"Marvellous," Alec said. "Absolutely marvellous. I saw my father and it went marvellously. Do we have to stay here?"

"Where would you rather go?"

"The place you took me after Lady Sefton's soirée. The second one. Let's do that again. Let's do it now."

"Will you have a drink first?"

"I'd rather not unless I have to," Alec said. "And I'm a little tired of doing things that I'd rather not, but have to."

Jerry contemplated him for a second, then pushed his half-finished drink away and rose. "Quite right, it is awfully slow in here." He tossed coins on the table. "Let's go."

It wasn't far to the little hotel. They walked in silence; Jerry spoke to the desk clerk in a low voice; then they were in the room, and Jerry was locking the door. The curtains were drawn.

"Right," Jerry said. "And?"

Alec opened his mouth, but he couldn't speak. The sheer boiling rage and misery and shame had choked him for a day and a half, so that he could hardly control his voice to ask for a cup of tea, and his mind had raced with imaginary conversations, with George, with Cara, with Jerry, with his father. He didn't want to say any of that now.

"Alec. Talk."

"It went extremely well," Alec gritted out. "I grovelled. I have a second appointment to grovel to Her Grace on Monday. My father couldn't remember which of his sons I was and forgot that his daughter is dead in his hurry to tell me about how we have wronged him, a poor hard-done-by duke, left all alone after his wife— Christ. *Christ.*"

Jerry stepped close and put a hand to his face. It wasn't an embrace, or even a comforting touch; more a steadying one, as though he were getting the right angle for a portrait. "Angry?"

"Yes."

"Humiliated?"

"As badly as I have ever been in my life."

"And you asked to come here."

Alec shut his eyes briefly. "Yes."

Jerry nodded. "Strip, and get on the bed."

He didn't speak much: none of those arousing promises, or threats. He made Alec kneel; he knelt behind him, pushed him face down on the covers, and stroked him to whimpering arousal, hand commanding.

"Are you close?" he whispered, as Alec moaned.

"Yes, but—"

"Shh."

Jerry let his stand go, leaving it painfully rigid, and then Alec felt light fingers sliding between his legs, over his balls, up and back to stroke his arse, setting off a new wave of sensation. A slick finger pierced him, sliding in and probing upward to find the point of pleasure. Alec yelped.

"Shh," Jerry murmured again. "Keep quiet until you're close."

His movements were tormentingly accurate, pressing inside Alec to toe-curling effect. Alec had never spent from this kind of stimulation alone; nobody had ever tried to make him. He rather thought he could. "God. *Jerry*."

"Close?"

"Yes."

Jerry gently withdrew his finger. Alec almost sobbed, and as he did he felt Jerry's other hand running up his chest, pinching a nipple, bringing a new set of nerve endings to life.

And it went on. Jerry's hands worked him, place after place, moving on every time the arousal brought him close to release, until the need was coming close to pain and Alec was begging aloud.

"Please. Please let me. I can't."

"Not yet."

"Please!"

"You can come when I fuck you. Not before."

"Jerry—"

"You don't have a say in this. You wanted my control; you have it now."

Alec closed his eyes, let himself slip into sensation. The feeling was dreamlike, lying naked in a darkened room, his world shrunk to nothing more than Jerry's fingers and voice, aware only of touches, the throbbing need, and a dizzy sense of floating. When Jerry finally pushed him flat on the bed and thrust in, he felt oddly remote, as though the rough usage were happening to someone else; when he came, prick untouched, he thought the climax might kill him with its force. He sobbed and gasped, spending helplessly over the counterpane as Jerry fucked him, and when at last Jerry gasped his relief and collapsed over his back, sweatily naked, Alec realised his cheeks were wet.

They lay in silence for several minutes. Alec felt emptied, as if the boil of seething emotions had been lanced and the poison drained away. He felt purified, almost, if that was the appropriate word for being buggered into insensibility.

Jerry crawled off him, and returned with a washcloth. He cleaned Alec up with gentle strokes, tossed the soiled cloth into a corner, and lay down beside him.

"Well," he said. "Do you want to tell me about it?"

Alec stared up at the ceiling. The cornicing needed sweeping for cobwebs, and the plaster was cracked. Probably too much hard use of the room upstairs. A dingy hotel, the smell of fucking thick in the air, Jerry's body warm beside him but not touching.

Did he want to tell him?

Perhaps he did. Perhaps the best thing he could do with the gnarled, poisonous, thorny secret around which he'd huddled for years was to take it out and give it to someone who'd kick it like a football. Perhaps he couldn't bear to carry it any longer.

"My mother was ill for years." He wasn't sure if that was the place to start, but it had to be somewhere, and if you could say anything for Jerry, it was that he was an active listener, sorting, thinking, probing. "She was never strong but after Annabel's birth, she was, if not bedridden, certainly unable to do much at all. George was at school, but the rest of us were in Castle Speight, where we stayed because Mother couldn't travel. Father—well, by then he'd met Mrs. Clayton, the estate manager's wife. I was only seven, I had no idea what was going on, but I knew things were wrong. The servants hissed and muttered. Mother cried a great deal. It wasn't a happy place."

"I dare say adultery is very trying."

Alec ploughed on. "It was more than mere adultery. Father was in love with Mrs. Clayton, passionately. I remember him shouting how Mother had never cared for his…needs, complaining about her weakness as though she'd decided to be ill to spite him. He told her—Cara and I were in the next room, listening—that she was denying him happiness with every breath she drew."

Jerry sucked in a breath. "Ah. I begin to see."

"You don't. Because—" Was he going to say this? In this room, to this man, his body still stinging and marked by hard usage?

"It was in the night," he said. "Cara had a nightmare. The rest of us were asleep so she went to Mother's room, intending to slip in for comfort—Mother didn't sleep well either—but when she was in the corridor outside Mother's room, she heard Father coming. He'd have been furious if he saw her up, he'd have told Nanny to beat her. So she hid behind a sort of pedestal that held a bust. And Father went into Mother's room. And—and she heard Mother say something to him, and he shut the door. Cara wanted Mother, so she stayed and waited for him to go. And in due course Father came out, and Cara waited a few minutes while he went away, and then went in. And Mother was dead."

There was silence for a second. Jerry said, carefully, "When you say dead—"

"She was lying in bed, staring up. Cara said it was quite unmistakable. There was a lamp, burning low. And there was a pillow next to Mother's head, and, uh, it was warm, and Cara said it was wet. A stained wet patch in the centre."

Jerry sat up, a sharp movement that brought him into the corner of Alec's eye. "Are you serious?"

"Cara thinks she fainted. The next thing she remembers— remembered—was a housemaid screaming, in the morning. She was taken out and the doctors were called. They said Mother must have had a seizure in the night and that it was her constitution failing at last."

"What did your sister say?"

"Nothing," Alec said. "She was ten. She had found her mother dead, and she'd seen—Jerry, he had our lives in his hand. You can't blame her for not speaking out, for not saying, *I think my father murdered my mother* when he was a duke, for Christ's sake, and we were all in that bloody shadow-filled castle full of echoes and medieval weaponry, and—"

Jerry's hand closed over his arm. "Hey. Hey. Look at me. I said, look." Alec forced his eyes to move. Jerry was staring down at him, and the tilt of his brows gave him an expression that was for all the world like concern. "How long have you been sitting on this?"

"Years. Cara didn't say anything for a long time. It affected her terribly, I think in part because she was already sickly and people used to say all the time that she'd end up like Mother—"

"Dear God."

"She became very withdrawn, very angry. She didn't speak at all for a month, and then only in monosyllables. We thought it was because of Mother's death; we were all devastated. But then, only a few months later, Clayton died. And once he and Mother were both dead, Father and Mrs. Clayton could marry. So they did."

"Alec," Jerry said. "You told me that Clayton's death wasn't ruled a suicide."

"No." Alec's lips felt stiff. "And I don't believe it should have been."

"Your father—"

"He was at a public meeting some miles away. It wasn't him. I think it was her."

Jerry whistled. "He was shot, yes? His own gun?"

"Or one that used a similar bullet, and his gun had been fired. There were no footprints, but it had been a dry summer. He was shot from under the chin, where he might have held the gun himself. He bled to death, perhaps choked on his own blood, and was found a couple of hours later."

"Did anyone ask Mrs. Clayton for an alibi?"

Alec snorted. "As though a lady would shoot her husband at point blank range. Poison is the woman's weapon, everyone knows that."

"Or a straight razor. And I know at least one who favours a broken bottle."

"Yes, well, Mrs. Clayton wore black to the inquest, and claimed that she had been at home by herself, and nobody could prove she hadn't. One police officer did ask questions—after all, it was common knowledge her husband had refused to grant a divorce—but he was very severely slapped down. There was an acting Chief Constable at the time, you see, hoping to be confirmed in the role, and my father extended his patronage."

"In my experience the long arm of the law usually has its palm out, but I'm a little surprised they'd cover up a murder."

"I'm sure they thought they were covering up a suicide," Alec said. "Mrs. Clayton's affair with my father was ruled to be irrelevant gossip. The missing ring was used to demonstrate that someone else had been in the area while Clayton was dying or dead, and was thus the prime suspect, and an open verdict was recorded. And six months later they were married."

"Do your siblings know of all this?"

"Cara spoke to us about Mother after the wedding," Alec said. "It was difficult. She'd been half mad, you see; we were used to her shouting and storming off. George took a while before he believed her—he didn't want to, quite understandably. And when he did, he was furious all over again because she hadn't told anyone. It wasn't fair. She was ten, she'd had a terrible breakdown, and in any case, what could she have done? Mother was dead, the doctors had called it a seizure, and anything we said against the Duchess was ascribed to malice. George tried, even so. He went to the Chief Constable and asked him to reopen the investigation into Clayton's death."

"Any good?"

"God, no. The man went straight to Father to assure him he didn't place any credence in this silliness. That didn't go pleasantly, afterwards."

Jerry took that in for a moment, then he lowered himself to lie on his side, propped on an elbow, his other hand still on Alec's arm. It was almost, not quite, like being held. "Does your father know you suspect him?"

"Cara accused him to his face, in the end. That was what happened eight years ago. He told us all that she was no longer his daughter, not until she apologised, and that we had to cut her out of our lives or we would be nothing to him either."

"Which would be the response of an innocent man as well," Jerry said. "To be offended rather than afraid. I suppose you're quite sure of your sister's testimony."

"Yes. I believe her absolutely. And the reason he behaves as though he's been insulted is because he feels it. We've been so unpleasant to him, we didn't appreciate his need, his *right* to marry Mrs. Clayton; we don't understand that his first marriage was inadequate and things had to go as they did. Do you know, the doctors had told him Mother shouldn't have another child after me? He was told it might endanger her life, but he still got Annabel on her. He ought to have everything he wants, it's as simple as that. He spoke to me as though he was entirely the wronged party. He said I owed him and the Duchess a humble apology for my obdurate refusal, for making her life difficult, and—and I did, I apologised—"

"Shit." Jerry's hand tightened, and Alec found himself pulled over, so that he was pressed against Jerry's bare chest, an arm over his shoulders. Jerry holding him close, for comfort. His heart thumped. "Shit and derision, Alec, all this would have been useful information before I sent you off there. How the devil did you get through that?"

Alec tried to smile. "Cheap tart under Waterloo Bridge, remember?"

"You bloody fool. What the devil are you playing at? This isn't a robbery."

"It is." Alec reared back in sudden panic. "It has to be."

"It is not. The point of a robbery is that whatever you might invest in the job, you come out making a profit. What the merry hell do you think this is going to cost you, between your siblings and your self-respect? Do you propose to do this till August? Is a handful of jewels worth this?"

"It's not about jewels."

Jerry made a sound in his throat that was very close to a snarl. "No, it's not. It's about revenge, and I am not a revenger. I'm a jewel thief, and if you're using me as a tool for your vengeance, you and I will not be working to the same end, and we are going to get caught. I'm not having that."

"Jerry." Alec pushed himself up urgently, staring into the dark eyes. "I want you to rob the Duchess. I will do whatever I have to so that you can do that. I've said so all along. You knew I hated them—"

"It makes a significant difference why!"

"It shouldn't to you. You aren't sorry, you don't believe in repentance, you think consequences only matter if you get caught. Why do you care if my father's a murderer?"

"I—" Jerry broke off. They were very close, his hand still resting on Alec's back, tension thrumming through it. "For one thing, I have never smothered the invalid mother of my children. That may not be much of a moral high ground, but I'm standing on it. For another, you've made me a participant in torture that I had no desire to inflict. I sent you off to do that. We could have played it differently."

"I doubt it. And it was my idea, my choice."

"And for a third," Jerry went on, "I meant what I said. If we aren't working towards the same end, we're going to fail."

"I want you to rob the Duchess," Alec said as steadily as he could. "I want to bring you into the house where my father killed my mother, and I want you to steal the diamond parure he had made for his wife while his daughter lay dying. He forgot Cara was dead, you know. He kept mentioning her in the present tense, talking about my 'sisters', because he doesn't even care enough to remember one of them is *dead*, so I want you to take the jewellery that was so damned important to him that he didn't pay for her funeral away from the wife who was so damned important to him that he killed my mother to get her. Do you understand? I want you to steal the fucking jewels, and if I have to humiliate myself for months to make that possible, then I will do it. You *said* I was determined. Were you lying?"

"I was not."

"Then don't let me down. Don't make me waste what I did yesterday, what I've done to my siblings. I've put skin into this. And you said yourself you've never been able to get at the Ilvar jewels. Are you really going to let diamonds worth eleven thousand pounds slip through your fingers?"

Jerry narrowed his eyes. "I'm not sure how I became the one who needed persuasion to commit a crime. It's all very well to say you won't fail, and I'm damned sure it won't be for lack of effort, but you're only human. You've considered going to the police?"

"I gave up hoping for justice some time ago. And I'm not exacting vengeance either. What kind of vengeance is stealing a necklace and ruining an anniversary, compared to two deaths?"

"Then what is this for, if it's neither justice nor vengeance?"

Alec shrugged. "Spite."

There was a brief silence, then Jerry laughed. "Spite. Yes, that's reasonable. Entirely so." He lay back, tugging Alec with him, so he ended up lying with his face on Jerry's hard shoulder. "If you're determined to see this through—"

"I am."

"Then we need to make it possible for you to do that without too much strain on the nerves. You might be over the worst, if you've had that particular talk with your father?"

"I don't know. I'm to make my apologies to the Duchess on Monday."

"Ah." Jerry's hand brushed his face. "Unpleasant, unwarranted, humiliating, and degrading."

"Yes."

"But, as you indicated, unavoidable. I'll just have to make it worth your while."

"Please do," Alec said. "I'm sure it's exactly what you intended, and I shouldn't be surprised, but it did help when I remembered—you know, Waterloo Bridge. If I actually think about what I'm doing—"

"I can quite see why you wouldn't want to do that."

"No. But acting Lord Alexander made me remember I'm playing a game. Thank you."

"I'm not sure why you're thanking me," Jerry said. "I'm doing exactly as I choose to a delectably pliant bit of stuff. Did you like being made to wait?"

"Christ, yes. Well, it was agony, but—yes."

"Fortunate for you. I think I've given you quite enough pleasure, Lord Alexander. Next time, you're going to serve me."

Alec's breath caught. He'd never so much as touched Jerry's body yet. Truth be told, he'd barely seen it, since Jerry seemed strongly to prefer handling him from behind. "What—what would you like me to do?"

"You say that as if you have a choice. How sweet." His fingers trailed over Alec's neck. "Let's say, whatever you have to swallow with the Duchess will be as nothing compared to what I'm going to make you do afterwards. Hold that in mind. Oh, and that will be after dinner, by the way, I won't have a repetition of tonight. You'll trot out a lot of meaningless flannel to a stupid, greedy pair of swine that we're going to rob blind, then come out to some very respectable place for dinner with me, and smile as you do it."

Alec took a deep breath. "Right. Yes."

"It's the least you deserve," Jerry said. "If people flaunt jewels, they may expect to be robbed; if they attempt blackmail they may expect to be kicked; and if they're quite so beautifully willing to make themselves my plaything, then…" He flicked Alec's nipple. "They may expect to be played with. You bring it on yourself."

"I dare say." Alec managed a smile.

Jerry's arm tightened a little. "Now. What else haven't you told me?"

Alec couldn't help the jolt. "Sorry?"

"The Duke and Duchess's alternative to divorce was relevant information. I understand you wouldn't spread it around lightly, but I needed to know. Have you told me everything? Is there something more troubling you? Because I don't like surprises. I don't want to make my plans and then find some new piece of trouble bobbing up like a corpse in the river. If we're working together—"

"Yes, I understand that. And, uh, nothing. It's fine."

"That could have been considerably more convincing. Let me ask you again."

"There's nothing else," Alec insisted.

"I don't believe you." Jerry's voice had an edge to it now. "What is it?"

Alec took a deep breath. "Why don't you look me in the face?"

"Sorry?"

"This is, what, our fourth time and you haven't once looked me in the face, still less kissed me. I mean, you don't have to— I'm not asking—" He could feel himself going scarlet with embarrassment, which, considering the things Jerry had done to him, was ridiculous.

"Right. Yes." Jerry sounded as though he'd been wrong-footed. It wasn't a tone Alec had heard from him before. "That's concerning you?"

"I just wondered why you wouldn't want to," Alec said wretchedly.

"If you're worrying you're hard on the eyes, there's a mirror over there. Believe me, there is no possible objection to your face. I assumed—well, never mind my assumptions. You want me to look at you?"

Alec did, desperately, want Jerry to look at him, or see him; he also, at this moment, wanted nothing more than to disappear. He stared fiercely at the ceiling, wishing to God he'd never raised the damned subject. "Really, I don't mind. If you don't want to, it doesn't matter."

"And you want me to kiss you?"

"I truly don't mean to be demanding—"

"Alec?"

Alec twisted round at the note in his voice. Jerry took hold of his jaw, light but commanding, lowered his head, and kissed him.

Alec opened his mouth more in shock than anything. Jerry's lips held his own without pressure for a moment, and then moved, and Alec found himself straining up into the kiss. Jerry's beard rasped his skin, his tongue tangled with Alec's, and they were kissing ferociously, Jerry's hands in his face and in his hair, Alec gripping his back and shoulder. Jerry moved over him, body to body, and there was nothing but closeness, and hungry, open-mouthed kisses, and the slide of hands on skin, stroking and holding, until Jerry broke off and pulled back, propping himself on his arms. His dark hair was tangled; his mouth slightly open, slightly wet; his brows slanting up at an angle that looked for all the world like confusion. He was hard again. So was Alec.

"Jerry?"

Jerry shook his head, a tiny movement. He shifted up onto his knees, and this time when he leaned in to kiss Alec once more, his hand came between their bodies to hold both stands together. Alec made a noise in his mouth.

"If you want it like this, you can have it like this," Jerry said against his lips. "If this makes you hard." His hand was moving steadily. "If this is your pleasure." He licked Alec's lips, urged them open for a kiss, moved his mouth a fraction away. "Because if I know your pleasures—"

"In the palm of your hand," Alec gasped, moving his hips on the words.

"Kissed." Jerry mouthed his earlobe. "And fucked. And controlled. Is that what you want of me?"

"All of it."

"Then you're mine." They were thrusting against each other, against Jerry's encircling palm and fingers. "Mine to use. Aren't you, my beautiful dukeling?"

"Christ, yes. Please."

Jerry's mouth hit his again, and this time he didn't move away. They were kissing greedily as Alec came, in pulses on his belly and over Jerry's fingers.

Jerry let go and sat up, straddling Alec, his eyes very dark, unreadable, his mouth red. He was still holding his own stand. Alec watched, his chest heaving, and Jerry's glinting-wet hand moved, stroking his hard length, up and down.

"Please," Alec said. "Can I—"

"No."

Alec could feel the aftershocks in his groin still. He watched, silent, watched Jerry bringing himself off and watching him back, and then Jerry knelt up straight so he was off Alec's supine body. His hand moved faster. Alec licked his lips and opened his mouth, blatantly inviting, and Jerry came with an incoherent noise, splattering over his chest.

Jerry let himself go and doubled over as if something hurt. Alec watched the dark head for a moment, in silence, and a moment later Jerry straightened and sat back on Alec's thighs. He didn't speak. Neither of them spoke, their eyes locked in something like shock at what had passed between them, and then Jerry took a very deep breath and exhaled deliberately.

"God." He sounded slightly hoarse. "I think I startled myself. Christ, Alec, I want to do the most appalling things to you. Are you sure you want to be kissed while I do them?"

"Especially while you do them."

"Well, in that case." Jerry leaned in for one more deliberate, open-mouthed kiss, then rolled off him to lie on his back, shoulder to shoulder, and Alec felt fingers tangling with his own. "My God, you go straight to my prick. How are you within my reach? Why is there not a queue?"

The idea was absurd, the compliment enchanting. "I think you might be unusual," Alec said.

"I'm unique," Jerry corrected him. "And it takes one to know one. Ah, well, everyone else's obliviousness is my advantage." The usual casual confidence was returning to his voice. "I'm starving. Let us leave this den of iniquity before I surrender entirely to voluptuousness, and get something to eat."

# Chapter Seven

The next few weeks were some of the best and worst of Alec's life.

He made his humble apologies to the Duchess of Ilvar, who regarded him with a chilly eye and gave him a lengthy prepared speech of rebuke for his unfilial behaviour. Alec stood through it, eyes submissively lowered, and went to his knees later that evening with Jerry gripping his hair, spending in his mouth and over his face, then kissing him till his lips felt raw. He presented his father, on instruction, with a list of small debts and a wholly fictitious note of hundred and twenty pounds owed at baccarat to one Templeton Lane, and received a banker's draft via Merrow, Ilvar's secretary. This he sent to Annabel, who sent it back by return and without a note.

"Don't try that again," Jerry said, without sympathy. "You can bend without breaking, but it's not in everyone's power. Don't ask your siblings to do that for you."

Alec spent the money on new clothes instead. He needed them, since the Society columns had all mentioned the rapprochement between Ilvar and his wayward younger son, and he found himself once again receiving the invitations that had dried up years ago. It was early July now, the social season coming to its close as minds turned to the grouse shooting due to start on the Glorious Twelfth of August. His father would go up to Castle Speight on the first of

August, hosting a small group of people for a few days, then there would be a grand dinner for forty, a mixture of politicians and aristocrats who were willing to overlook the Duchess's origins and manner. Alec was yet to be invited.

"Give it time," Jerry said.

"I'm not worried."

"You look preoccupied."

They were at the races. Alec would normally have attended professionally for the illustrated papers, but that was impossible. People would notice him now, and to be seen working might be construed as a reproach to his father. He felt rather sick at the number of commissions he had to turn down for the illustrated papers, but at least he'd won the fairytale book job, which was something to fill his time. He was here as an idler now, overdressed for the general crowd in his smart new morning suit, with Jerry at his side, but he still couldn't stop himself looking for faces, scenes, details.

"It's habit," he said. "I like doing sporting scenes. Crowds and action."

"Ah, is that it? I thought it looked like your fingers were itching."

"Are yours?" This wasn't Royal Ascot, with expensive finery on display, but Alec still felt the need to say it, to remind himself that his sharp, attentive, understanding lover was a thief.

"Heavens, no. This is all bustle work. The chap over there— soft brown hat, Harris tweed—is dipping. He had a fob watch off the portly gentleman and if he doesn't take the fuddled youth in the grey suit while he's passing—ah, there goes the wallet, smooth as butter. It's a pleasure to watch."

Alec had never seen a pickpocket in action before, or never noticed one. "Goodness. Are there any others?"

They watched the crowds for a good hour while Jerry pointed out thieves. It was far more interesting than the horse racing, and

Alec found himself planning sketches of pickpockets in action, and composing the captions in his head. He wanted a pencil and sketchpad with a sudden, agonised yearning to get to work. Was this meant to be entertaining, drifting around a racetrack, gambling money you could afford to lose, which was trivial, or couldn't, which was stupid?

Not that they were here for gambling, or at least not that sort. The Duke of Ilvar owned several racehorses, two of which were running today. He was in the owner's enclosure, and Alec felt a new kind of nervous excitement as they headed off in that direction. He wanted this to work for the sake of the long game; there was no denying that he also wanted to impress Jerry.

He gave his name to the man at the gate— "Lord Alexander Pyne-ffoulkes, with Mr. Gerald Vane"—and they were admitted. The enclosure was all morning suits and finery. Jerry plucked two glasses of champagne from a passing waiter with his usual insouciance and they strolled through the crowd, approaching His Grace of Ilvar as the half-hour chimed.

"Lord Alexander!"

Alec swung round, and smiled as he saw the oncoming woman, her husband in her wake. The Countess of Moreton was tall and statuesque, with thick brown hair pinned in elegant loops under an extremely dashing hat. She was in her early forties, and three children had thickened her figure, but she still had an unmistakably athletic look and a long stride. She had once been a music hall trapeze artist, just as the unassuming man by her side had once been a clerk, before a sequence of family disasters had left him with the coronet.

"Lady Moreton," Alec said, taking her hand. "And Lord Moreton, how lovely to see you. May I introduce my friend, Mr. Gerald Vane?"

Jerry bowed gracefully. Lady Moreton gave him three fingers and a smile, gently passed him over to her husband, and asked Alec about his well-being. He in turn conveyed his regards for Lady Penelope, the oldest Moreton girl, and they were chatting amicably when the Duke of Ilvar came past.

This was the tricky part. Alec hadn't known if his father would greet him, command his attention, wait to be approached, or acknowledge him at all. He'd kept the portly figure in the corner of his eye, and he noticed as Ilvar slowed. Not stopped—of course he would not stop and wait to greet his son—but definitely slowed.

"Oh," Alec said. "Sir—"

"Your Grace," Lady Moreton said, turning smoothly. "How lovely. Is the Duchess with you?"

Ilvar bowed, a small movement making his own superiority clear. "She is not, Lady Moreton."

"What a shame. I met her recently and I was hoping to pursue our conversation. Will you be in London a little while longer, sir?"

"Until the end of the month, when we will return to Castle Speight."

"Oh, how delightful. I am chafing to be at Crowmarsh for the summer, as are the boys, but there are two more parties that absolutely *must* be attended lest my daughter go into a decline." She struck an attitude, eyes brimming with amusement. "On which— may we hope to see you at the Cirencesters' ball, Lord Alexander?"

"I don't think I have the honour."

"You will," Lady Moreton assured him. "I shall speak to Tommy Cirencester at once, and I'm claiming at least two dances from you on Penelope's behalf. Now, I will leave you to your father. Delightful to meet you, Mr. Vane—are you of the Cirencester family too?"

"Not a member of whom her ladyship would have heard," Jerry said with a smile. "The connection is some way up the family tree."

"Which is exhaustingly large, I know. We will see you at Cirencester House, Lord Alexander. Duke, I will venture to call on

Her Grace very soon. And if I don't have the honour of meeting you before then, may I wish you many congratulations on the anniversary of your nuptials. Moreton and I celebrated our twentieth anniversary last year—a very small event, with our family and dearest friends. Two decades of marital harmony is something of which we Darby and Joans should be proud."

The Duke drew himself up slightly. Alec suspected he was not entirely pleased to be grouped with a mere earl and countess, but at that moment a man's voice said, "Greta, how lovely! Hello there, Tim."

Lady Moreton's face lit up at the sight of a very handsome young man of Indian looks in a remarkably well-cut suit. He was accompanied by an even younger woman who bore a strong resemblance to him, in a gloriously frothy white dress with a huge feather curling from her hat. "Freddy, Sophia, how delightful to see you! Now, I am sure you know the Duke of Ilvar."

The young man inclined his head. "I don't believe we've met."

"I beg your pardon," Lady Moreton said. "Your Highnesses, His Grace the Duke of Ilvar. Sir, Prince Frederick and Princess Sophia Duleep Singh."

"Your Highnesses." The Duke bowed, somewhat stiffly. He wasn't often obliged to do that.

Alec and Jerry bowed as well, in silent unintroduced obscurity. The Prince and Princess were children of the last Maharaja of the Sikh empire, with Princess Sophia the goddaughter of the Queen herself. Their father had signed away his empire to Britain as a child, but his offspring still had its titles, even if they were empty, and its coffers, which weren't.

"Delighted to meet you," Prince Frederick told the Duke graciously. "I believe you've a horse running?"

He and the Duke exchanged a few words about odds and the state of the ground, while Lady Moreton engaged Princess Sophia in conversation that quickly became animated. The royal siblings moved on after a few moments, taking the Earl and Countess with them, and the Duke gave Alec a look in which he was sure he detected a glimmer of approval. "I wasn't aware you knew the Moretons."

"Yes, sir. The Countess is charming, and Penny—Lady Penelope—is a wonderful young lady. There are twin boys as well, who are rather a handful."

"Hmph," Ilvar said. "Not much to them in the way of land, is there? And some sort of trouble, I recall."

"There was a bad business with the previous Lord Moreton. Bigamy," Alec mouthed, for discretion, though the scandal was two decades old. "The current earl inherited unexpectedly. They're not great landholders, but Lord Moreton's known for good management and they're widely liked." He hardly needed to point that out, considering Lady Moreton was on first-name terms with marchionesses and princes, but the Duke's instinct was ever to dismiss those lower than himself.

"And you'll be dancing with their girl at the Cirencesters' ball."

Alec attempted an embarrassed smile, very conscious of Jerry's silent presence. "If she'll have me. And if I receive an invitation, naturally, but Lady Moreton is very close to Lady Cirencester, and very practical."

"Well." The Duke seemed to be considering. "Good company to keep." He gave Alec a nod, seemed about to move on, then said, "By the way. Have you arrangements for the summer?"

"None, sir."

"I'll have Merrow write to you."

He passed on without further acknowledgement. Alec and Jerry spent a little longer in the enclosure, then sauntered out. They chatted idly on the way to the railway station, and in the crowded compartment, then once they were finally in a hansom cab, Jerry let out a long breath. "That was promising."

"I think it was," Alec said. "I think he's going to invite me."

"Did you plan to meet the Moretons there?" Jerry slanted a brow.

"I found out when they'd be going. I did think, if Father saw me with the right sort of people, it might help. The royals arriving was an unexpected stroke of luck."

"Wasn't it. You know, if you're such pals with the Moretons, who are such pals with the Duleep Singhs—"

"I've never even been introduced to Princess Sophia so no, I can't help you rob them."

"Oh, well, worth a try. You were saying?"

"Only that Lady Moreton is awfully good friends with Lady Cirencester, and that's the kind of connection I think Father wants. I'm not sure how he feels about Indian royalty, but the Duchess would very much like to condescend to Lady Cirencester without the risk of being cut dead in return."

"Ouch," Jerry said. "So what's the lure you're trailing with the Moretons' girl?"

Alec made a face, feeling vaguely embarrassed. As if Jerry would care. "It's not really a lure. It's—well, the thing is, Penny is still very young, and I'm afraid she has developed rather a novelistic view of me."

"Novelistic?"

"Living in an attic, simultaneously well born and utterly unsuitable, a starving artist, yes I *know*, don't laugh. She'll grow out of it. Lady Moreton, who is enormously sensible, would far rather Penny realised for herself that I'm not an interestingly romantic figure at all, so she's made a point of being friendly. She says Penny would like nothing more than for her wicked parents to oppose the match."

Jerry raised a brow. Alec sighed. "It's nothing to do with me at all, not really. Penny just wants a romance. A proper melodrama with hearts and souls everywhere. Her twin brothers want to be circus performers."

Jerry snorted. "I see."

"They're quite a family. But meanwhile—well, if my father thinks I might be on the verge of a society wedding, if he believes he could find advantage in that, it might help."

"Your brother's married, isn't he?"

"Father didn't attend," Alec said. "It was before the final estrangement but things had been worsening for a while and Melissa's aunt very helpfully died—that sounds dreadful—anyway they had a small private ceremony and George didn't ask him to come. I'm sure he'd see the advantage in a big wedding now, with an earl's daughter and the Cirencesters present and so on."

"Clever."

Alec ducked his head. "Well, it's what you said. Giving him what he wants."

"Mmm. You don't think the Moretons might actually consider you eligible, once you're back in your father's favour? He could settle a very nice income on you if you wanted."

"Possibly, but it's not something I'd consider," Alec said. "I couldn't give Penny a normal marriage. I've no inclination that way, and even if I did, I'd still be what I am, and I can't imagine any woman wanting *that* in a husband."

Jerry's brows drew together. "What do you mean, what you are?"

"You know very well. All the things you like about me. Passivity and pliancy and helplessness—"

"Wait a moment. For one thing, there are plenty of women who like the whip hand in the bedroom. For another, why the tone of voice? What's wrong with you?"

Alec almost laughed. "Well, I'm not precisely manly, am I?"

"Perhaps not, by the usual definition. Would you say I am?"

*Manly*. Alec thought of Jerry's contained violence, of his dark lust for control, and the way he'd probed into Alec's needs to satisfy them both. "Well, yes, of course. You're the very opposite of me. You know what you want and you do it without hesitation. You take charge."

"How flattering. So Lady Penelope would be better off married to me?"

"Christ!" Alec found himself genuinely appalled. "Don't say that."

"Why not? Because I'm a dangerous degenerate who oughtn't be allowed near an innocent virgin?"

"Well, without putting it *quite* that way…"

"Indeed. This isn't about 'manliness', whatever that may mean. You ought not to marry any passing girl, not because you're lacking in some way, and certainly not because you don't have sufficient character, but because you have particular tastes that require a particular partner. That's all, and it's hardly unusual. I'm not sure how anyone expects a marriage to succeed when the couple are obliged to unite for life before finding out whether their desires are compatible."

"It probably explains why there are so many unhappy marriages."

"And you refuse to add to their ranks, even though you have wealth, social position, and your father's approval for the taking." Jerry's brows twitched. "I don't know about manly, but I'd call that decent."

Alec felt himself blush. "Hardly. I'm not doing something good, only refraining from doing something bad."

"Trust me, most people don't refrain. Talking of which, I should like to know what it is we do, or what I might make you do, that you consider particularly unmanly." He rolled his tongue over the word.

Alec swallowed. "Er, why?"

Jerry's grin was satanic. "Guess."

The invitation to the Ilvars' anniversary celebration came at last. Alec's attendance was commanded from the first of August, for the whole period from the small house party to the grand dinner.

"Now we need to get me in," Jerry said. "It's not a disaster if you can't, you can take Templeton as your valet, but two of us will be a great deal better than one. Will there be any other young men there? If there aren't you can hint you need company, and if there are, you can suggest I'd add to the gaiety of the event. But let's see you ingratiate yourself with your father first."

Alec did his best, thanks to the promised invitation to the Cirencesters' ball, where he duly danced with Lady Penelope. She was a tall buxom girl, almost his own height, who would probably be called handsome rather than pretty, but she had her mother's eyes and smile, which in Alec's opinion qualified her for beauty. Her sparkling looks and blushing giggles as they danced three times produced a crop of arch speculation about Lord A.— and Lady P.— in the society columns.

"I am considering extending an invitation to the Moretons to the celebratory dinner," the Duke of Ilvar informed him. "While not of the highest rank, they are acceptable, and your stepmother has been most pleased with Lady Moreton's recent courtesies."

"That is very generous of you, sir. Uh, do you—do you propose to invite Penny?"

"I do not," Ilvar said majestically. "It is not a gathering of young people and I should rather not give rise to the inevitable speculation that such a visit would create. A wise man considers before linking his family to another."

Alec had to dig his nails into his palms, and even so it took him a moment before he could say, "Yes, sir. Will there be any other young people in attendance, may I ask?"

Ilvar gave him a knowing look. "Worrying you'll be bored, boy?"

"I'm looking forward to seeing the house again, sir. But, well, I'm more considering if I'll have much to contribute to the conversation."

"Very true," his father said, unflatteringly.

"Just a thought, but my pal Vane—you've met him once or twice, sir; he found Her Grace's bracelet? He's going up to Scotland for the grouse shooting at much the same time. Perhaps, if it wouldn't be overburdening the staff..."

And that was Jerry's invitation to the house party secured. Not to the formal dinner, but he seemed unworried. "We'll aim to take the thing before the great unveiling. Frankly, I'd rather be gone before the Moretons arrive."

"Oh. Why?"

"Templeton," Jerry said elliptically. "Wouldn't want them seeing him. Warn me if they're liable to arrive before the rest of the guests for the grand dinner, won't you?"

Alec nodded. They were strolling in Hyde Park, taking advantage of the morning before the heat became intolerable. London was baking in the mid-July heat, and it had been a dry spring; the grass was yellowing, the flowerbeds wilting. He found himself thinking of Castle Speight. His childhood home was not a place of happy memories, but the grounds were extensive, lush and green, cool and damp in the mornings, and the moors above them stretched for miles. One could breathe clean air there, at least outside the castle.

"Not long now," Jerry said. "Are you prepared? Anything worrying you?"

Alec almost laughed. "Well, a few things. No, I'm ready."

Jerry didn't respond immediately. Finally he said, "When we embarked on this I told you we wouldn't be open to changes of mind or heart. In or out."

"I know. I'm in."

"I'd like you to consider that again."

Alec blinked. "I told you—"

"No. Listen. I'm not suggesting you're not committed. I understand you want to strike at your father. I know how much this has already cost you. But one thing I have learned in this game is that sometimes you have to walk away from an investment."

"Wait," Alec said. "Is there a problem? Are you backing out?"

"No, I'm not, but I would like to be sure the cost isn't too high for you. Look, everything you have done so far is Lord Alexander. Apologising to your father, alienating your siblings, seeming to disregard his actions for profit: you know it's all lies. But if you abuse your father's hospitality to help me rob him, that is not Lord Alexander, and it won't be a lie. That will be you, Alec. You'll be a traitor and a thief."

"You're a thief."

"Yes, and I'm not a good man." Jerry was looking away, tapping the path with the end of his walking cane in a light manner that suggested he was making an effort not to do it harder. "I'm not a good man but you are. And this is a betrayal."

"Sorry?" Alec said. "You do remember what my father did?"

"Your father is a piece of shit, and you aren't. I've forced you into enough things—"

"You have not. I made my choices."

"I don't want you to force you into this," Jerry went on over him. "I want you to consider that, no matter what, this will be a betrayal and to be sure that won't eat away at you, because betrayal does. It's one of those sins that sits in the gut."

"I find it hard to believe you're warning me about sins."

"Who more qualified?" Jerry asked, with a mocking twist that Alec didn't feel was directed towards him. "I'm not moralising; that would be a ridiculous spectacle. I just wanted to say that you can change your mind. You don't have to; I am very ready for the job. But if you've had second thoughts, if you fear this will damage you, if you want to stop for any reason, I won't hold it against you, and I will make sure Templeton doesn't either."

Alec licked his lips. "Do you think I should stop?"

"I fear this will hurt you. That's not the same thing. Look, betrayal is the great unforgivable in my line, and, not unrelatedly, common as hell. When I go down, it will be because someone I trust sells me out, and I only hope it's not Temp. It's—ugh, how can I put this? Corrosive to the soul, even souls as tarnished as mine. I'd rather not see you suffer that."

"But don't you feel, if someone has done something terrible, one should take whatever steps are necessary?"

"Of course I do. You can't betray someone to whom you owe no loyalty. But it's probably quite difficult to tease out what loyalty means when it's one's father. I think he—if he were to find out— would feel betrayed. Don't you?"

"Why should what he feels matter to me?" Alec demanded. "Why should I care?"

"You shouldn't in the slightest, but I'm not certain you won't. God damn it, I'm not trying to persuade you of anything. Left to myself I'd clean out Castle Speight of everything down to your father's false teeth. All I'm saying is that I don't want this to hurt you—*I* don't want to hurt you—and if we go ahead, I don't want it to be because you were afraid to ask me to stop."

Alec stared ahead at the park, the trees, a swirling flock of starlings. He couldn't look at his companion.

He was going to commit a betrayal. Jerry was absolutely right about that. The months of lies were going to reach a culmination in

Castle Speight, the trap he'd helped build would be sprung. He'd embarked on this path certain in his soul that it didn't matter what he did so long as his goal was clear, his heart pure. The lie of that had become clear weeks ago.

Jerry was right. If he did this, he wouldn't be able to forgive himself. It would be unforgivable.

He made himself think of holly berries squashed on the floor, the sharp smell of greenery and church candles, and the terrible void in his heart left by Cara, who had made them all promise never to forget what Father had done, and he took a deep breath. "We're going to do it."

# Chapter Eight

They had first-class tickets up to Broughton. The Duke of Ilvar paid for it all.

Alec arrived at Euston in a hackney, and a sweat. A railway station on a hot day was always a little bit like Hell and this was no exception. Whistles screamed and wheels screeched like souls in torment; steam billowed across platforms; the heat radiated out from the great black iron demon-steeds and beat down from the iron-girded roof, which lay suffering under the relentless sun. Ladies' finery drooped; men's collar-points wilted; bouquets and buttonholes lost their freshness as quickly as their wearers in the grimy, sweaty streets. Men and women hurried by, craning their necks to catch sight of clocks, platform signs, trains, or loved ones. And in the middle of it, cool, unhurried, in a light summer jacket and a very dashing grey soft hat, was Jerry, with an impassive black-clad clean-shaven attendant by his side. It took Alec a second look to recognise the well-built serving man as Templeton Lane.

"Alec, old man," Jerry hailed him. "You cut it fine. Let's take our seats. Leave your bags with Fanshaw, he'll deal with it all."

Alec indicated as much to the porter, tipped him, and followed Jerry down the platform. He didn't dare look at Lane, who would doubtless be travelling third.

The coach was one of the older style, divided into compartments of two facing benches. There were already two suited men in there. Alec nodded politely and seated himself opposite Jerry.

It would be a long journey: two and a half hours to Crewe, then a change to Broughton, where they would use the Castle Speight private line that the Duke had built at heaven knew what expense. He was not sure if he was glad or sorry they couldn't talk openly.

He'd brought pencils and a sketchpad, but he felt a little self-conscious taking them out in the company of businessmen. He settled with his new book instead, a collection of short stories, read the first three, confused and increasingly disturbed, and looked up to see Jerry watching him.

"Are you enjoying that?"

"I wouldn't say enjoying, precisely."

"Your face has suggested as much. What on earth are you reading?"

"It's a new thing. *The King In Yellow.* Good in its way, but I don't know if I like its way. Weird and macabre and feels rather like an opium dream. It's about a play that induces madness in anyone who reads it."

Jerry slanted a brow. "Sounds like the author's been at the St. James's Theatre recently."

One of the businessmen guffawed, and added, "I beg your pardon." Jerry waved a graceful hand.

Alec hid behind his book again, feeling rather self-conscious. Jerry's remark had been an allusion to *The Importance of Being Earnest,* a smash hit earlier in the year, until the author had been arrested for gross indecency. Taking his name off the programme and advertising hadn't saved the box office from the taint of scandal, and the play had closed. Wilde had only been in prison two months, the scandal had yet to fully subside, and Alec was rather conscious that *The King in Yellow* had a similar sort of atmosphere to Wilde's work. Perhaps he should have brought something less decadent. Perhaps Jerry was angry he'd given them away.

No, he was being absurd. The book was a legitimately published popular hit that anyone might read, and Jerry wasn't sniping at *The Importance of Being Earnest* for any reason other than that he loathed all Wilde's plays. And yet Alec still felt snubbed, self-conscious, uncomfortable. It was an all-too-familiar sense of nauseous anticipation, dreading the disapproval and rebuke and condemnation he knew would come, and, now he'd recognised it, he knew just why he had it. It was what he'd felt each time he'd come back to Castle Speight—home—from school. He wondered how old he'd be when that dread went away, if it ever did.

The businessmen left the carriage after Tamworth. Nobody else got on. The guard slammed the doors, the train moved off, and Jerry let out a sigh. "Alone at last."

That they were, since the only access to the compartment was the platform door. They would be entirely free from eavesdropping or interruption until the next stop.

"Is there anything we need to discuss?" Alec asked.

"I don't think so. Try to relax."

"Of course. We're off to a marvellous party. What fun."

"It will be." Jerry tipped his head back, eyes narrowing a little. "We've a week to play with and a hell of a game to play in it. And I like a challenge."

"I thought you liked to be in control."

"That, too, but there has to be something *to* control, doesn't there? Something that takes effort to master." His brow tilted in a very familiar way, sending a shiver through Alec. "Do you know what I regret? That I didn't have you at Lady Sefton's soirée."

"There was hardly an opportunity. Was there?"

"I could have made one. Taken you upstairs into some room."

"And?" Alec asked, holding his gaze.

"And pushed you against the door," Jerry said, low. "Pulled your trousers down and your shirt up and had you there and then. No preparation, nothing but spit, and you'd have had to be silent as the grave. Not even a gasp, far less a cry, while I had you as I pleased."

"Have you had this in mind for a while?"

"Since Lady Sefton's soirée. I've had you on my mind since Euston."

"The next stop isn't till—"

"Stafford. That seems to me long enough for one of us to have his cock sucked."

Alec went down onto his knees, between Jerry's legs. Jerry shifted to make room, and Alec ran his hands over the grey cloth of his light suit, the hard-muscled legs.

"Forward," Jerry said softly.

He wasn't sure if it was an observation of his behaviour or an order. He leaned forward anyway, pushing his face between Jerry's legs, mouthing him through the cloth, and felt a hand in his hair. Jerry's fingers drove down to the nape of his neck, and stroked up against the grain of the small hairs, making Alec shiver.

He dealt with the buttons, fingers a little clumsy, freed Jerry's stand. He'd had that in his mouth a few times now, on order, but not had much chance to explore for himself. He stroked the length of it, ridged, smooth under his fingers, a little curved, and felt Jerry's hand tighten.

"Right, Your Graceling. I want you to pleasure me like you're getting paid for it."

Good God. Alec leaned in and gently closed his mouth over the head.

"Yes." Jerry's fingers were moving, pressing into Alec's scalp, not quite pulling his hair but certainly holding it tight. "Oh, yes. We were discussing you getting fucked at the most inconvenient possible juncture, weren't we? So that you'd have to clean yourself off and rejoin the party with your arse aching and your prick throbbing. I wasn't planning to let you come, you understand. Are you hard now?" Alec grunted affirmatively. "Good. Don't touch yourself. Christ, you're beautiful."

Alec looked up sharply. Jerry's eyes were wide and startled, as if he was shocked by his own words, then his lips curled deliberately. "With a cock in your mouth, I meant to say. I'm not sure if I prefer making you whimper or not letting you make a sound. Yes, like that. Deeper."

Alec worked his hands into Jerry's clothing. Skin on skin, feeling, caressing, stroking as best he could given the constriction of cloth, using his tongue the way Jerry liked, swaying with the movement of the train. Jerry's hands were moving urgently in his hair. "Dear God, Alec, my noble plaything. I will have you unrelentingly when we next fuck."

Alec made a noise around his mouthful that sounded in his own ears like a sob. He leaned in, taking Jerry as deep as he could, his cheeks and jaw burning from the movements, and felt strong fingers tighten on his scalp.

"Oh God, the feel of you, the way you suck me. The way you want me— Alec!" Jerry came, gasping, in his throat, pulsed once, twice, jerked Alec's head back, and let the last spurt hit his face.

Alec knelt, mouth open. The spend was wet on his cheek.

Jerry leaned forward and wiped it up with one finger. He pressed it to Alec's open mouth, and Alec closed his lips around it as though it were a sacrament.

They stayed like that for a long silent moment, eyes locked, then Jerry straightened. He pulled out a handkerchief, wiping Alec's face first, then tidying himself, all the time watching Alec as he knelt on the jolting floor.

"We've a few more minutes to the station, I'd think." He sounded raspy.

"Yes."

"Stroke yourself," Jerry said. "No, don't touch your buttons. Through your clothes will do."

Alec moved his hand between his legs. His prick was trapped and painfully needy.

"Lightly. Widen your legs." Jerry was watching, eyes intent. "Christ, I love watching you pleasure yourself. The look on your face. Rub harder."

The train lurched slightly. It was slowing. "We're stopping."

"Good."

"Jerry—"

"Don't stop until I tell you. Keep your hand moving."

"Jerry!" Alec didn't know if he was going to come, if he wasn't, or what he'd do. His arousal was painfully close; so was the next station. "Please!"

"Keep going."

"I'm going to come." In his clothing. The humiliation burned.

"Don't you dare stop touching yourself until I tell you. Now, or I take my pleasure on you tonight and you get nothing. Understand?"

"Yes. Oh God." He was so close, his own hand's pressure and Jerry's words reducing him to nothing but sensation, he was reaching the peak—

"Stop."

Alec jerked his hand away. The train whistle screeched, the carriage jolted, his prick throbbed with furious need.

"Up." Jerry looked wild. He shut his eyes, and Alec could see his face smoothing back into a calm mask. "Quick. And brush off your knees.

Alec's knees weren't the problem; he could hardly stand. He managed to get his bag on his lap—carefully—before the platform guard pulled open the compartment door with a cry of "Stafford!" The blood was thumping in his ears.

Jerry had brought him to the edge and made him wait before, but this felt different. A new level of the control he used to reduce Alec to helpless wanting, but also, perhaps, a warning. If you knew a man's desires, you had him in the palm of your hand. Had Jerry given away a little more of himself than he'd intended?

Under other circumstances the very idea would have been a thrill. As it was, the thought gave Alec a slightly sick feeling.

He liked Jerry enormously: he was amusing, intelligent, a good conversationalist, a superb listener. He wanted him physically more than anyone he'd ever known, and not just because he was hopelessly enslaved to dark eyes, absurdly mobile eyebrows, and a wicked mouth. It was the way Jerry fucked that made him irresistible, teasing out Alec's desires and taking such dark enjoyment in fulfilling them. That intense attention was something Alec tried not to think of, because he wanted it so much. He felt like curling up around it and hoarding it as the Duchess did her jewels.

In fact, Jerry was like nobody else he'd ever known, and Alec would have counted himself absurdly fortunate if all they'd had was the companionship and the fucking. But when the mask slipped, revealing the man underneath; when Jerry cared what Alec thought and wanted him to be happy; most of all when he startled himself with uncalculated truths…

That Jerry could break Alec's heart. That was the man he barely saw, which was good, because every glimpse of him was a danger. There was no happy ever after to be had with Jerry Crozier, there would be no future, and if Alec ever forgot that and let himself hope, he'd be lost.

He'd known it from the start and if he had any sense he'd have resisted his own treacherous desires—which was about as useful as saying that if a gambler had any sense he wouldn't have staked every penny he had on the fall of the dice. He'd wanted to play, and by God he'd had value for his stake, but the game didn't have long left to run.

There were other men in the carriage all the way to Crewe, and on the smaller train to Broughton. Alec tucked himself in the corner and hid in his sketchbook, not caring any more if it looked odd. He'd drawn Jerry's face in there, over and over, sketches from memory and doodles in odd moments. Images of Jerry laughing, of that cold, remote expression that betrayed fury, of his eyebrows at a dozen angles. Of his face when he'd looked down at Alec after they'd kissed for the first time. He'd worked on that and made it a full-page piece. It was one of the best things he'd ever drawn.

They changed again at Broughton to take the Castle Speight spur. A uniformed man ushered them to the private train, informing them that there was one more passenger to come. It was a single car, so Templeton Lane joined them with the baggage, sitting silent and severe in the black garb of a manservant, which Alec noted was cut to diminish his broad shoulders.

"This is very fine," Jerry remarked, looking around the upholstered coach with its brass fittings and mahogany. "Is it used for anything but Castle Speight?"

"I don't know. It's after my time really. Father started the work about ten years ago."

"Must have cost a few bob."

"I expect so. Oh, I think our fellow traveller is here."

A gentleman who looked to be in his thirties but was almost entirely bald hurried down the platform, holding a large document case. He exchanged a brief word with the railwayman, and sat down with a gasp. "Gentlemen. Please excuse my heat."

"It's warm to be hurrying," Alec said sympathetically.

"Really a matter of some inconvenience," the man mumbled, mostly to himself as the doors were slammed. "Am I correct in thinking—Lord Alexander?"

"Yes, and this is Mr. Gerald Vane, my guest, Mr.—?"

"Merrow. Frederick Merrow. His Grace's confidential secretary. I, ah, if I may say so, Lord Alexander, I hope that my role in communicating the Duke's wishes has been, or will be, understood as merely the obligation of my position and in no way an expression of my own opinions. His Grace prefers me to *digest*, if I may so put it, and *express* his wishes, which are phrased and communicated entirely in line with his command. I pray I may be understood."

Alec shot a look at Jerry, whose face was unhelpfully blank, then worked it out. Merrow, the writer of those casually dismissive letters to the Duke's children, including the one that had given Cara her death sentence, was feeling uncomfortable at meeting their recipient. That was probably a good sign as to Alec's increased favour in his father's eyes.

He made himself smile at the man. Merrow only did what the Duke told him, like everyone else. "I'm very pleased to meet you, Mr. Merrow, and don't worry in the slightest. I quite understand your role. Oh, we're moving, marvellous," he added with hearty meaninglessness in the hope of heading off any further conversation.

"What a delightful thing." Jerry came in over Merrow's reply, greatly to Alec's relief. "How convenient to have one's own private railway."

"The road down from Castle Speight winds a great deal. I dare say it saves a lot of time."

"The railway takes twenty minutes, where the road journey is an hour and a half," Mr. Merrow interjected. "His Grace's wisdom and foresight in the investment are remarkable."

"And is it just for the Duke and his guests?"

"There is a goods carriage which His Grace very obligingly permits to be leased for the benefit of the nearby villages if he does not require the line."

"Most generous," Jerry murmured.

"May I ask, Mr. Merrow, who will be in residence?" Alec enquired. "I believe my father has a few guests present before the grand dinner."

"Indeed, Lord Alexander. There is Miss Hackett, the sister of the Duchess. Sir Paul Maitland, chief constable of Cheshire, and

Lady Maitland. Two gentleman of industry, Mr. Forbes and his wife, and Mr. Pelham. Tomorrow we also welcome Mr. Ayres, a magistrate and highly respected gentleman of the county and Mrs. Ayres, and Sir William and Lady Cooke."

"All the dignitaries, in fact." Clearly his father was throwing crumbs to useful people with this house party, the better to avoid cluttering up his grand dinner with provincials. "Well. That sounds very… I look forward to it."

Jerry's eyes hooded, indicating near-fatal boredom. Alec pressed his lips together and looked out to admire the view.

The Castle Speight station was some five minutes' journey from the castle by cart. That took Templeton Lane, Mr. Merrow, and the luggage; Alec and Jerry agreed they would stretch their legs. It was a warm afternoon but breezy, without London's heat, and the grey-green-yellow slopes of the Bowland Fells made his breath hitch. He loved the fells, and it had been too long.

"I like the railway line," Jerry observed. "It's nice to see a rich man make use of his money. I'd definitely have a private railway line to my castle."

"It makes the whole business of travelling far more pleasant. It was such a slog back from school for the holidays—you'd get off the train and still have hours to go, and they only ever sent the second-best carriage, not the one with modern springs and proper upholstery. That was reserved for the Duke and Duchess."

"Naturally. It's rather bleak round here."

"It's beautiful," Alec said. "Or I think so, at least."

"Eye of the beholder. I like landscapes where one can't be seen for miles. I also like houses that one can leave slightly more easily than by a train that belongs to one's host, or alternatively a two-hour slow passage down a hill where one may expect to find the police waiting to examine one's pockets."

"I did tell you it was inaccessible," Alec said guiltily.

"I already knew, but there's nothing like sight of the ground to clarify the problem. Don't worry, I have all sorts of ideas. Are you ready for this?"

"Yes. Of course."

"Mmm." Jerry didn't push him. "And is there anything to fear in the guest list?"

"Death by anecdote, I should think," Alec said, eliciting a bark of laughter that sent birds flying off the fence posts. They walked companionably up the incline, and Castle Speight came into view. Alec heard his companion's soft hiss.

He'd forgotten what an imposing building it was. One did when one grew up somewhere, but he contemplated the building now with fresh eyes, and found himself rather embarrassed.

"Good Lord," Jerry said. "How medieval."

"Gothic Revival, actually. It's the fourth castle on the site. The first was Norman. The second was destroyed by the Parliamentarians—we were Royalist—and the third more or less fell down. This one was built around 1794."

"Mid-French Revolution. You have to wonder why our peasants weren't busy at the guillotine as well. Look at it."

Castle Speight was, architecturally, something of a monstrosity. The towers on the left of the main hall were broad and squat with stubby crenellations; those on the right resembled a Gothic cathedral with soaring arches, spires, and flying buttresses. Somehow, the heavy side entirely overwhelmed the attempt at grace. The building sat bleakly on the hilltop, glowering out over the valley with grey stone aggression.

"I don't think it wants to be robbed," Jerry said. "Well, life is hard. Do we enter by the steps?"

"I suppose we must. I always went in through the gatehouse but you are a guest. So am I, really."

The great oak door was opened for them by a footman, and the butler was there to greet them with a deep bow. Alec recognised neither, which was no surprise; the Duchess did not retain staff long. He didn't really recognise the hall, either.

The old threadbare tapestries and weapons had gone, replaced by oil paintings of horses, most of them Stubbs. The rugs were new; the furniture looked like Pugin's work, finely wrought pieces rendered trivial by the echoing stone hall that demanded great hulking furniture. There had used to be a huge Jacobean carved dresser, and a suit of armour at the foot of the great stair.

"Oh," he said. "It's been redecorated."

"Yes, Lord Alexander," the butler informed him with a nicely judged inclination of the head. "All the main apartments have been entirely refurbished in the last five years under Her Grace's direction. John will conduct you to your room."

Alec wandered upstairs, following the footman like any guest, since his father was not available to be greeted. The busts and their pedestals had gone too, replaced by glass jars of stuffed birds and animals. As with the furniture downstairs they were excellent pieces, the creatures bright and clean and posed with striking beauty, but not quite right where they stood in the stone halls.

"She's changed everything." Alec felt numb. It was a peculiar thing to come home and discover so little of it left. He had not thought of Castle Speight with fondness in his years of exile, but he hadn't wanted it all to be changed.

"It's delightfully modern," Jerry said with the faintest note of warning in his voice, and Alec pulled himself together and let the waiting footman show them to their rooms.

They were both in the Upper Corridor West, in adjoining guest bedrooms. The rooms he and his siblings had had as children were probably in holland covers. His bags had already been unpacked and his evening dress laid out, reminding him, rather jarringly, that Templeton Lane was acting as his valet as well.

There was hot water in the jug; it was past six. Alec washed off the smuts of the railway, plus a remaining trace of dried spunk on his cheek, with some relief. He got dressed in his new finery, and had just satisfied himself that he looked respectable when a knock came at the door.

"Come in," he called.

It was Jerry, looking extraordinarily good in evening dress. He shut the door behind him. "All right?"

"Yes. Fine. No, not really. I don't know why I thought it would be the same. It's not my house; they can do as they please. But..."

"Why does it bother you?"

Alec wasn't sure how to answer. "I don't know. It's been a certain way for a hundred and fifty years, but you might well think a fresh look was overdue. The history of the family..." He tailed off.

"What?"

"Mother," Alec said. "That's what's gone. She's gone, and now the place she lived, where I knew her, is gone. He took down the paintings of her long ago when the new Duchess came. There's nothing left."

He couldn't say anything else. Jerry hesitated for a second, then came over. He put a cautious hand on Alec's shoulder, the barest touch of comfort, and then he gave a very quiet sound of exasperation and pulled him into a one-armed hug. Alec held on, breathing deeply, face in Jerry's shoulder.

He lifted his head after a moment, feeling rather self-conscious. Jerry was looking at him with a little frown.

"Thanks," he said. "Sorry. It's all rather much."

"I know." Jerry's arm tightened slightly. "What's the programme now?"

"We should go down for drinks soon." He'd imagined on the train how they might spend the pre-dinner interval, and he wondered if Jerry wanted that. He didn't in the slightest any more. What he wanted was to be held like this, Jerry's arm strong and comforting around him, a tiny refuge from the bruising world outside.

"Whenever you're ready. No hurry." Jerry brushed a kiss over his cheekbones. "Ah, you poor bastard. This is not right."

Alec tried for a snort. "Are you really offering sympathy because my father the Duke bought new furniture for his castle?"

"When you put it that way, no." Jerry didn't let go, all the same, and they stood together for a moment more until the clock chimed the half hour, and Alec disengaged himself with reluctance. "We should go."

Jerry contemplated him, frowned, and smoothed one of his eyebrows with a careful finger. "Tsk. Better."

"I bet you comb yours."

"And wax them. Come on, Lord Alexander, we've flats to kite."

"We've what?"

Jerry grinned. "We've local dignitaries to meet, is what I said. Let's go."

"Jerry?" Alec caught his hand. "Thank you. You aren't obliged to nursemaid me."

"That is not what I'm doing."

"You've been far kinder to me than most people ever are. And, whatever happens, I wanted to tell you now—"

"Don't," Jerry said, voice harsh.

"Don't what?"

"Anything. I'm not a good man, Alec. If I have redeeming features, they are few and far between. You deserve a great deal better than—than you've had, but don't put me on a pedestal because I'm not as shitty as some others. And while I'm giving orders, stop telling yourself you ought to be stronger or more manly or feel less, or whatever it is now." His fingers tightened on Alec's. "You don't need to be different. It would be a crying shame if you were."

*Will you still be saying that in a week?* Alec didn't ask, didn't press for more. He hadn't meant to push Jerry into any sort of admission, even a guarded one; he wished he hadn't, given that any self-betrayal would inevitably be resented later. The thought of what might have been if only they could have met another way, without any of the theft and lies and treachery, was almost unbearably painful.

He released Jerry's hand. "Let's go down."

The drawing room had been completely refurbished too, this time in French Style, with swags of rich red velvet, ornate decorative scrolls wherever they could be fitted in, and gilt. The mirrors, picture frames, tables, and chairs all gleamed gold; the place looked like a throne room.

"What a magnificent setting," Jerry murmured. "Fit for kings."

The Duke and Duchess had not yet descended. The drawing room held two gentlemen in their sixties, one tall and gaunt, the other shorter and giving evidence of a lifetime of good dinners, and a third, slightly younger man with a sun-darkened complexion and a somewhat tense air. There were four women, two dressed with suitable elegance for the setting. The third, in an aggressively plain dark brown gown, had a marked resemblance to the Duchess, and Alec realised she must be the sister, Miss Hackett. The last was an unremarkable woman in her mid-thirties with hair of an intermediate shade between brown and blonde, drably clad in dove-grey with a modest collar. She looked like the Platonic ideal of a single lady's companion, like boredom on two sensibly-shod feet.

"Good evening, ladies, gentlemen," Alec said, deciding he had to take the bull by the horns. "I'm delighted to meet you all. I'm Alexander. His Grace's second son," he felt compelled to add, in case none of them had heard his name before. He wondered whether to address Miss Hackett as "Aunt" and decided that would be overdoing the bonhomie.

There was a round of introductions, which identified the tall thin man as the retired Chief Constable Sir Paul Maitland (wife in green), the fat one as the retired businessman Mr. Wykeham Forbes (wife in blue) and the tanned one as Mr. Pelham (no wife). Alec received two fingers and an icy look from the Duchess's sister, and a small inclination of the head from the younger woman, introduced as her companion Miss Roy.

They chatted awkwardly for a little while. Mr. Forbes was excessively friendly, and took to calling Alec "Lord Alex". His wife wore what looked like a habitual pleasant smile but said little. Sir Paul clearly had a lifetime's experience of municipal socialising: he made polite conversation of the kind that kept going for hours without ever veering into the personal or interesting. Jerry was pleasant but not nearly as charming as Alec knew he could be, and apparently happy not to attract attention. Miss Hackett sniffed disapproval whenever she found an opportunity; Miss Roy remained silent, but Alec felt her eyes on his face more than once.

It was awful. The party was too small to be made up of people with nothing to say to one another, and was all too obviously an exercise in ticking necessary guests off a list. Things could have been rescued by a charming hostess, but the Duke and Duchess did not come downstairs until almost half past seven. They greeted their guests with suffocating condescension and the Duke gave Lady Maitland his arm into dinner, causing Miss Hackett's nostrils to flare a little.

The meal was excellently cooked; the wines well chosen. The conversation dragged on. His Grace pronounced on various political issues of the day and received agreement as no more than his due. When he'd finished, the Duchess observed to the table in general, "You will note that the castle has been much improved in recent years," and embarked on a lengthy monologue enumerating the renovations. Alec had wondered if Jerry would lead the conversation to topics such as the Duchess's jewels and the security precautions for the grand dinner. He didn't, and nobody else mentioned the dinner either, presumably because they were all aware they were not in the group selected for that honour.

After dinner the ladies retired. Jerry asked the Duke about his racehorses, starting a sporting conversation that lasted for what felt like hours, considering that the group was too small for the remaining men to start a conversation of their own. By the end of it, Sir Paul was rather flushed with port, which he had consumed at a startling rate; Mr. Forbes evidently felt snubbed and irritated; Jerry was basking in the Duke's approval thanks to an impressive body of knowledge about racing; and Alec was glazed with boredom. If he'd actually sacrificed his self-respect and his siblings' love in order to win a place at this table, he was pretty sure he'd have needed to drink the decanter dry to prevent himself breaking down in tears.

They joined the women for a little more uninteresting chat. At ten o'clock precisely, the Duchess announced she was retiring, very much as though she'd been waiting for the chimes, and bade her guests to stay up and enjoy themselves as long as they chose. The Duke accompanied her out, and Mrs. Forbes let out a long, shallow breath as their hosts departed. "Well. We've two fours; would anyone care for a hand of whist?"

"Oh, yes," Lady Maitland said thankfully.

"I do not play cards," Miss Hackett announced with a freezing look.

"Then we shall make up one four," Mrs. Forbes returned, still with the pleasant smile. "Mr. Vane? Lord Alexander?"

Jerry glanced at the Maitlands and Mr. Forbes, none of whom looked willing to forego the chance of some entertainment. "I will deny myself the pleasure this time. A game of billiards, Alec?"

Alec accepted, and led the way to the billiards room. Jerry set the game up with swift movements. "One and then bed for me, I think."

"Very wise. It was a long journey."

Jerry hit the cue ball with some force, scattering balls. Alec took his shot and missed. Jerry made a winding gesture that clearly said, *Hurry up,* and potted the next four in a row. Alec didn't bother trying after that, letting Jerry clear the table and replying at random to his idle chatter as he did so. He was rather more concerned with the icily murderous expression he read in Jerry's dark eyes.

Jerry sent the last ball to its doom with a stab of the cue that came within a whisker of ripping the baize. "Bad luck, old fellow," he announced. "Well, I'm for bed. What about a nightcap?"

Alec topped up their tumblers from the whisky decanter and followed him up the stairs. The whist game was still in full swing.

Jerry led the way to his own room. "Since we're sharing Fanshaw, you might as well stay for that drink." He rang the bell as he spoke.

Alec had wondered if his peculiar mood would be the precursor to something. To Jerry fulfilling his promise on the train, taking Alec over the billiard table or here, up against the door, whispering obscenities, making him writhe. He wanted that, painfully. He knew he wouldn't get it.

He sipped whisky for Dutch courage until Templeton Lane arrived, a picture of the respectable upper servant. Lane murmured "Good evening, sir," and shut the door.

"Anyone in the corridor?" Jerry asked.

"No."

"Good." Jerry knocked back a mouthful of whisky. "Gentlemen, I regret to announce that we're fucked."

# Chapter Nine

Alec felt his stomach plunge. Lane said, calmly, "Why?"

"I suppose it depends how far back you go, for example to the point when I asked you to do one simple task, you anthropoid ape," Jerry said. "Susan Lazarus is here."

"The devil she is. She's in Devon."

"So you assured me. Which makes me question why she's in the drawing room posing as the Duchess's sister's companion, *Templeton*."

Lane took the glass from his hand and drained it. "Fuck."

"Quite. Susan Lazarus, Alec, is the younger generation of a particularly tiresome and persistent detective agency. I am not pleased to see her."

"She was meant to be in Devon," Lane insisted. "I had someone approach the agency with a request for her services, asked the office junior, and paid the idiot housekeeper. They all said she would be in the wilds of… Shit." He rubbed a hand over his mouth and chin. "She primed them to tell the same lie. Of course. That's my girl."

"She wanted to conceal her whereabouts. And she got here before we did. Now, how would that come about?"

"Easy enough if someone talked. It wasn't me, and I doubt it was you." The big man turned, blue eyes glacial. "Any comment, Lord Alexander?"

Alec recoiled. "What do you mean?"

"Stop it, Temp," Jerry said. "All it would have taken is someone recognising me when I was squiring Alec about town. That was always a risk. Equally, it's possible the Ilvars hired her as discreet security for the event, and this is pure rotten chance. Posing as a companion would fool other thieves, but it's pointless if she's after us. I'm pretty sure that chap Pelham isn't a businessman, come to that; he dodged all Forbes' efforts to make professional conversation."

Lane scowled. "Did she recognise you?"

"I don't know," Jerry said. "I've never met her face to face but I'm sure she's had a look at me at some point. She didn't seem to know me, but—"

"Oh, that means nothing. She's worse than her old man for unreadability, and I wouldn't play cards with him if you paid me. Realistically, we're going to have to clear out."

"Or not," Jerry said. "Or, yes, but. Look, if she knows we're here, she'll be expecting us to operate according to our usual practice: get the lie of the land, plan it out, find a foolproof exit. And if she hasn't recognised me, she won't have any reason to be twitchy about Mr. Gerald Vane up till the moment she sets eyes on my valet."

"Therefore?"

"We do it right now," Jerry said calmly. "The parure is in the safe in His Grace's bedroom, yes? It'll be at least an hour's work to get into the thing—"

"I thought you said the safe's lock was unpickable," Alec said.

"No such thing. How does he sleep?"

"Soundly, according to the maid," Lane said.

"And if he doesn't, that's what chloroform's for. In, out, gone before morning, what do you think?"

"Dashing, but stupid. There's a reason we don't act without planning."

"Exactly. We never do, and Lazarus knows it."

"Are you literally saying, 'let's behave like lunatics, it's the last thing she'll expect'?" Lane demanded. "What about getting away?"

"If we move early enough we can be down at the station for the first train to Lancaster, well before any hue and cry. Look, the Bramah is famously impenetrable. Everyone knows you can't pick them. Therefore, if Lazarus is expecting us to crack the safe, she'll think it will be by flim-flam or drilling, neither of which can be done overnight. I say we take the risk."

Lane considered that, then a slow grin dawned. "You may have a point. Do it tonight and vanish. Why not?"

Jerry nodded. "The only problem is, it would leave Alec on his own to answer a lot of awkward questions. Alec, can you handle it if I disappear with Temp and the loot tomorrow?"

"I— Yes. Probably."

Lane gave him a narrow look. "Something wrong? You look queasy."

"I feel it," Alec said. "Sorry. I'll be back in a moment, but— I need to splash my face, I think."

Lane's hand came up, gripping his bicep as he tried to get past. "Wait a moment, friend. If there's a problem, I want to know about it."

"There isn't a problem. I just— Nerves, that's all. Let me go, will you?"

"I don't want to see nerves," Lane said. "Not in these circumstances."

"Alec will be fine. Let him go."

"*Alec* is a loose end, and I don't like loose ends," Lane said, almost mocking the name. "And we're depending on him not to fold when all hell breaks loose. Which—"

"Will be fine," Jerry repeated. "Don't piss about."

Alec tugged unavailingly at the grip on his arm. "I really do need to go."

"Get off him, you gorilla," Jerry said. "I'll speak to you later, Alec. It is all under control. Trust me."

It was a statement, with the faintest hint of a question, and Alec didn't think he could breathe. He wanted to say, *Always. I know you wouldn't let me be hurt. I can trust you, just as you can trust me.*

He couldn't.

He managed a smile and a nod, and hurried out. The nearest water-closet was at the end of the hall, near the main stairs, and he set off in that direction.

He returned about ten minutes later, knowing that they'd be wondering what had taken him so long. He knocked at the door of Jerry's room. Lane opened it a crack, face composed in a valet's expression, and stepped back to let Alec in. Jerry stood behind Lane. He started to say something, and then his face changed along with his partner's as Alec's companion stepped into the room after him and kicked the door shut.

"Good evening, boys," said Susan Lazarus.

There was a second's ringing silence. Jerry's face was the most unguarded Alec had ever seen it, wide-eyed with blank incomprehension turning to shock. Lane's expression was pure thunderhead. He gave Alec one look full of lethal promise and began to move—not even taking a step, but swelling—and Susan said, "No," pushing Alec to the side as she did so, revealing the snub-nosed revolver she held.

"Susan," Lane said, with a visible effort at control. "What a treat."

"James." Her tone was equally flat. "Sit down on the bed, both of you, with your hands palm up on your knees."

Alec saw Jerry take that in. Saw him realise that she wasn't including Alec; saw the momentary look of devastation before the rage ignited.

"*Now*, Crozier," Susan told him. "Don't try my marksmanship. I have been taking lessons since I missed James last time."

"Ah, so you admit you missed me," Lane said.

"I will shoot you in the face and not regret it for a second. Alec, why don't you come behind me and get in the opposite corner by the door, to keep everything tidy."

That meant "get out of lunging range". Alec did as bid, though he'd rather have kept walking, shut the door behind him and never looked back. He could feel Jerry's eyes on him as he crossed behind her, and when he turned, his lover's expression was everything he'd imagined.

"Well." Jerry's voice was thin. "I said it always ends in betrayal, and I was right. Out of interest, did you only now lose whatever excuse for a spine you possess, or have you been a treacherous little cunt all along?" Alec couldn't hold back the flinch, and saw Jerry's nostrils flare. "You have, haven't you? You played me like a fiddle. I take off my hat to your dedication to the role. I quite thought you were the hapless tart you pretended."

Lane half turned to look at him, looked back at Alec, and said, "Christ, Jerry. You arse."

Susan's eyes narrowed. "You didn't, Alec. Did you?"

"Of course he did," Jerry said viciously. "Really, Alec, you ought to be on the stage. Or give up the doodling and dedicate yourself to selling what you're actually good at. They could use you on Cleveland Street, and you do make yourself available for use, don't you?"

Alec set his back teeth. He couldn't help the colour flooding his face, but he was not going to react; he was *not* going to cry.

"Shut up, Crozier," Susan said.

"No. Now, kindly explain why you're holding a gun on us when no crime has been committed and you're not an officer of the law."

"That's a very good question," Lane said. "Because if all you have to go on is the accusations of a spurned boy friend—"

Susan gave him a look of startling contempt. "If I wanted you two arrested I wouldn't need Alec's help. I'm not here to gaol you."

Jerry's face tensed. "Then what are you here for?"

"I want you to open the Duchess of Ilvar's safe."

There was a short silence. Jerry's mouth moved slightly as if trying out the words. Lane said, "Not to put too fine a point on it, but you do realise we were going to do that anyway?"

"No, you were going to open the Duke's safe, which is why Alec and I had to intervene. Why do you think we brought you here?"

"You didn't—" Lane began and then, "Really. Did you, now."

"I put Alec on to you two in the first place," Susan said. "Lady Moreton endured hours of condescension in order to persuade the Duchess to hire me, and young Penny's going to have people teasing her about Alec for months. A *lot* of work has gone into getting you two into Castle Speight. I hope you're flattered."

"That's not my overriding emotion," Jerry said. "Why?"

Susan gave him one of her blank looks, which Alec knew from experience could cut through steel plate. "Work it out. Bearing in mind I know you two bastards are behind the Milner and Cyrus-Price robberies."

Lane's brows drew together. "You're serious? You want us to rob the Duchess?"

"Nobody in the country can get into a Bramah lock without drilling," Susan said. "The only time a Bramah was beaten, it was that fellow who set himself to do it as a stunt and took fifty hours. But the Milner and Cyrus-Price safes were both unforced, both Bramah locks—"

"Which is why the police concluded both were inside jobs," Lane remarked.

"A little bird told me about Stan Kamarzyn's trip to Antwerp and what he shifted in the way of uncut gems. I know what was stolen from those two safes; Kamarzyn doesn't fence for anyone but you; QED. No, don't argue, James. Your only value to me is your ability to open a Bramah lock, and if you can't, I'm going to hand you over to the police along with whatever exciting toys we may find in your luggage, including safecracking kit and chloroform. So if I were you, I'd stop trying to persuade me of your innocence." She let that hang a moment, eyes on Lane, as if neither Alec nor Jerry mattered at all, then cocked her head. "Between us, how do you do it?"

"Magic fingers," Lane said. "I think I'm hallucinating. Susan, dear, *why* do you want us to rob the Duchess?"

"I don't want you to rob her," Susan said. "I want you to open her safe in my presence. After that, you can go."

"Right." Lane was going a little red. "Right. One more question: do I look like your fucking lackey?"

"What are you after?" Jerry asked. He was watching Alec, not Susan.

"Nothing that concerns you. Oh, and you're not going to take a halfpenny that doesn't belong to you. Sorry about your loss on this job, but I'm sure you have a few bob put aside. That might change if someone laid information and Stan Kamarzyn's shop was raided by the police."

Jerry's nostrils flared so wide there were white marks at the sides of his nose. Lane said, with a creditable attempt at joviality, "You know, if you wanted my help, all you had to do is ask."

"I remember the last time I asked you for something," Susan said. "Do you?"

The smile died on Lane's face. He didn't reply.

"You owe a debt, James," she went on steadily. "Your payment is, in fact, very seriously overdue. Consider this a visit from the bailiffs."

"I'm not aware *I* owe you anything," Jerry said.

"Unless James needs you to open the safe, you can piss off," Susan told him with total composure. "If I don't get what I want out of this visit, you two and Stan Kamarzyn will all be turning the crank before Christmas, so it might be in your interest to help out, but otherwise I don't give a damn. Scarper if you like."

"No, I won't do that," Jerry said. "I don't believe in betraying my friends."

"Oooh," Susan said, mockingly sing-song, as Alec dug his nails into his palm. "Stay, then, but don't do anything stupid. My firm knows exactly what I'm up to here, and we've got eyes on Kamarzyn." She glanced between the thieves. "I'm not asking much, really. Open a safe, don't steal anything, and disappear. I know the first and last of those are second nature, so if you can manage the part about not stealing, we'll all be happy."

"Will we?" Jerry enquired.

"Happy enough. Do what I want the way I want and we—the guvnors and I—will consider the slate wiped clean."

Lane's eyes widened slightly. Susan gave him a single nod. "Wiped clean, up to and including the Milner and Cyrus-Price jobs. You won't get a better offer in your life. Mess me about and there's a pair of crosses ready-built, just waiting for me to nail you to them. Come on, Alec."

He followed her out, and shut the door. Susan's gun had magically disappeared somewhere about her person.

"Right," she said. "Which is your room?"

"This one."

"Neighbouring?" Susan grimaced, led the way in, and checked the door handle. "I'd suggest you use the lock, except that Crozier could get through it easy as breathing. Put a chair under the handle. Are you all right?"

"No." Alec sat on the bed. "I think I might be sick."

Susan sloshed some water from the nightstand into a tumbler. "Sip. Also, please tell me Crozier was lying."

"No."

"Alec." She sat down beside him. "You did not have to do that."

"Of course I didn't have to," Alec said drearily. "I wanted to."

"But it was pure recreation, no finer feelings involved, yes?"

Alec shook his head. Susan made a despairing noise. "You berk. You absolute berk." She put an arm round his shoulders, pulling him close, and Alec leaned on her, feeling the sobs in his chest, refusing to let them out. "What a pig's ear."

"He's not what you think," Alec said, and winced at the feebleness of the words.

Susan snorted. "You've got no idea how many times I've heard that, usually from women with black eyes. Look, you did your part, and superbly. Hurt feelings aside, those two know what side their bread is buttered. They'll do it. A few more days and we'll have what we've been working towards all this time, and as much of a case as it's possible to make at twenty years' distance. Isn't that worth it?"

It ought to be worth it. Alec had been telling himself it would be worth it for months; he'd shoved away every fear and doubt behind the great boulder that was his conviction. His father and stepmother had taken two lives and Cara was dead by their negligence. Nothing had mattered as much as fulfilling Susan's plan, and the wreckage of whatever lay between him and Jerry had always been an inevitable consequence, a price that had to be paid for the great aim.

And now he'd done it, and the wrongs of three dead people no longer seemed to be the only thing that mattered, because one live man had looked him in the eyes and hated him for his betrayal. He wished more than anything in the world that he hadn't done it, but it was too late. He wondered if his father had felt the same way as he walked back down that dark corridor twenty years ago.

He curled down over himself, as if that would help the terrible pain in his gut. Susan sighed heavily. "I'd sympathise, but you're an idiot. Alec, you can't tear yourself apart over Crozier. For one thing, he's just another tea-leaf with a bit more class than most. For a second, you've done him no harm and some good. The guvnor's been making a case against the Lilywhite Boys for a couple of years now. They're slippy, but nobody's slippier than my old man, and he doesn't like James Vane one bit. He'd have sent Crozier down with him, but if they do what they're told he'll let it go, and Crozier should be thanking you for the reprieve."

Alec blinked at her. "James who?"

"Vane. Templeton Lane. Doesn't matter."

"No, but...what?" he demanded, briefly distracted from his misery. "Templeton Lane is a *Vane*? A real one? As in the Cirencester family?"

"Oh, yes," Susan said grimly. "Grandson of a marquess, all that, don't talk to me about noble blood. Right, I'm going to bed. I need my beauty sleep if I'm not to strangle the Hackett before breakfast. And, Alec? I meant it about your door. Those bastards bear grudges."

She left on that note. After a moment Alec got up to put a chair under the door handle, at once feeling like a swine for thinking it was necessary and miserably aware that it was. He heard Susan's voice next door, pitched quiet and unmistakably menacing. She was probably threatening Jerry on his behalf, he realised, Cara's best friend taking care of her little brother now that Cara was dead and gone, and on that thought Alec slid to the floor, his back against the door, and wept the great airless sobs of misery for which there could be no relief and no redress.

He woke up lying on his bed, still clothed, his throat dry and painful. Heaven knew when he'd gone to sleep; he'd cried himself to exhaustion for everything that was lost. It ought to have been cathartic, but in fact he merely felt parched, and nauseous at the prospect of a new day in which he and Jerry would have to pose as great pals.

He washed the salt from his face, shaved, and dressed, praying that they could drop the pretence of Templeton Lane acting as his valet because he suspected he'd end up garrotted by his own necktie. Once he could no longer put it off, he headed downstairs to the breakfast room.

Susan was there, eating kippers in a demure manner. Miss Hackett was consuming dry toast and tea. There was no sign of Jerry. Alec took a seat opposite Susan with his back to the door, and helped himself to a boiled egg, but couldn't stomach the wobbling whiteness, the too-vivid viscous yolk. This was how he'd felt after Cara, repelled by food, by physicality, by everything that pinned him to the world.

"Let me butter you a slice of toast, Lord Alexander," Susan said in a mild voice that he knew contained an order.

"Thank you," he made himself say.

"Marmalade?"

The thought of its cloying sweet-bitterness clogged his throat. "No, thank you."

Miss Hackett sniffed deeply, as though his rejection of marmalade confirmed all her worst suspicions. Alec bit, chewed, swallowed.

"Would you care for tea?"

"There's no need for you to serve Lord Alexander, Roy," Miss Hackett said. "You are neither the lady of the house nor its maid."

Susan gave a single slow blink, then asked Alec, in exactly the same tone as previously, "Would you care for tea?"

Miss Hackett stiffened. Alec cringed internally in anticipation as she drew a breath, and then almost dropped his toast as a cheery voice rang out behind him. "Ah, marvellous, tea. Are you being mother, Miss Roy? Milk, no sugar, how kind. Good morning, Miss Hackett, I trust you've made an excellent breakfast." Jerry went to the chafing dishes as he spoke. Susan poured him a cup of tea, blank-faced. "Devilled kidneys, what a treat. May I make you a plate, Miss Hackett?"

"Certainly not. I do not consume anything but a little toast at breakfast time and I never eat red meats. That is an indulgence that leads to gout, corpulence, and unpleasantness of temper."

"Really?" Jerry said, piling his plate with bacon, kidney, and sausage. "I like nothing more than laying into a pig or two at breakfast. Are you sure I can't offer you a nice plump sausage?"

Miss Hackett gave him a freezing look. "I prefer not to witness carnivorous displays, Mr. Vane."

"Sorry about that," Jerry said. He sat down opposite her, cut off a large chunk of sausage, and speared it on the end of his fork. "What's everyone up to today? Miss Roy?"

"I shall be attending to my duties."

"Can we persuade you to a walk? All work and no play makes Jill, or Susan, a dull girl. Lord Alexander has promised to show me the gardens after breakfast; perhaps you will accompany us? I'm sure Miss Hackett can do without you for a little while."

"Very kind," Susan said tonelessly. "And what will you do after your walk?"

"Oh, we'll come up with something, won't we, Alec?" Jerry's knife sliced into the sausage, sawing through the taut skin, so that clear hot fat oozed from the flesh beneath. Alec put down his half-eaten slice of toast. Jerry looked up and gave him a desperately charming smile that didn't touch his eyes. "Oh dear, Lord Alexander. Has something put you off your food?"

They went out into the gardens. Castle Speight lay in the foothills of Bowland, at the point where the lush green lowlands turned into high, bleak gritstone fells. The gardens were well maintained but not extensive; one could not keep a lawn given the wind and the tendency of everything to be coated by moss. Alec led the way to the walled rose garden with Susan walking between him and Jerry. Alec felt like he was hiding behind her, because he was.

They proceeded in silence on his and Susan's parts, Jerry keeping up a flow of light, inconsequential chatter that grated on Alec's nerves. The garden seemed a long way.

He reached the entrance and stopped. Jerry took two steps onward, looked around irritably, and said, "What?"

"It was a rose garden." Alec's mouth felt odd. "Just roses, always. My mother had it all replanted, new varieties, but it was always roses."

The walled garden was now Italianate. There were vines stretched over the walls, busts in alcoves, a gleaming-new fountain, and the roses were gone, all gone, replaced by…other flowers, bushes, he didn't care. There was still the hum of insect life busily working and fragrance in the air, but it wasn't right. It wasn't the mass of roses in which his mother had sat every day of spring and summer until she was bed-bound, among which he and Cara had played hide and seek, where they had later fled to weep. His mother's garden was entirely gone.

"They've dug up the bushes," Alec said numbly. "They haven't left a single one."

Jerry glanced at him, looked away, said nothing. Susan took his arm. "Come on. In."

Alec forced his feet to move. The old gritstone walls had been faced with something pale gold, presumably for the Italian look. A tiled path led to a fountain, which was all rococo nymphs and wide-mouthed angry fish in white marble. Someone probably had to scrub off the moss and lichen every spring.

"Christ, that's hideous," Jerry said. "And with the artistic appreciation out of the way: I want to be clear on the deal here. You want the safe opened, and that's all?"

Susan nodded. "Opened in my presence, the contents left intact, closed again, and nobody knows we were there."

"And in return you offer…?"

"Amnesty. We, Braglewicz and Lazarus, will forget what we know about you. Open that safe as demanded, everything up to today is—" She made a wiping gesture with her hand. "That's not a trivial offer. My guvnor would be just as happy to send James to gaol and you with him, and don't doubt that he could."

"I'm sure," Jerry said. "Well, you have us over a barrel. You needn't expect us to like it—"

"I don't care if you like it."

"As I was about to observe." Jerry's brows were at a dangerous angle. "We'll open this safe, once, and that will be the end of it. We will not be your personal skeleton keys again. And on that note, let me observe that your 'guvnor' and his journalist friend aren't untouchable either. You leave us alone and we'll return the favour."

"Don't," Susan said, very softly. "Don't even *voice* a threat. I will ruin you."

"Oh, you don't like the idea of being struck at through one's affections? Yes, what utter shit would do that. And by the way, you forget about Stan Kamarzyn too, not just me and Templeton. Now and for the future."

"No," Susan said. "I'm not here to give you carte blanche for crime. We won't go after any of the three of you for what's done, but next time we get hired to one of your jobs, you can all take the consequences. That's the best offer you'll get and a damned sight better than what you'd have been facing if we didn't need you."

"And yet you do need us. Evidently quite badly, given the lengths you've gone to, because I'm quite sure forgiving Temp is sticking in your throat."

"Did I say I'm forgiving him?"

They were looking at one another like dogs, ready to snarl and snap. Alec felt he was going to snap in quite a different way. He wanted to demand they stop *talking*, and kept his mouth shut with an effort.

"Very well," Jerry said at last. "Amnesty for all three of us, up to and including this job. Agreed?"

"Agreed."

"But this will happen only if you make it possible for us to do our end. We'll need a solid hour to get into the safe, at least. My preference would be to go in at two in the morning and do the work before the Duchess's tweeny maid comes in at five, but that has its own problems, especially if we bring two people in. The Duchess is a light sleeper, and chloroform isn't nearly as convenient as the ill— the illustrated papers would have you believe." He didn't look at Alec in that brief stutter. "It can leave burns, and there's a good chance she'd remember being put out."

"We can't have that. It has to be discreet."

"Then give me a daytime option. You're here for security. You can demand a list of the Duchess's movements."

"Unfortunately, when she isn't in her room, the servants frequently are," Susan said. "She doesn't want to see them, but she does want her room cleaned twice a day."

Jerry hissed. "How important is it that nobody knows the safe was opened?"

"Critical."

"Must you be present? It doubles the risk and noise. What are you looking for?"

"None of your business," Susan said. "Why does it take an hour to open the safe? I thought you two were good at this."

"Are you familiar with the operation of a variable key for Bramah sliders?"

"No."

"Assume I explained how it works and you grasped that it takes an hour. Look, I need to get the lie of the land. I suggest we both seek a way for us all to be done with this ugly little situation. Meanwhile Alec is going to take me round the house."

"You're not going to spend the next week torturing Alec to improve your wounded self-esteem," Susan said. "If you have a bone to pick, you can pick it with me."

"On the contrary. We're not going to waste all the hard work we put in. Alec and I are as close and friendly as we ever were. Aren't we, Alec?"

Susan's eyes narrowed ominously. Alec said, "It's all right."

"It had better be," Susan said. "I don't like you, Crozier."

"The feeling is entirely mutual." Jerry gave her a small bow, then crooked his arm. "Come, Lord Alexander. You've done so well getting me to your childhood home, you may as well give me the tour."

Susan hissed like a cat. Alec shook his head and took Jerry's arm with deep reluctance, and they walked back to the castle together.

"Well," Jerry said after a moment. "You'd better find something to say. About the castle, that is, or perhaps your noble family's history of heroic deeds or something, because I'm not doing all the work here."

Alec took a deep breath. "Is it any use to say I'm sorry?"

"I don't give a shit if you're sorry. I want to do the job you trapped me into and get out before the Lazarus bitch changes her mind. So walk me round this temple to the Great God Mammon with a smile on your face, and don't forget the Duchess's bedroom."

*Breathe. Breathe. You've done worse.*

It didn't feel like that. It felt as humiliating as the interview with his father, and he had no persona to hide behind, no excuse. Jerry had warned him that he wouldn't be able to live with himself if he became a traitor, and, as in so many other things, he'd known Alec to the bone.

But it had to be done, so Alec summoned up the few reserves he had. He smiled. He dredged up whatever he could recall of family history and indicated notable pictures, pieces of furniture, or carvings that he recognised. The Duchess had done a thorough job in sweeping through Castle Speight and making it her own. He tried not to point that out. There was no reason for Jerry to care.

The tour took an agonisingly long time, since there were some thirty rooms on the ground floor. They greeted fellow guests, kept up a light stream of conversation whenever they were observed. It was surprisingly easy, since Jerry was very good at light conversation, except that they were next to one another, shoulder to shoulder, the faint smell of his cologne in Alec's nose.

"And this is the library," Alec said, pushing open yet another heavy oak door. "Oh."

"Oh?" Jerry repeated, stepping in after him.

"Just— It hasn't changed." It was not a particularly noteworthy library compared to some of the great houses, nothing compared to the Cirencester collection, and mostly made up of leatherbound almanacs and collections of dusty sporting periodicals rather than anything one might want to read. If the Duchess had filled it with modern novels he wouldn't have objected. All the same, it was the library, where he'd sat and read or drawn, and he shut his eyes and inhaled the dry, dusty scent of books.

"This doesn't look much used," Jerry remarked.

"Father prefers his own study. We used to play or read in here. I wonder—" He went to the great, heavy wooden desk and pulled open a drawer, the feel of the carved knob familiar to his palm yet oddly too small. It held only a few oddments, a pen wiper and knife, a piece of string. He pulled open the next drawer, empty, then all of them, faster. There was nothing.

"Well," he said.

"What were you expecting?"

Alec shut the last drawer carefully. "Cara put things in here. It was hers, really, Father gave her permission to fill the drawers. Special oddments like lucky stones, and all my best pictures, and a doll George carved her and cut his thumb making, and dried flowers when Mother had picked us each a posy. I suppose it would have looked like rubbish. I suppose one would naturally throw that sort of thing away, if one wanted to use the desk. It's just empty now."

He looked up then. Jerry was two feet away, looking at him, expressionless, and Alec felt suddenly dizzy, as if he'd snapped from one reality to another, because he'd forgotten. Jerry didn't care if his father had thrown away his childhood drawings. He would have cared before, but now he didn't, and Alec had earned that.

"Anyway," he said. "I think that's all. Shall we go upstairs?"

Jerry didn't reply. He just looked at Alec, watching him with that intent gaze, unblinking, and it was all Alec could do not to shift awkwardly where he stood.

"What I struggle with," Jerry said at last, "is why you gave me so much truth while also lying to me so extensively. Because you did, didn't you? That wasn't all an act. If you had the capacity to run a game so convincingly for so long, you wouldn't be living in an attic."

"I wasn't lying about anything, apart from—that one thing."

"The small matter of entrapping and grassing me up. Indeed."

"I wasn't, though." Alec wanted to beg Jerry to believe him, as if it would do any good. "I lied about the job, and Susan, and I'm sorry, but everything else I told you—everything we did—it was true, Jerry. It was all true."

Jerry's lips tightened. "That seems to me quite extraordinarily ill-judged."

Alec couldn't find an answer. "I don't think so," he said at last. "I don't regret it."

"Really?" Jerry said. "You should."

# Chapter Ten

Jerry disappeared after they'd walked the upstairs, having particularly noted the main corridor past the state bedrooms. He didn't emerge till luncheon, another endless, dreadful meal with the ill-assorted company. Jerry was charming, inevitably. Susan sat, uninteresting and invisible, not speaking until spoken to. Alec made courteous conversation with his fellow guests, asked polite questions and pretended to listen to the answers, smiling, smiling.

He was going back to his attic after this, he decided. He would settle back into illustration, make up the ground he'd lost with the picture papers in the last couple of months of inaction, build his reputation with the book publishers. He'd forget his title and position; their price was far too high. He never wanted to come to this house again.

After lunch he settled in the gardens—not the walled garden—with a sketch pad, in the hope that it would discourage people from approaching him. He had about half an hour of peace, and then footsteps crunched on the gravel, and Miss Hackett came up with Susan.

"Lord Alexander." Miss Hackett looked down at the pad on his knee. "In my day, drawing was the pursuit of young ladies. I was under the impression your father preferred you not to indulge this hobby."

Susan shut her eyes. Alec said, as calmly as possible, "I like to draw and I don't think it's harming anybody if I do so."

Miss Hackett sniffed. "My sister the Duchess might differ, considering the unfortunate past to which I should not care to refer. Come, Roy."

"I think I'll stay outside," Susan said. "You go in."

"Miss Roy—"

"We had this conversation," Susan told her, very softly. Miss Hackett drew herself up and marched off. Alec let himself sag.

"Good God, she's awful," Susan said, sitting by him.

"I don't understand it. Why can't people let everyone else get on with their lives? What possible reason is there for seeing someone not doing any harm, taking a bit of pleasure, and deciding to ruin it, for *nothing*?"

"It's not for nothing. She can tell herself she's better than whoever she's condemning, and get a thrill of power while she does it. It's not about principles, or people, or anything except a demonstration that she's higher on the ladder than whoever she's picking on. If I were actually her companion I'd have put a pillow over—" Susan clamped her mouth shut, too late.

"It's all right," Alec said.

"No, it isn't. Sorry. That was awful."

"Then it fits right in with everything else. I don't know if I can do this much longer."

Susan scowled. "What's Crozier done?"

"Nothing. I almost wish he would. I feel so guilty."

"I really do think he'll survive," Susan said drily.

"Oh, I'm sure he will. Only, he trusted me. I think he…cared, even, and I don't think he does that often, and I shouldn't have spoiled that. Not for me, but for him. He was kind to me, and this is what I did in return, and I'm afraid he won't be inclined to kindness again."

Susan was uncharacteristically silent for a few moments. At last, and carefully, she said, "You do know that bad people aren't generally redeemed by the love of a good woman, or man, don't you? Most people don't change, and if they do, it's not because of someone else. Crozier's acts aren't your responsibility."

"I don't agree. What we do affects other people. If we teach other people that they won't be loved, or they can't trust anyone, then that's how they'll be."

"Your father did his damnedest to teach his children that, and I don't recognise you or Cara in that description," Susan said. "We're not helpless. Do you know about my guvnor?"

"Only that he's a private detective."

"He is now, but he was a flim-flam man before that, in the Spiritualist racket. Bloody good, too. People called him the Seer of London and believed he had magic powers. Made a fortune."

"Good heavens. Really?"

Susan nodded. "I grew up in the Golden Lane rookery. My mother died when I was, I don't know, six or so, and then I was on my own until Justin took me out of the gutter and made me his accomplice. I was eight or nine by then, probably. He taught me how to pick pockets and fool marks, how to do the tricks that made the fraud work. We took hundreds of pounds off people who thought he could talk to the dead."

Alec's mouth was hanging open. He closed it.

"And he also taught me to read and write and talk proper," Susan said. "He fed me and housed me and looked after me—and took in my friend too, when I asked, even though she wasn't any real use to him. I wanted to work with him forever, to become a medium myself. I can still do it, you know. I could hold a seance now and you'd swear the dead were speaking."

Alec had a sudden picture of Susan presiding at the seance table, summoning up his mother's spirit, or that of the Duchess's first husband, intoning ghostly accusations. He almost wished she would. "So how on earth did you become private detectives?"

"Long story. We got mixed up in a murder case, and everything went arsewards in the most spectacular way. But as part of that, the guvnor met a good—well, a good man, actually." Alec swung round at that. She gave him a quick smile. "Nathaniel, the other guvnor. He's got principles, and lives up to them, and once they'd found each other, it changed everything. The guvnor walked away from spiritualism, from all of it, went straight, and the next thing I knew he was sending me to school. He paid for me to have the best possible education so I could have a respectable occupation or a nice middle-class marriage. And then he took me on in the agency anyway because that was what I wanted."

"But he and, uh, your other guvnor. Are they still together?" *Please*, Alec found himself thinking. He wanted to know it was true, that it was possible. *Please.*

Susan grinned. "More than twenty years, and they haven't stopped arguing yet. But listen, Alec. Anyone would look at all that and say, well, the good man reformed the bad one. Yes?"

"I suppose so."

"But everything Justin did for me, he was doing it long before he met Nathaniel. He looked after me in his own way from the moment he saw me, even if it wasn't the right way by most standards. Nathaniel didn't find one single thing in Justin that wasn't already there, and nobody on earth could have redeemed my guvnor if he hadn't felt like redeeming himself. I say redemption," she added, "but he's still the devious bastard he always was. He just turns it against different people now."

"I see," Alec said, nonplussed.

"The guvnor never changed: he just did things differently. And if I'd told him to stick his school up his arse and gone to work for another spiritualist—and I could have, I was really good at my trade—or even if Nathaniel had walked out on him, I don't think he'd have gone back to the table-rapping. He made a decision and he stuck with it, and that was all him. And the reason I'm telling you this is, when someone was going to become a better person, but you didn't do what they wanted, so now the rotten things they do are your fault?" She tapped Alec's knee lightly. "Pile of shit. If Crozier wants to dig up some human decency from under whatever rock he's buried it, he'll do it with or without you. And if he doesn't, nothing you could say or do would change him. Don't flatter yourself."

Alec blinked. "You don't mince your words, do you?"

"You should meet the other guvnor."

He could see why Cara had liked her so much. Susan's sharp intelligence and fearsomely uncompromising nature must have felt like a lifeline to a woman raging against a wrong the world refused to acknowledge. "I'm still not sure I agree, though. It's asking a lot to say people shouldn't be affected by others."

"I didn't say not to be affected. You might feel and think a lot of things you can't help. But the only thing that counts is what you do, and we're all capable of controlling that. Crozier, and my guvnor, and the Duchess, and you."

Alec rubbed his face. "Yes. Maybe. I don't know if I've done terribly well. Certainly not by Jerry."

"Crozier's first instinct when he realised what was going on was to hit you where he could hurt you worst. I dare say he knew I wasn't going to make a fuss about who you share a bed with, but that was still the act of a stone-cold bastard, and I'd bear that in mind if I were you. He's lost nothing but a bit of pride and a lot of diamonds that weren't his to take. Don't waste any tears on him. He's not worth it."

Alec sighed. "I'll try."

"Good. May I see your drawings?"

Alec handed over the sketchbook. Susan flipped through it, and Alec winced to see quite how often he'd drawn Jerry's face, but she made no comment until she came across a pencil sketch of Cara. "Oh. When did you do this?"

"Last month. It's from memory."

"It's very good." Susan looked at the pencil image, the corners of her mouth pulling down for a second. "Very like her. At least, in some moods."

"Like Mother too," Alec said. He hadn't intended it, but he'd thought of Cara on that evening when he'd haltingly confessed kissing another boy and the growing, terrifying certainty it had brought. She'd held him then, whispering comfort and reassurance, just as Mother had when he'd fallen and knocked out a tooth. They'd both said, *I love you,* and *Everything will be all right,* and even though he'd known the words could do nothing, they'd meant everything. "They were very alike."

"She looks tired," Susan said. "God, I miss her."

"So do I."

Susan touched the corner of the picture. "We'll nail them, Cara, me and your brother." It came out *bruvver,* her accent slipping steeply and unexpectedly down the register. "Like we promised."

"Yes," Alec said. "It's what we're here for."

They sat in silence together, then Susan gave herself a brisk shake. "Right. I've a meeting with the steward to talk about security for the dinner. Chin up. We'll be through it soon."

She left Alec sitting in the garden, wondering what to do. He'd known he had no part to play beyond getting the men they needed to Castle Speight; for all Susan's "me and your brother", he was just one of the tools with which she was constructing her trap. Even so, excluded from Jerry's council and with nothing to offer Susan, he felt himself to be as useless as any Lord Alexander drifting around the clubs and racetracks, and that feeling didn't dissipate throughout the afternoon.

More guests arrived: a railway magnate named Ayres who seemed overwhelmed with the grandeur of his surrounds, and Sir

William Cooke. The latter was standing in the hall as Alec came downstairs, miserably arm in arm with Jerry, for pre-prandial drinks. He was looking at the Stubbs paintings, and Alec recognised the expression on his face at once.

He disengaged himself from Jerry and went up to the older man. "That is rather a beauty, isn't it?"

"The racehorse?" Sir William enquired with a touch of sarcasm.

"Well, yes. The anatomical accuracy, the sheen of the coat, and on the hooves. I've heard a story that when Stubbs was finishing his painting of Whistlejacket, the canvas was propped against the stable wall and the horse took one look at the raging stallion depicted and tried to attack it."

"It's certainly a masterpiece of realism."

"More than that, though. There's the emotion, the sensitivity. We can see the feelings in his animals' eyes, as well as in the twists and tensions of their bodies." Alec indicated the canvas. "This isn't only a racehorse, it's a sportsman, or even a performer. Poised to run, all tension and excitement.

Sir William's brows were raised. "You seem to know what you're talking about. Lord Alexander, is it?"

"Alec. And yes, I studied at South Kensington. I do illustration work for some publishers." He didn't mention the papers.

"That's right," Sir William said. "His Grace mentioned that. You know I bought these for him?"

"I did not." Cooke was an art dealer, one of the "gentlemanly patron" sort rather than the "sordid financial transaction" variety. He looked prosperous on it, nevertheless. "I associated you more with the Peaks and Lakes painters. Romney, Raven, Ansdell."

Cooke nodded. "That's right. Ansdell is sadly underrated to my mind."

They moved into the drawing room, discussing landscape artists. Lady Cooke, who was evidently as knowledgeable as her husband, joined in, and so, somewhat to Alec's surprise, did Lady Maitland, who turned out to collect watercolours. Since the Ayres and the Forbes were acquaintances, by the time the Duke and Duchess made their entrance, the party was lively and even noisy.

It continued so. Alec rather thought that Mrs. Forbes had had her fill of patronage yesterday, and simply having more people present made it harder for their Graces to insist that everyone hang on their pronouncements. Sir William Cooke even made some remark congratulating the Duke on Alec's knowledge, and suggesting that artistic sense must run in the family, which the Duke greeted with a small bow and the Duchess with a stony lack of response.

"I'd be proud to think so," Alec said. "I must say, the Castle Speight collection has become something quite extraordinary under Her Grace's direction."

"You don't have anything on the walls yourself?" Sir William suggested jovially.

"Oh, I don't think I could aspire to any such honour."

"You do underrate yourself, old fellow," Jerry said, across the table. "I dare say you haven't told anyone that Sir Frederic Leighton himself advised you to submit to the next Royal Academy show."

Alec had indeed not told anyone, because it wasn't true. His immediate open-mouthed reaction was drowned in a chorus of congratulations; he clamped his lips shut and tried to look modest.

"And you probably haven't mentioned the portrait either," Jerry added as the hubbub died down. "Really, when it comes to hiding one's light under a bushel—"

"What portrait is this?" Sir William asked.

"Of the Moreton family," Jerry said promptly. "I believe Alec drew Lady Penelope—for some reason." He flickered a wink. "The Earl was immensely taken with the work and has asked him to paint the whole family."

"You are a portraitist?" the Duke asked, with a little frown. Alec saw Miss Hackett draw herself up, anticipating.

"That's very interesting," Sir William said. "Very interesting indeed. Do you work with an agent?"

"Er, no," Alec said, with perfect truth. He had no idea what Jerry was doing. "Really, I haven't done many at all. The Earl is very kind—"

"Undue modesty again, old man," Jerry said. "I do *try* to tell him. Sir Frederic said you had a natural skill at seizing a likeness that he'd rarely seen."

"But there's so much more to portraiture than likeness," Alec protested. He was beginning to panic.

"I'm sure you're right. I make no claim to artistic appreciation; I only know what the experts say."

"That's a shame," Lady Cooke remarked. "I was reflecting you'd make rather a good art dealer."

Jerry joined in the general laugh at his expense with apparent good humour. "I don't know about that, but I may tell you, I've had Alec sign a couple of sketches for me as an investment for my old age."

That got another laugh. Jerry smoothly moved the conversation on to the Stubbs painting, and thus to racing. Alec sat back, wondering what that had been about, aware of his father's eyes on him. It felt like he was being regarded with approval.

When they went up to bed at last, Jerry paused in the corridor and said, "Nightcap?"

"I think I've had enough."

"Keep me company then," Jerry said, with a friendly smile, and opened the door to Alec's room, not his own.

Alec went in; Jerry shut the door behind them and turned.

"Right," he said. "You need to draw the Duchess, or rather to have her sit for you. Talk to your father and confirm everything I said. He needs to think of you as an up-and-coming artist, not a jobber. Keep up the good work with Cooke. He'd give good money to act as agent to a lord painting lords, and your father trusts his judgement. Tell him about your paintings, get him on your side."

"You seem to have missed something," Alec said. "I'm an illustrator, not a portraitist! I haven't completed a canvas since I was twenty."

"Balls. You're good enough."

"Yes, well, thanks, but since you don't know anything about the subject—"

"I know *my* subject. I need uninterrupted access to the Duchess's rooms for at least an hour and a half, so you are going to pin the bloody woman down for me, however it suits you. Preliminary drawings for an oil painting, charcoals or sculpture: I do not care, so long as you keep her out of her damned rooms."

"What if the servants come in?"

"Leave that to us. You just handle the Duchess."

"But she hates me," Alec said. "She truly does, she can scarcely look at me. She won't want to sit for me."

"She won't want Lady Moreton having something she doesn't, or for you to paint someone else here before her. Especially if there are other people clamouring to see you draw, which there will be. This is the dullest house party I've ever encountered: there's no shooting, or hunting, nothing organised, and we're miles from anywhere. Offer something interesting and people will leap on it. Get her jealous."

Alec tried to imagine a scenario in which the Duchess would sit for him. "I could ask Father if I could draw her, as an anniversary gift?"

"Do that. And take your sketchbook downstairs to be admired tomorrow. Don't wait to be asked."

"Right." Alec couldn't stop his eyes from darting guiltily to the book. Jerry followed his gaze and picked it up. "It's not ready!" he blurted. "I mean, I can't, I need to—"

"Rubbish," Jerry said, flicking back through the pages. "This looks just right. You can simply—" He stopped. Of course he did, because he was looking at a picture of himself.

Alec gave a second's thought to wresting the book from him physically. He knew damned well he couldn't, and in any case, he seemed entirely unable to move.

Jerry leafed through the book, page after page, unspeaking. There were the face studies, various sketches of eyes and eyebrows, and then he turned the page to reveal that accursed full-face drawing, and Alec decided he really did now want to die. He'd tried to catch Jerry's expression in that long moment after they'd made love kissing—that intent look, the tenderness—and he'd put so much of his own yearning on the page that he didn't believe any viewer could miss it.

Jerry looked at that picture for what seemed hours, face unreadable. He didn't speak, he didn't move, and Alec watched him, throat as constricted as though Jerry's hand was gripping it tight.

At last he closed the sketchbook, though he still didn't look up. "You'll have to take a few of those out."

"Yes," Alec said, stifled.

Jerry nodded slowly, and then his head rose, his eyes met Alec's, and Alec couldn't breathe at all. They stared at each other for seconds, or hours, and then Jerry stepped forward, taking Alec's chin in his hand, forcing his head up.

"You owe me," he said, very softly.

Alec tried to nod against the pressure of the firm hand. Jerry's eyes narrowed. Alec swallowed, and felt his throat move against Jerry's palm. "Yes."

Jerry was entirely still for a few seconds longer, poised and tense, then he released Alec's neck, grabbed his shoulder, turned him and pushed. Alec found himself stumbling against the door, bracing himself with his hands.

"Just how you like it," Jerry said in his ear, almost below hearing, and a hand came down to his waist buttons.

"There's people," Alec breathed. This was a corridor of guest rooms; the Maitlands and the Ayres were both along here.

"Then you'd better not make a sound." Jerry's fingers were working fast, pushing Alec's drawers down. He kicked off his shoes and trousers, widened his stance, braced his forearm against the door, pressed his mouth against it. His heart thumped as though he'd been sprinting; he felt airless, overheated, and he couldn't help a hiss as Jerry's palm drew over his prick.

"I said quiet." Jerry was barely audible even with his mouth at Alec's ear. His hand slid over Alec's stand. "I see you've been waiting for this. Are you going to be silent? It's your disgrace at stake." Alec nodded frantically. Jerry snarled in his throat. "Good. Stay."

He stepped away. Alec stood, braced, bare, and as Jerry came back behind him, he heard voices in the corridor.

"Good," Jerry said again, in his ear, and Alec felt the pressure of his prick seeking entrance. No preparation, except that he'd slicked himself liberally with something, and Alec bit down on his forearm, because the Chief Constable of the district was on the other side of the door, just up the corridor, chatting to Mr. and Mrs. Ayres. He could hear them quite clearly, and if he or Jerry made the unmistakable, guilty sounds of sex they'd hear him.

Jerry thrust, hard. Harder than you would if you wanted your partner to be quiet; punitively hard. Alec bit back the noise he wanted to make, aware of his breathing as horribly too loud, and felt Jerry's arm round his chest, his other hand gripping Alec's thigh. Jerry pushed in until he had Alec pinned, and then he started moving, in and out, and Alec couldn't help a whimper.

Jerry let go his thigh, tugged at his hair to bring his head off his arm, and Alec had half a second to inhale before a hand came over his mouth.

And this was real control. Jerry was at once pinning him, silencing him, taking him ruthlessly hard, so all Alec could do was brace himself against the door and try not to let it bang. Jerry fucked him, his hand a hard intrusion over Alec's mouth, his arm round Alec's chest so tight he feared for his ribs. Nowhere near his stand, no relief given to Alec's desperate need, and he stood used and helpless as Jerry drove savagely into him, and bit down on his shoulder as he spent.

It had taken no more than a minute or two. The other guests were still talking in the corridor.

Jerry took a long, soundless breath, his chest heaved, then he pulled out. Alec didn't move. He didn't think he could bear to turn and see Jerry's face; he didn't want to know. He was painfully hard, and he wasn't sure he wanted Jerry to know that.

He heard the sound of water—Jerry cleaning himself up—and felt a wet cloth pressed into his hand. He'd be doing that himself, it seemed.

When he did finally turn around, gathering his clothes up in front of his groin as though that might confer some sort of decency, Jerry was leaning on the dressing table, both hands braced on the surface. His head was bowed.

"Er," Alec said.

Jerry's shoulders rose, taking a breath, then he straightened, turning away from the mirror. "Well," he said, voice cheerily casual. "Thanks for the nightcap, old man, but I'm for bed now. Sleep well."

"Goodnight," Alec said automatically, and Jerry slipped out into the now-empty corridor without meeting his eyes.

Alec stood in his room, alone, naked from the waist down, aching and aroused. He'd expected to be left that way; he wished to God it had been accompanied by the menacing promises Jerry had given him on the train, the ones whose taunts were bound up in the fact that there would be a next time and something to wait for. Had Jerry denied him pleasure because he wanted to leave Alec frustrated, or simply because he didn't care?

It didn't matter. Or if it did, there was nothing to be done about it. Alec stood for a few moments, breathing deeply. Then he opened the window to let the smell of sex dissipate overnight, sat carefully down on his bed with his stupid bloody sketchbook, and began the slow process of tearing out everything that didn't fit.

In the morning he spoke to his father.

"You did not mention work as a portraitist," the Duke said. Alec had hung around near the breakfast room until his father had emerged, and asked him for an interview. "I understood you were…" He made a little distasteful gesture to convey the degradation of paid employment.

"Yes, sir. I've been supporting myself with illustration, which hasn't left as much time as I'd have liked for painting of this sort, but it's something I have a great ambition to pursue, having had such kind responses to the work I have done."

If they didn't pull off their intention, this was going to be the most embarrassing and easily identified lie in the world. He couldn't believe Jerry had let him in for this. Or perhaps he could.

"I hope that meets with your approval, sir," he went on. "I don't presume to compare myself with Sir Frederic, naturally, or Sir John Everett Millais. But they have both been honoured by Her Majesty for their art, and I do believe it isn't an inappropriate field for a gentleman. As a, an interest, an occupation, rather than a livelihood."

"I am glad you understand that," the Duke said. "You say you are to paint the Countess of Moreton?"

"And her family, yes."

"Hmph. I suppose this is related to your interest in the Moreton girl."

"It all rather came up at the same time," Alec said, with an embarrassed smile.

"You realise you will need my support for this marriage, if it is to take place. Or is she wealthy?"

"Not by your standards, sir. The estate is prosperous but not a great holding. I...would, yes, sir. I should wish to keep my wife in the manner to which she has been brought up. Of course, this is all rather thinking ahead; I haven't yet spoken to her on the subject."

"More importantly, I have not been fully consulted," the Duke reminded him. "I shall consider the Moretons and let you know my opinion in due course. Meanwhile, I suppose there is no harm in you pursuing this interest. Many Pyne-ffoulkes have taken an active and distinguished role in public life."

"Sir," Alec agreed. "Thank you. Uh, there is one more thing. I wondered if you would consider it appropriate or welcome if I sought permission to paint Her Grace."

"My duchess?" The Duke looked, for once, slightly startled. "Why?"

"Well, I would like to offer my effort as a token of my respect on your wedding anniversary. It won't match your own tribute, but I can't help that." Alec actually elicited a small smile at that bit of flattery. "And for another—well, to be honest, sir, I'm desperate to paint her. She has such a fascinating face, from an artistic perspective—the planes of her cheeks, the character expressed in her features, along with the beauty of maturity, which is so much more interesting than young women's beauty because it's, oh, personal, and shaped by experience and by her innate nature. Do you know what I mean, sir?"

The Duke did not look at all as though he knew: he was staring at his son as though Alec were speaking Greek. Alec cursed internally: he should probably have praised the Duchess's beauty as untouched by the ravages of time and left it there, instead of getting carried away. He pressed on. "It's why I'm looking forward to painting Lady Moreton much more than Penny, because Penny is a blank canvas still, really, and her face shows that. Whereas a woman like the Duchess, grown into her character through adversity, in the dignity of her position and the experience of her life—well, that's where faces become truly wonderful. Developed beauty. Don't you think?" he finished desperately.

The Duke didn't respond for another moment, then shook his head. "That is… That is extremely interesting, Alexander. Women are so determined to keep their youth, but I have always said my wife becomes more beautiful by the day. I have told her again and again that she is lovelier now than when we met. I didn't realise other people saw it, that anyone else might recognise…" His voice trembled slightly as he tailed off. "Could you paint that? Her?"

"I don't know if I'd be able, sir. But I can see how she should be painted—the spirit within the features, the eyes. I know exactly what I'd do, if I had the talent to match my subject."

The Duke nodded. "We have never had a satisfactory portrait. She greatly dislikes the Burne-Jones work."

"Could I do a sketch? If she'd sit for that, for me, and I could show you both what I mean?"

"I shall speak to her." The Duke hesitated, then added, "Thank you, Alexander. I am most pleased we had this conversation." He offered a small smile, one that looked almost hopeful, and Alec looked at his father and smiled back.

# Chapter Eleven

He was sitting in what was no longer the rose garden, looking at the walls as the Forbes and Maitlands pottered around him admiring things, when Jerry came up to him.

"Morning. What are you up to?"

*Not what I was ordered to do.* Alec blew out his cheeks. "Just thinking. I had an interesting chat with Father earlier."

"Come for a walk," Jerry said. "You can tell me all about it on the way up to one of those hills."

"You want to go fell walking?"

"Yes. Let's."

"But I thought I should—"

"A walk," Jerry said. "Please."

Alec didn't even know how to respond to that. He didn't have the strength to think it through. "All right."

They took the route behind Castle Speight. The air buzzed with life around them, the striation of crickets, the low hum of bees. "That's Speight Peak," Alec said, pointing to the bare outcropping that rose ahead through the scrubby moorland. "Is that where you want to go?"

"As long as we can see anyone coming. What was that about your conversation with your father?"

"I told him I wanted to paint the Duchess, as you asked."

"He wasn't amenable?"

"No, he was. I told him that she has a wonderful face, that I thought women, people, grow into their faces and become far more interesting to look at as they age because of the way character comes through. And he told me that he thinks she's lovelier now than when they met. He adores her. He thought I could see what he sees, her inner beauty or whatever you call it, and he was so pleased. He *thanked* me. It meant something to him, how we spoke. Oh Christ."

Jerry's feet crunched on the dry, loose scree of the path. He didn't speak.

"I feel like a swine," Alec said. "I know what he did, and what she did. But he loves her. And he wants, I will *swear* he wants to repair relations between us. He all but offered to give me an allowance so I could marry Penny. And he let Cara die in London. Oh God, I don't know what to do."

"If you could work out a way to remove half your heart and soul and lend them to me, we might both be normal people. Jesus Christ, Alec." Jerry kicked a stone out of his path with some force. "All right, before anything else, we need to straighten this out. To recap: you and Lazarus needed me and Temp here because we can get into the Duchess's safe. When her late husband was shot, a valuable emerald ring was stolen from the corpse, and the ring probably points to the killer. She has jewel mania, and an overweening sense of entitlement. I think you believe that the Duchess killed him, you expect to find the ring in her safe, and your plan all along has been to retrieve it to use as evidence of murder. How am I doing?"

Susan hadn't wanted to share any of their mission with the Lilywhite Boys, but there was no point arguing. Alec nodded. Jerry gave a sharp puff of breath. "Lazarus will use the ring, if it's there, to demand a new investigation into the death, one not directed by the Duke. You won't get him for what he did to your mother, but you'll get the Duchess, and that will be punishment."

"We may get him too," Alec said. "Susan found the maid who discovered Mother's body. She said that when she came in, the pillow on the floor was stained in the middle, but by the time she returned to the room, the pillowcase had been removed. She asked about it—it was her job to account for the linen—and was given her notice the next day. She made a statement to a policeman at the time of Clayton's death because she wasn't ready to believe in two dead inconvenient spouses. That was the officer to whom the coroner gave short shrift at the inquest. Susan's found him too, and they're both ready to take the stand. All together there might be enough for a prosecution, especially if the Duchess admits anything. I don't know if there's enough to convict, but—if we're right—at least there will be a trial. At least people will know what they did."

"And that's what you want?"

"It's what I wanted," Alec said. "It was the only thing I wanted for so long. I loved Cara, you can't know how much. She was my best friend. She knew me, and she loved me, and she's gone just as Mother's gone and—I needed him to pay for what he did."

"And now?"

"You were right. I had no idea what it would cost."

Jerry nodded, pacing at his side, apparently tireless as the path began to rise. The air was so clean here, so clear. Alec didn't think he'd feel clean or clear ever again.

"Is this what Cara would have wanted?" Jerry asked after a while. "You to act as her avenger?"

"God, yes. She saw Father go into the room and leave Mother dead and it affected her life more than any of ours. She made us all promise we'd never forget, that if there was ever a chance to make him pay we'd take it. She was talking to Susan about it before she died. Susan came up with the plan, and asked me if I'd be willing to play my part, and I said yes."

"It seems to me that you're more than playing a part," Jerry said. "How did Lazarus come into it in the first place?"

"She and Cara were friends—through a women's suffrage group, initially. They became very close. Cara always made her laugh."

"Good Lord. I didn't know she could."

"Susan's marvellous," Alec said. "I don't think I would have managed after Cara's death without her. I couldn't eat or sleep, and she was the only person who understood that it wasn't just grief. Annabel was devastated, and George was guilty, but Susan was *angry*. I needed that."

Jerry nodded slowly. "And it didn't seem like a good idea for you to tell me the truth at any point. Not at first, I quite understand that, but—not later, either?"

"You told me you aren't a good man. You said you were in it for the jewels."

"I'm not. And I did say that."

"Should I have ignored you?" Alec asked. "Should I have taken a risk that you'd be the man you've barely let me see, rather than the one you keep telling me you are? That's not a rhetorical question, Jerry; I want to know. Should I have wagered everything on whether you'd forgive me for deceiving you? Whether you'd put yourself into Susan's hands for my sake? Whether Mr. Lane would?"

"No. Obviously not. Of course you shouldn't have."

"I wish I had," Alec said more quietly. "I wish I'd told you anyway."

"So do I. I wish you hadn't lied to me over months. I wish you hadn't deliberately set me up to walk into a trap, and once you had done so, I wish you had given me a choice instead of forcing me into a corner."

"I know." Alec's throat hurt. "I'm sorry. I've let the ends justify the means all the way through this. I shouldn't have."

"Of course you should."

That was so entirely unexpected that it took Alec a second to make sense of the words. "What do you mean?"

"I may wish you'd done things differently, but you shouldn't have," Jerry explained, as if to a slightly slow pupil. "What else were you to do? I would unquestionably have been a shit about it if you'd told me, just as I have been at every single opportunity when a better man might have understood, or listened, or thought of you instead of himself. I knew damned well there was something up: it was staring me in the face all along. You wouldn't have been in a position to betray me if I'd thought about matters, rather than contorting myself to avoid facing up to what was between us, and you couldn't possibly have told me the truth until I had done so."

"But—"

"Tell me something. Suppose I had said to you, 'I don't believe in this jewel theft of yours, I know you're up to something, but let me help you anyway.' Would you have told me the truth then? If I had told you that you could trust me, or asked you to?"

Alec thought about it and, reluctantly, nodded. "I...think so. Probably. Yes."

"Quite. But I didn't. I'm sorry, Alec."

"I thought you were never sorry."

"So did I. Apparently I was wrong, because I am, though I don't see any reason in the world that you should forgive me."

"For what?" Alec asked, somewhat breathlessly. The hill was steep, and Jerry's pace wasn't slackening.

"Christ, do you have to ask? Going backwards: I'm sorry about last night, that I manhandled you because I couldn't find words to talk to you. I'm bitterly sorry for what I said when you came in with Lazarus. I haven't been ashamed of myself in years, but I'm ashamed of that. I'm sorry you couldn't tell me the truth, and I'm sorry to be a man to whom you couldn't tell the truth, and I'm sorry you had to ask me even to look at you because I didn't have the spine to kiss you. Is that everything? No: I'm sorry about that incident under Waterloo Bridge, which put you in entirely unnecessary danger for my enjoyment. I don't know why you haven't pushed me off this hill yet."

"I don't want to."

"And that's the problem," Jerry said. "Don't think I am dismissing your sister, or the wrong done to your family, but you shouldn't be doing this, Alec. You should *never* have done this. You have a heart and a soul, and neither of them ought to be soiled with this filthy business of betrayal and incrimination. Lazarus is a ruthless woman—"

"She's my friend."

"She may be, but I've tangled with her and her father or whatever he is before now. They use people."

"So do you."

"It takes one to know one. I promised you I don't spoil my tools, didn't I? I didn't manage to keep that either. Ah, Christ. What can I do?"

"In what way?" Alec asked cautiously.

Jerry grabbed his hand, tugging him to a stop. They stared at each other on the hillside, the breeze whispering at the damp curls at Alec's neck, over his face.

"Whatever you want. If you want to pull out now, to find a way to explain to your siblings and try to put Humpty Dumpty back together, I'll do my best to help. If you insist on proceeding, I will open the damned safe, and do whatever I can to shield you from the consequences. If you would prefer never to see me again, I'll heed that. Tell me what you want, Alec. Not what Cara would have liked, or what Susan Lazarus dreamed up, or what your father deserves, and least of all what you think I hope to hear. Just what *you* want. Tell me, and I will do anything in my power to bring it about."

"Why?" Alec whispered.

"Because you made me sorry. Because I want to know what it's like to kiss you when we're not fucking. Because I'd like to be the man you draw. That is, to be the man you think of when you're doodling, but even more, to be the man in that picture, the one who looks as though he deserves you. When I looked at that—when I saw how you see me and I realised—" Jerry tipped his head back, staring at the sky. "Oh, damnation. I am not going to say I want to protect you from the cruel world because I'm not entirely witless yet, but if I don't do something to right things between us I'll go mad. Because I love you."

Alec stared. Jerry grimaced. "Christ, your expression. Is it really that implausible?"

"Uh." Alec had no idea what to say. He'd never heard *I love you* except from his mother and Cara. He'd never expected it this way. He wouldn't in a thousand years have expected it from Jerry. "I..."

"You don't need to say anything; I wasn't expecting you to fall into my arms. This mess is my fault, I'm well aware. You've been open all along—with one significant exception, of course—whereas I've done nothing but hide my face from you. A face which had to be very firmly rubbed in the mess I helped create, I may add, before I understood why my whole world turned to ash when I thought you'd betrayed me."

"But I did betray you," Alec said. "That's exactly what I did. I lied to you, and I misled you, and I brought Susan down on you, and—and when I asked you to look at me, that time, it wasn't out of courage or anything like. It was because you knew I was hiding something, and I couldn't think what else to say."

"I'm well aware of that. I'd have known it at the time if I hadn't been so keen to believe that you wanted my kisses. You couldn't have lied to me if I hadn't been lying to myself."

"No," Alec said. "That's not right. I did want you to kiss me, to look at me, even if I didn't ask it for the right reasons. I wouldn't have had the nerve to say anything if I hadn't had to."

"And yet you found the nerve, which is more than I did," Jerry said. "Damn it, Alec, you've been telling me the truth since we met—the real truth, not nonsense about rings and murders. You kept other people's secrets, but you gave me your own."

"But my secrets don't matter."

"They're the only ones that matter," Jerry said with breathtaking certainty. "To hell with dukes. You gave me your truth all along, with a courage I can't begin to match, and I don't have anything to offer in return except my own stab at honesty for what it's worth. And the truth is that I love you. That I've been coming to love you for so long, and with so little care and attention on my part, that by the time I realised you'd walked off with my heart and soul it was already too late." He gave Alec a smile that looked almost embarrassed. "A pathetic performance considering I pride myself on my sharpness, but they do tell us pride comes before a fall. And thus I find myself in Othello's position, like the Indian who 'threw a pearl away richer than all his tribe', because I'm a fucking idiot who needs kicking. Please don't say anything," he added, unnecessarily, because Alec could barely breathe. "I don't want you to. I'm not asking, and you're not obliged. But you've trusted yourself to me in too many ways and I would feel a great deal happier if you'd let me earn some of that trust, if only belatedly."

Alec took off his hat, shoving his hair back from his sweaty forehead. "I. Uh."

Jerry gave him a wry look. "Should we get up this hill?"

"Let's," Alec said, with relief.

They climbed in silence, taking the path as it curved, pushing on as earth turned to stone and scrubby grass to heather, yellow and purple. The path opened at last, and Jerry whistled softly as they came onto the height of the Peak.

"My God," he said softly.

The country spread around them. Castle Speight below, more convincingly medieval from this distance and angle; below it the downlands opened out, bright green, traced with drystone walls. Behind them were the Bowland fells, barren-looking moors studded with gritstone, rising and falling jaggedly, stretching out and up forever, bleak and empty and beautiful.

"God," Jerry said again. "A man could be happy here."

"That's not what most people say."

"Isn't it?"

"Most people want flowers and gardens, or trees. Or at least a landscape that cares if you live or die."

"But that's what's so marvellous," Jerry said. "It truly doesn't. This is… Christ, it makes one feel tiny under the heavens."

"That's what I love. You can't be consumed with your problems up here, in a landscape that hasn't changed in thousands of years. Everything down there is awful and complicated, but up here it's stripped back to bare bones. Back to what matters."

"And what is that?" Jerry asked.

Alec tipped his face back, feeling the sun. "You said you wanted to kiss me."

Jerry contemplated him, face very serious. He stepped forward and took Alec's face in his hands with intense care, and their lips met almost chastely. A soft exchange of touch and breath and warmth, a gentle movement to find the connection. Alec let his hands rest on Jerry's hips, opened his mouth to the kiss. Jerry groaned quietly, but he didn't press further. He seemed content to kiss, slow and intent, hands sliding to Alec's shoulders, and Alec sank into the sensation, feeling his battered heart open like the moors under the sky.

He had no idea how long they kissed. Jerry took his hand at one point and led him to the big flat stone that topped the peak. They sat together, shoulder to shoulder, looking out over the moors and the empty land in silence until Jerry tugged up his hand, kissed it, kissed him again, and Alec ended up sprawled over the sun-warmed stone as blissfully as on any feather-bed. Jerry lay over him, braced by an arm, and there they were, as gently together as though there were no fear of interruption, no safe to crack, nothing but two sets of need and longing, melting into one another and soothing each other's sores.

"God," Jerry said at last, brushing the hair out of Alec's eyes. "Out of interest, what happens if we head out over the fells and don't stop walking?"

"A cliff edge."

"Damn." He sat up, and gave Alec a hand to do the same, then moved to brush the lichen off his jacket. "I have no idea where my hat is."

"Down on this side." Alec had put both hats out of the way of the treacherous wind. "Jerry?"

"Mmm?"

"Do you mean it?"

Jerry rested his elbows on his thighs. "Everything I said on the way up? Yes. I love you. I don't know if you want me to, or if you even believe me, and I don't blame you if you don't."

"I want you to. I...think I believe you."

"Don't rush into it. I've no idea what I'm doing, and I don't deserve you anyway. I can't imagine why you haven't been swept away by someone honest and decent and just perverse enough for your enjoyment."

"Honest, decent people probably aren't that perverse."

"Nonsense. There are dozens of perfectly good respectable men who'd enjoy taking you in hand. And, conversely, dozens of thieves and fences and magsmen who would shudder at the idea. Your tastes don't require a criminal mind."

"Your criminal mind does very well." Alec brushed his finger over a little bloom of yellow lichen, growing outward in round scabs. "Are you truly not angry about what I did?"

"I'm not going to deny I found it somewhat trying," Jerry said. "I shall consider it a salutary reminder that you're a bad man to cross."

Alec's mouth opened. "I am not. That's you."

"Alec, my sweet, you trampled me, Temp, and your family underfoot, and no less effectively because you did it in velvet slippers. I'm genuinely impressed. And, let's face it, I'm in no position to complain about other people's wrongdoing."

"There is that," Alec agreed. "You never said why you do it—your line of work, I mean."

"Oh, well." Jerry leaned back on the stone, propped on his elbows. "Idleness, disinclination to sell my labour to a plutocrat, spite. Ha. Do you know, I actually believed you when you told me that was your motivation?"

"Why is it yours?" Alec pushed.

"It's the usual tedious tale. Do you really want to know?" Jerry clearly read the answer in his face, because he sighed. "If you must. How it started... I joined the army at eighteen. The devil with university, I couldn't wait to go. I had ambitions for Afghanistan, the North-West Frontier, the Great Game. Grammar-school boy on the make, you know."

Alec could imagine it: Jerry, weatherbeaten and keen-eyed, on some bare mountain peak, looking over the world, scheming for his country. "Oh."

"Mmm. But then—well, bluntly, my commanding officer selected me for the honour of being his latest fuck, and made it clear that my life would become unpleasant if I didn't oblige. I should doubtless have reported him for improper advances, but I couldn't. For one thing, it would be my word against his and he was well connected; more, though, I harboured some sort of fellow feeling for a fellow queer, even if he was a prick. It seemed wrong to ruin a man's career for tastes I share myself. And, since I'm confessing, I had some idea that ploughing my CO—that being very much what he wanted—might in some way make up for being ordered to do it. Well, it didn't. And the fellow feeling was just as much a figment of my imagination, because once he'd had enough of me he threw me to the wolves without a second's hesitation."

"How do you mean?"

"I found myself hauled into a room of senior brass, informed that allegations had been made but the matter was to be handled privately for everyone's sake, and given a choice between accepting a quiet dishonourable discharge or facing an open court which would be heavily rigged against me. The reason he was untouchable, I may say, is that he was a marquess's heir, and a royal cousin. Apparently I was one in a long line of juniors through his career, used and removed with the quiet connivance of people paid to clear up this particular officer's mess. 'Weeding out the sodomites,' someone called it, as if he were performing a public service by seeing who he could screw."

"My God," Alec said. "But that's—"

"All of a piece," Jerry said over him. "The nobleman does as he pleases and discards his leavings. My commanding officer, your father, Lord Alfred Douglas walking away as Wilde stands in the dock. One law for us and another for them, every time." He exhaled hard. "I sound like a social reformer, don't I? If I were a different man I might have become one. As it is, I was fucking furious. I had nowhere to go and an invisible, indelible mark on my record, of the kind that can't be erased or challenged because it's a matter of *a quiet word, old chap* and the job offer is withdrawn. I could have gone to India, as the usual dumping-ground for the Empire's black sheep, but I didn't feel like exiling myself, or bullying natives. I wanted to take it out on people who deserved it.

"And then I had word of a man who needed someone to pass as a gentleman, for a job. You might have heard of Harry the Valet?"

"The jewel thief?" Alec said. "I've read about him, in the papers."

"Hasn't everyone. Yes, well, he needed a hand, I needed money, and I felt like sticking it to the upper classes, so I helped him out and got two hundred pounds for my efforts. I did a couple more jobs with him, since it seemed better than work, but he was too fond of seeing his name in print for my liking and has a weakness for the ladies that I suspect will be his undoing one day. So we parted ways, I met Templeton, and here we are."

"Yes. Um. Jerry? Were, or are, you and Mr. Lane, uh, together?" He'd wanted to ask that for some time and hadn't previously found the nerve.

"Lovers? Christ, no. He doesn't incline that way, and wouldn't be to my taste if he did. Not only is he a gorilla, he's a romantic."

"Mr. Lane? Really?"

"Under the hulking exterior beats the heart of a boy who never sodding grew up. With all that's past, Templeton still dreams. I stopped dreaming a long time ago." He paused. "At least, I thought I had. It might be possible to argue I've started again." He smiled at whatever Alec's face showed, and brushed a quick kiss over his lips. "Anyway. My bond, if that's the expression, with Templeton is probably that we amplify one another's more objectionable qualities. He was looking to score points against the world as much as I was, and the idea of living off the idle rich appealed strongly to us both."

"That sounds rather Robin Hood."

"Robin Hood gave to the poor. We give to ourselves. Also to locksmiths, servants, police officers et cetera, in vast profusion. The variable key for the Bramah lock cost us a fortune; we had to do those two jobs Lazarus was boring on about to pay for it. Bribes cost; our fence takes, and deserves, a big cut; and jewellers are as much thieves as anyone. You wouldn't believe the mark-down on gems without provenance. Plus all the effort in learning to drill safes, to pick locks, memorising railway timetables and the layout of stations, dah di dah. Really, a life of crime is not the primrose path it's cracked up to be."

"I wish you'd write it up for the paper," Alec said wistfully. "True Revelations of a Jewel Thief, illustrated, in ten parts. Honestly, it would sell like hot cakes."

Jerry grinned. "It would certainly dispel anyone's idea of glamour. I don't mean to complain; I've done very nicely. But that's it. If you were hoping I'm secretly funding an orphanage or some such, I'm sorry to disappoint: I steal because it pays. Granted, I only steal from people who can afford to be robbed, but that's not a moral principle. It's just that poor people don't have jewels."

Alec nodded. The breeze had picked up a little; it ruffled his hair and kept the sun from being too oppressive. It would still burn him, no matter how good it felt.

"I think I understand. You were angry, you're still angry. I'm angry too. I'm just wondering—"

"If the game is worth the candle. I know."

"If you go to gaol for theft," Alec said, looking out over the moor. "Or if I see my stepmother in the dock, perhaps even hanged, and know I brought that about, and have my father know it."

"Not quite the same thing," Jerry pointed out. "If I'm gaoled it will be because I commit crimes, and that goes for your father and stepmother too. Their acts, their consequences."

"But it's my acts if I make them face the consequences they'd otherwise escape."

Jerry nodded. "It's as per that chap under Waterloo Bridge, isn't it? You didn't want his head kicked in, despite the fact that he clearly deserved it and the lack of other options."

"There was always *not* kicking him in the head."

"No, I can't see that working at all. Whereas this… I don't know, Alec. Your mother was murdered, and the fact that it was twenty years ago doesn't make her less dead, or your father less guilty. But you aren't an impartial dispenser of justice. This is your father."

"Cara died. If he hadn't cut her off—"

"Oh, I'm not arguing. He ought to face justice, if one believes in justice at all. But you'll be actively responsible for the consequences, you'll be playing a part in destroying an old man's life, and while there are people who could count themselves an instrument of Fate, or say, *He deserves it* and feel nothing more, I don't think you're one of them. Ugh. I don't know."

"Nor do I. If making the Duke and Duchess face justice could bring Cara back, I wouldn't hesitate for a second, but it won't. Susan's an avenger, she's quite ready to see him punished—"

"He's not her father," Jerry said. "It's harder to see someone pay for their crimes when you have family feeling, or indeed fellow feeling, for them. The trick is to ascertain whether they have the slightest feeling for you."

"Yes. That is the trick, isn't it? What would you do?"

There was a long silence. He twisted round to see Jerry frowning, his eyebrows at a Mephistophelean slant. "Jerry?"

"I'm thinking. Let me mull that one over. Is that a hawk?"

"A red kite." Alec watched the bird hanging in the sky, riding the air apparently without effort. "I love the way they float."

"I like the way they drop. Straight down on a mouse which, one must assume, has no idea of the predator fifty feet overhead. Death from above, in a second."

Alec shuddered. Jerry watched the kite a moment longer, then pushed himself up. "I suppose we should go down for lunch shortly. It strikes me that whatever you decide, the first step is for me to get into that safe and see if the ring is there, because if not, all this soul-searching is moot. Can you go ahead with the sketch?"

Alec nodded. "If she'll let me. This is probably a stupid question, but could you not steal her key?"

"It's not a stupid question. I know people who've spent hours working on doors while there was a window open in the next room. Sadly, no; her key is treated as the key to a fortune should be. It's locked in the Duke's own safe, of which the key is guarded by the butler. The palaver involved in breaking that Russian doll of security would take as long and risk more attention. No; I'll open the safe while Temp intercepts the servants. What would be ideal is if Lazarus could be persuaded not to be there. It doubles the risk, and frankly, if she's caught opening the safe, there goes her credibility in the entire business."

"Yes, I see that. She doesn't trust you, though."

"In other circumstances she'd be right not to." Jerry took Alec's hand, running his thumb along the knuckles, then brushed a kiss over it. "I meant what I said: I will do what you want through this. I think it would be better to persuade Lazarus to be entirely elsewhere with witnesses while I open the safe, but if you have even the slightest fear I'm running a con on you, then don't. And this is not a test, Alec, or a challenge, or a request for you to prove something. I'm a dishonest man and you are well within your rights to treat me as such. But I'm also a practical one, and I can see multiple possible outcomes, all of which will go better if Lazarus doesn't appear to be involved in this game. I suspect she knows that. Decide as you wish."

Alec wanted to say, *I trust you.* He almost did. Jerry tugged his hand and rose. "Come on. If you're sure we can't walk into the blue, we'd better get back down there."

Alec stood too. "I suppose so. Jerry? I do want you to love me. I don't think there's anything I want more—up here."

Jerry cupped the back of his head, kissed him gently. "Then you're in luck. Now all I have to do is make you believe it down there."

# Chapter Twelve

That afternoon, Alec took Susan for a walk around the garden, and filled her in on the events of the morning and Jerry's request. It went down as well as he'd expected.

"You want Crozier and James to open the safe, unsupervised, while I make myself scarce. Right. And what do you think are the odds of them emptying it and vanishing before the Duchess opens it for her evening toilette?"

"It's not easy to vanish from Castle Speight," Alec pointed out. "And I don't think Jerry would."

"James would."

"I don't think Jerry would let him."

"You mistake me," Susan said. "James would cheerfully make whatever assurances and promises Crozier has made to you, and then empty the safe and disappear. Crozier has been his partner in crime for years. They're two of a kind. QED."

"I don't think it has been demonstrandumned, though. Demonstrated. Jerry isn't James."

"Give it time, and him a chance," Susan said grimly. "I'm sorry, but if you expect me to believe that he's looking out for your best interests—"

"Why is that hard to believe? Is it so entirely impossible he might care about me?"

Susan's mouth opened slightly. "No, of course not. This isn't about you, it's about him."

"But you don't know him. You know me."

Susan put her hands on her hips. "I know his sort."

"People like your father?"

"Guvnor. Yes, like him, because he's a bastard too. Alec, you want to see the best in people."

"You mean I'm gullible."

"I mean what I said. You're worrying over whether you can turn the Duchess over for the murder of her own husband because your father's given you the time of day for once in a decade. The first spark of human feeling you get from him, the first sign he's noticed you exist, and you start fretting about how he's going to feel when his chickens come home to roost. Whereas if he had cared about not even your feelings but your *lives*, Cara wouldn't be dead. Caring about people who don't give a curse is a fool's game."

"And you don't think Jerry gives a curse for me."

Susan exhaled. "I have no idea. I've had two conversations with him and found neither of them impressive."

"I've had a lot more than that. And he's right, anyway. He has to get into that safe, and he has to do it without being caught, and if something goes wrong and you're caught with him—"

Susan set her teeth. "Granted. Nevertheless—"

"No, not nevertheless," Alec said. "I think you should let him do it alone. I want you to. And I think it should be up to me to decide."

"You started this conversation by asking me what I thought," Susan pointed out.

"And now I know what *I* think. What you said about my father is absolutely right, but it isn't everything. Because this isn't only about my father. It's about me."

"And Cara, and your mother, and Mr. Clayton."

"And me," Alec repeated doggedly. "I count. Maybe I count more than the others, because I'm still alive, and I have to live with myself after all this. You may think I'm too soft; perhaps I am. But I have to decide for myself what to do about my own father, and I have to decide whether I'm going to trust people—"

"Crozier's not *people*. He's a thief."

"You lived on the street, and when you were eight you found someone you could trust completely," Alec said. "Someone who saved you and loved you and looked after you. I lived in a castle, and when I was eight my father murdered my mother. I don't think we're going to agree on learning to trust."

"Do you know, Cara said something very like that to me once? Except she was saying, *And yet we completely agree*, which disproves your point somewhat. If you want to take a leap of faith on Crozier, does it have to be this one?"

"Yes," Alec said. "I think he's right. I think he needs to get into the safe with the most secrecy possible, and if he gets caught I'll need you to get him out of trouble somehow." Susan choked. "And in any case, I want to try. I've spent my life hoping people don't let me down and waiting for them to do exactly that and believing it's inevitable and thinking it's my fault. I don't want to do that any more."

"I grasp that you want to trust him, but he won't become any more trustworthy for the wishing it. For God's sake, Alec. We have put too much into this to make a mess of it now."

"We don't even know if the ring is in the safe," Alec said. "Let's get past that hurdle first."

They cleared a preliminary hurdle that evening, at pre-prandial drinks. The Duchess gave Alec her usual cold nod, then crooked a finger for his attention. "Alexander. The Duke tells me you have requested permission to paint my portrait."

"If that meets your pleasure, ma'am." Alec could feel Susan and Jerry in the room, circling like sharks, well out of one another's range.

"It is His Grace's wish that I grant your request," the Duchess said in measured tones. "Naturally, I shall do as he asks. You may begin after dinner."

"That's very generous of you," Alec said, bowing. He could see Jerry in the background, casually sliding a finger across his neck. "Unfortunately, the light of candles is not nearly as good as daylight."

"Some of us ladies prefer candlelight for that very reason," Mrs. Forbes remarked archly. She was well into her third drink of the evening. "Of course Her Grace isn't *quite* at that stage yet."

The Duchess stiffened. Alec said, "A final portrait can be in whatever light and to whatever style one wishes, but I'd never do a preliminary sketch by candlelight. The essence of a face lies in the bones, and the eyes. That's the underpinning of a portrait, and what needs the most accurate observation. If the artist doesn't have the real essence of the face first, I don't believe any portrait can succeed in capturing what makes the person unique, and beautiful."

"I shall be interested to see your theories in action, Lord Alexander," Sir William said. "Do you tolerate observers when you draw?"

"That's entirely up to the Duchess," Alec said, cursing everyone.

Her Grace waved a hand, and the appointment was made for ten-thirty the next day.

"Well done," Jerry murmured in his ear as they retired for a game of billiards after dinner, mostly on the grounds that nobody else played it.

"It's all very well for you to say," Alec remarked bitterly. "I'll have Sir William Cooke watching me as I try to pretend I'm the new Millais."

"Oh come." Jerry had a cue in one hand, the other resting casually on Alec's shoulder. It felt very warm, and so did his breath on Alec's ear. "You're good, very good. Do you need me to demonstrate how good you are?"

"Not in here."

Jerry leaned in and drew Alec's earlobe between his teeth, scraping it gently. Alec shivered. "Perhaps not. Why don't I teach you to play billiards half-decently instead?"

"Or we could go upstairs?" Alec suggested. It was far too early, he knew, but he wanted closeness. He wanted to be with Jerry because it was so much easier to believe him when he was there, overwhelming Alec's senses, and indeed sense.

Jerry shook his head. "I think I'd rather watch you bending over the table. That is a very nicely fitted pair of trousers. Take your coat off first, though. And then I'm going to teach you how to play billiards, and you're going to learn, if you're not too distracted by wondering what I'm thinking, and what better uses I could find for the table. Or the cue."

"Jerry!"

"I want to watch you," Jerry said softly. "I particularly want to watch you when you know I'm watching you, and you're all too conscious of every movement."

"We are playing billiards, yes?"

Jerry grinned. "Think of it as a metaphor. And get your coat off."

Alec stripped off the black coat, and his necktie, then removed his waistcoat as well. He had always felt there was something particularly appealing about a man in braces, and the slant of Jerry's brows suggested he might agree. He rolled up his sleeves. "Well, then. Shall we begin?"

"Let's see you handle the cue."

Alec picked up the cue and leaned in, bending over the table with legs braced wide. He circled the smooth length of wood with thumb and forefinger, then slid his hand deliberately along it and back, up and down.

"I think I see where you're going wrong." Jerry's brows were raised in a sardonic way, but a smile twitched at his lips. "Here." He came up behind Alec and leaned over him, hands meeting Alec's. "Relax your grip, it's very tight. And you don't need all those fingers. Two will do very nicely to ready you for the push."

Alec bit his lip savagely, but he could feel the giggle rising, bubbling in his chest. Jerry added, sounding somewhat stifled, "Line yourself up, nose to ball," and that was it. Alec collapsed, howling. Jerry staggered to brace himself on the edge of the table, and they were both still shaking with stupid, wonderful, happy laughter when Sir William and Mr. Forbes came in to see what all the noise was about.

And then came morning, and the Duchess.

They'd ended up staying late in the billiard room, and Jerry had actually got him handling the cue properly, albeit with some further outbreaks of mild hysteria. They'd kissed goodnight afterwards—nothing more, just long, slow kisses, bodies warm and together—and Alec had fallen into bed and slept like the dead for the first time since he'd got to Castle Speight. He woke past eight, refreshed and ready to face the day, at least until he remembered what it held.

He had to spend perhaps two hours with his stepmother, long enough to make the sitting seem real, while Jerry broke into her safe in broad daylight. Marvellous. He sat up, aware of a sick anticipatory feeling in his stomach, and took a few deep breaths, then went to the window and looked out. The room was on the side of the castle but there wasn't a single window without a view. He could see the downlands rolling away, the distant smudge of Lancaster's dirty air on the horizon, and directly below, Jerry and Susan, walking together in what appeared to be civil or at least non-violent conversation. That was promising.

Breakfast, a solitary stroll in the gardens, some deep lungfuls of clean air. He set up his drawing things in what had been the Blue Morning-Room, but was now primrose yellow, pulling the curtains back fully to let the light flood in, and choosing a position for the Duchess's chair that would illuminate her face without the inconvenience of sun in her eyes. He donned his spectacles, sharpened his pencils, took out his new unused sketchbook, and waited.

The Duchess came in at a quarter to eleven, accompanied by her sister. Alec stood hastily. "Good morning, Your Grace, Miss Hackett."

The Duchess tensed her face, drawing her lips into a flat line which Alec assumed was to suffice for a smile, and looked around. "It is very bright."

"Wasteful. The sunlight will sadly fade the upholstery," Miss Hackett observed.

"Then we shall have it replaced," the Duchess informed her crushingly. Alec didn't harbour any hope that was a defence of him; he recognised the Duchess's tone. Anyone who spoke would be rebuked, ridiculed, or denigrated, until sullen silence and the Duchess reigned unopposed. That was how it had been in every school holiday for ten long years.

He took a moment to work out the best possible phrasing, knowing it was futile because she'd find something to be insulted by, and said, "When it suits you to begin, ma'am, I have positioned this chair for the light. I hope it will be comfortable."

"Of course it will be comfortable," the Duchess said, stiff with offence. "I chose the furniture myself. I hope I am capable of selecting a chair fit for its purpose." Miss Hackett sniffed in agreement. Alec bowed in lieu of an answer that would be wrong whatever he said, and couldn't help a swift glance at the clock. Two minutes down, one hour fifty-eight to go.

"If you're ready to begin, madam?" He went to the chair, moving it an entirely unnecessary inch because gentlemen moved chairs for ladies. The Duchess seated herself in a rustle of stiff skirts. "Thank you." He moved his own chair slightly rather than ask her to look round. "I'd like to do some preliminary sketches today, for your approval and to make sure I have the right approach."

"What possible approach is required? You paint a picture of my face and attempt to achieve an accurate likeness."

"There's a little more to it," Alec said mildly. "A portrait tells us all sorts of things about the sitter. The expression you wear, the background, the clothing, the pose. We—you—need to consider who the portrait is for."

"What do you mean, for? It is for the Duke. Who else would it be for?"

"Well, it might be for the public, or for posterity. It might be your record in the family gallery, the image by which you will be remembered in a hundred or two hundred years—"

"You think very highly of yourself," the Duchess remarked.

"I'm speaking generally, madam. A portrait might be aimed to hang in the Great Hall, a blaze of ducal magnificence, or it might be for your husband's rooms, a private, domestic image rather than a public one. The clothing, the setting, the pose will all be part of the message any portrait conveys. That's what I mean about who it's for."

The Duchess apparently had not considered that aspect. She frowned.

"There's no need to decide now," Alec added, seeing a way to kill time. "Perhaps I could do a couple of different sketches, to indicate what I mean? I find it much easier to decide these things when I have something to look at."

"Ilvar shall decide," the Duchess said. "Well, go on."

"Thank you, madam. Please, relax. Converse, if you choose."

The Duchess's nostrils flared. "I do not need your permission to speak to my sister in my home."

"I meant——" Alec began, and stopped himself. What was the point? "No, madam. I beg your pardon."

"Well. Get on." She put her chin up, mouth tight.

The stupid thing was, Alec thought as he let his pencil slide over the paper, she provoked the hostility she expected. She gave and took offence at every turn, constantly slapping people down in a manner that suggested she was retaliating, if one could retaliate for an insult that hadn't actually been given.

He had no doubt they had been given in the past. Her wedding celebration had been shunned, her name spoken with distaste, her character torn apart in gossip and the press as an adulteress who had driven her husband to self-murder, whatever the coroner had concluded. All the same, she'd been a duchess, one step below the Queen herself, for twenty years. Could it really be so hard to ignore insult, or rise above it?

He looked down at his sketch, up at the Duchess. He wasn't getting her, he knew it. Her face was set in the habitual mask, an impenetrable expression that reminded him a little of Jerry, somehow. It was how he looked when he didn't want his face to be read, how he'd looked when he'd understood Alec had been working with Susan all along.

*It's how he looks when he's afraid.* The thought came into Alec's head unbidden, and he blinked at it. That didn't make sense. Jerry had been hiding hurt then, and anger…

Except he'd said himself that he'd needed to have his face rubbed in the mess to realise he loved Alec. What if he'd realised then, at the moment of betrayal, that he was no longer in control of his feelings, or Alec, or any of it? Jerry didn't shy away from a fight, or a risk. But to find his heart in a traitor's hand—oh, that would have made him afraid, all right. Jerry had been terrified. No wonder he'd struck out; no wonder he'd defended himself with attack.

And the Duchess had been afraid for twenty years. The realisation dawned so blindingly bright that Alec's pencil stilled. Of course she was afraid. Of course she couldn't rise above the sneers, because every questioning of her first husband's death was a threat, every mention of her adultery a reminder of her criminal trespasses on the road to marriage. Any remark, no matter how innocent, that could possibly be construed as an attack on her position would be felt as one, because she knew in her heart the position wasn't truly hers. Because she was guilty as sin, and married to a murderer.

The last twenty years must have been hell.

"Have you finished?" The Duchess's impatient voice cut through his reverie, and Alec realised his hand was slack and unmoving.

"I... No. No, I'm only just starting." He turned the page to a clean sheet. "I had a thought, that's all. Inspiration, if you like. Artistic inspiration."

The Duchess made a scornful noise. Alec didn't care. He wanted to draw this. He wanted to draw the mask, and show it for what it was. He wanted to find the fear in her eyes.

There was a knock on the open door some time later. "May we enter the creative sanctum?" Sir William Cooke enquired.

"Please," Alec said, without looking up. His pencil skidded over the page.

"Alexander," the Duchess snapped. "You will greet the Duke with due respect."

Alec glanced round. Yes, his father was entering, with Sir William, whose eyes had snapped wide at the Duchess's tone, Sir

Paul Maitland, and Mrs. Forbes. "Sir," he said, bowing where he sat. "Excuse my informality."

The Duchess took a sharp breath. The Duke cleared his throat. Sir William, who had crossed to behind Alec, said, "Good heavens. Good *Lord*. Lord Alexander, may I ask—"

"Could we talk later," Alec said, not making it a question. He wanted them all to shut up. He had the Duchess in front of him but also in his mind: the years of slights and snaps and sneers, the unkindnesses large and small, the endless efforts to eradicate memories of her predecessor. Was that for herself, or for the Duke's sake? Did they speak of what they'd done to be together? When she slept badly and woke in the night, what did she see?

Sir William moved away after a moment. Alec heard him murmuring something that included "remarkable," and "awfully good", and ignored it. He knew what he was putting on the paper was good. It was *true*.

The watchers moved around behind him, muttering and whispering in a way Alec normally loathed. He ignored it, and when he heard a rustle of paper, people looking at his other sketchbook, he ignored that too. He only had eyes for the face emerging on his page, and for the Duchess, sitting opposite him, hands folded in her lap.

No, they had been folded. Now they were clenched, and the knuckles were rather pale.

*I see you*, Alec thought. *I see you and you know I see you, don't you? No jewels to hide behind now, no position to throw up as a shield, and I don't care for your contempt. I see you, madam. I see your guilt.*

He glanced at her face and her eyes met his. They had been averted until now, glaring over his shoulder. She looked at him, and Alec looked back, and her chin went up in a defiance that caught his breath. He could paint her like that, like Boadicea, a warrior woman who'd fight to the last, and it would be as true as the other.

Then there was a sharp gasp from behind them, and the Duchess's gaze snapped away. "Ilvar? Ilvar!"

"Your Grace?" Sir William asked.

Alec twisted round. The Duke was looking at his other sketchbook, face slack, mouth open. That was the one Alec had filleted to remove most of the pictures of Jerry, and he had a horrified second's doubt as to whether he'd left in a treacherously bare-shouldered sketch, or if his father had seen too much in the picture he hadn't brought himself to tear out.

"Ilvar!" The Duchess rose. Alec stood too, an ingrained courtesy, and saw what his father was looking at.

It was the picture of Cara, the one that looked like his mother. The Duke held it out in front of himself at arm's length because of his long-sightedness, thus allowing everyone to see it. His hand was shaking.

They stood around the picture, the Duke, the Duchess, and Alec, with the other guests looking from one to another in bewildered fashion, in a silence that stretched out endlessly, punctuated only by the Duke's harsh breaths, and then the Duchess moved. She took the sketchpad from the Duke in a single sharp tug, and ripped the page across.

Alec couldn't help the cry that escaped him. Sir William exclaimed too. The Duchess tore the remaining part of the picture off the sketchbook, dropped the book to the floor, ripped the two halves of the picture, ripped them again, and let the pieces flutter to the carpet.

Alec stared at her. She stared back, lip curling contemptuously, and it turned out Jerry was wrong about his ability to bend against pressure, because that was the point Alec broke.

"That was Cara's picture," he told his father, lips feeling a little odd. "Your daughter Caroline, sir, the dead one. She died in winter, gasping for breath in the fog because you wouldn't help her. Do you remember her at all, sir? Do you care? Sir?"

"And there it is," the Duchess said. "I knew he was deceiving you, Ilvar, I told you it was a pretence. They have always insulted you, and this is one more piece of malice."

"No, that was a picture of my dead sister," Alec said. "I'm surprised you even recognised her. Or were you afraid it was someone else?"

The Duchess's mouth tightened. "We have tolerated enough. You have chosen to continue your path of insolence and insult in the teeth of your father's forbearance, and you will leave this house at once."

Alec ignored her. His eyes were locked with his father's. "Did you think it was my mother's picture? They were very alike, Cara and Mother. Did you think it was the Duchess of Ilvar?"

"I am the Duchess of Ilvar!" That was a shout. "Get out, or I will have you thrown out!"

"I know what you are, madam," Alec snarled, but he didn't look away from his father. He could see the guilty horror on the man's face, and it was fuelling his rage, burning away the lifelong uncertainty. "Why were you shocked to see a picture of my mother? Why are there no portraits of her anywhere? Why have you dug up her garden and changed the house? Do you think you can wipe away your guilt if you obliterate every trace and tear up every picture and pretend she never lived?"

The Duke was breathing hard. "How dare you?"

"How dare *you*?" Alec shouted. He had no idea what the time was; he'd been caught up in his work and hadn't looked. He couldn't begin to guess if Jerry had been able to open the safe yet, and didn't care because he had the confirmation he needed. He'd always believed Cara, but now he knew for himself. "You rid yourself of my mother, and every trace of her after her death, and you even got rid of the daughter who looked like her. Did it work, pretending that Mother never existed? I bet it didn't. I bet she's been with you every night since the last one."

The Duchess slapped him. Alec didn't even see the blow coming, he was so focused on his father, and it sent his head snapping sideways and his spectacles flying. He straightened, shocked, hand going to his face.

"You miserable ingrate," the Duchess hissed. "You've always hated me, and your father for marrying me, and this is nothing but the vicious, contemptible spite to which you and your nasty siblings have subjected my husband for years. Ilvar should disinherit you all."

"Yes," the Duke mumbled. His lips were white, trembling. "Yes. Unfilial, unkind—"

"Oh, come off it," Alec said. "Self-pity, Father? Playing the victim? Really?"

The Duchess turned on her heel and stalked to the door, pushing Sir William out of the way with an angry hand. "Ho! Footmen! At once! At once, I say!"

"You deceived me, Alexander." The Duke drew himself up straight. "You promised me you had thought better of your obstinacy, you apologised—"

"I gave the word of a Pyne-ffoulkes," Alec said. Voice and body were shaking, but he was flying too, with a dizzy feeling of not quite being in control. "What's that worth, Father? What's that worth when your daughter is dead by your negligence, and your wife is dead by your hand?"

That got an audible gasp from the watchers. The Duke's face was a bad, congested colour. "Have a care, boy. The laws of slander—"

"Try it. Bring suit and let's do this in public, I've nothing to hide. We could call Sir Paul in witness. Do you remember, Sir Paul? That my sister Cara was ready to swear my father left Mother dead? That Hartington came to you for help, and you sent him away for a whipping without so much as investigating his concerns? And here you are now, dining with the Duke. Do you feel you earned your dinner?"

Sir Paul's mouth was open. The Duke said, "You will be silent!" It was clearly intended to thunder; it came out a little weakly for that.

"I won't," Alec said. "I'm tired of being silent while you shout. Do you think, if you make enough noise, it will drown out the sound of a woman with a pillow over her face, struggling to breathe?"

"Lord Alexander," Sir Paul said. "I must advise you to consider your words. This extraordinary accusation—implication—"

"We told you. Nearly two decades ago, we *told* you and you didn't listen. He can't even look at her picture!"

"As if that proves anything but that your father is exhausted by his children's scheming, plotting, and resentment," the Duchess said. She was at the door, two footmen standing behind her. They were both a good six foot four. "Their cruelty and malice has blighted a good, noble man's life. It has been like this since the day we married, and I will not have one more minute of this insolence. You will leave this house or John will remove you as he would any common brawler." *John* apparently encompassed both footmen. "Take him out."

Alec backed away. The Duchess came into the room to allow the two burly men access. Her eyes flickered down to Alec's abandoned sketch pad; she walked over to it, tore out the picture, and ripped it up into deliberate strips. Sir William made a stifled noise.

"You can keep on tearing them up," Alec said. "And I'll keep drawing."

"Get him out," she said, voice icy. "Out of my sight and my house. Ilvar, my dear, pray be seated."

"You needn't worry," Alec told the two footmen, as the Duchess went protectively to her husband's side. "I'll go. You know, if she's told you to manhandle me on the way out, I really wouldn't. She won't protect you if it comes to a lawsuit. I expect you know that."

"Nonsense," the Duchess said furiously. "How dare you."

Alec waved that away without answering. He could feel the rush of fury draining as quickly as it had come, leaving him exhausted. He picked up his pencils, paper, spectacles, watched by the fascinated crowd. There were people in the hallway too; it seemed that all the guests had gathered to hear the shouting match, even Susan. All except Jerry.

"Have him pack his things," the Duke said, his voice sounding old and thin. "Ring the bell for Merrow, my dear. Let the rail carriage be prepared."

# Chapter Thirteen

lec made his way to his room flanked by the silent footmen, followed by stares and an appalled hum of conversation that began as he ascended the stairs. He kept a stiff back and a stiffer upper lip until he got to his room, then he shut the door on his guards, attempted to turn the key, and realised he couldn't manage it because his hands were shaking so hard.

Christ, what had he done?

He wondered if Jerry had had enough time to finish his work and get away. It was almost twelve; he'd had an hour and ten minutes, and he'd surely have heard the commotion downstairs. He probably wouldn't be very pleased, Alec thought. Susan would probably be furious. He should have—

What? Smiled and nodded as the Duchess tore up Cara's picture, with the guilt written on his father's face? No, to hell with that. One could only play the villain or the coward for so long before it became true. He'd go back to London with his pride, even if he didn't have his father's approval, the proof he'd sought, or anything to excuse his behaviour to his siblings. Shit, shit, shit.

He desperately wished Jerry were here, to say something sardonic and hold him close, and that set him wondering where the devil the man could be. He surely wasn't still in the Duchess's room, with all hell broken loose downstairs, but if not, Alec might have thought he'd knock on the door. That he'd realise Alec needed him now.

All that aside, he ought to pack, and quickly, since the Duchess would throw him out shortly and probably cut up his clothes if he left them. He started that as soon as his hands had stopped shaking quite so much, and had half-filled his case when he heard the piercing scream.

"Thief! *Thief!*"

Oh, no. Alec dropped his little pile of neckties, fumbled with the door, and made himself stop.

*Think, man.* If it came out that he'd knowingly brought a jewel thief here, the Duke and Duchess would use that fact without mercy, and it would destroy any credibility he might still have. He would have to stay calm, not incriminate himself, pray Jerry would not incriminate him.

And he'd have to act naturally, which would mean responding to all the shouting.

The noise was coming from the Duchess's bedroom—shouts, now, male ones, and a heavy crash. Alec hurried out, almost colliding with Sir William, who was also on his way. "What on earth is going on?" he demanded.

"I've been asking myself that for the last hour," Sir William said fervently, then apparently realised to whom he spoke. "That is—ah—"

"Believe me, I know how you feel," Alec assured him. "But— Oh my God!"

They'd come onto the corridor that led down to the state rooms. The Duke and Duchess stood at the end, both drawn up in pure outrage. Mr. Pelham, the one who Jerry had thought was another private detective, had Jerry in a very competent-looking arm lock; two footmen were hanging onto Templeton Lane's arms. He had a bloody lip and his eyes were wide and dangerous. Susan had her revolver out, covering both Lilywhite Boys.

"What—" Alec's voice failed.

"My God," said Sir William.

"What is going *on?*" Miss Hackett almost shrieked from the stairs.

"This man had Her Grace's safe open," Susan said coldly. "Meanwhile his accomplice seems to have raided a number of the ladies' rooms." Mrs. Forbes, Mrs. Ayres, Lady Cooke and Lady Maitland all exclaimed at once. "I'm afraid you've been harbouring a serpent in your midst, Your Graces."

"More than one, it seems," the Duchess said, with bitter triumph, glancing over to Alec. "A thief, brought to your father's house? I should like an explanation of this."

Alec felt the blood rush to his face. "I— I—"

"In fairness, we've fooled better men than him, although I haven't met many more gullible ones," Jerry said. "You aren't any better at spotting a fraud in high society, are you, Your Grace? At least, not if they let you talk about racehorses." He winked at the Duke.

"Shut your mouth," Susan said. "We're going to go downstairs, all of us, so I can lock this precious pair in the cellar. I'm going first, and if you two try anything I will shoot. Sir Paul, please give Mr. Pelham a hand to restrain Vane, in the unlikely event that's his name. Everyone else out of the way."

"Miss Roy—"

"The name's Lazarus, Susan Lazarus. I'm a private detective," she added impatiently, as everyone stared. "We're going to need the police, but let's get these two securely locked away first."

Alec followed, numb, as the little procession moved awkwardly down the stairs, the other guests keeping a wide berth from Susan as much as from the two pinioned thieves. On the ground floor, Susan stopped.

"All right, thank you, Sir Paul, Mr. Pelham. I want the footmen holding them. Let's search them first." She jerked a thumb, and

Jerry and Lane were pushed into the drawing room. Susan glanced around the men, then passed Sir Paul her gun. "Keep it on them, if you would. Right, you pair, arms up. Try anything and you'll regret it."

"Witch," Lane said softly.

Susan gave him a long, blank look then punched him in the stomach, a swift, practiced jab. Lane folded over with an explosive grunt as the watchers all stepped back another pace, exchanging looks of alarm. "Right. Let's see what we've got."

She slipped her hand into Lane's pocket, whistled, and drew out a handful of blue glitter. Mrs. Forbes cried out. "My necklace!" and started forward.

"Stay back," Susan snapped. "These two are dangerous men, do not get in the way. And there's plenty more where that came from, so we'll sort it out once I'm finished. Someone bring me that little table."

She went through Lane's pockets ruthlessly, inside and out, extracting bracelets, rings, a fortune in sparkling gems and gold, piling it haphazardly on the table, then did the same for Jerry. The Duchess hissed through her teeth. Alec stared, unable to think. Jerry stood, unemotional, if anything seeming slightly bored as he was searched.

"Very well," Susan said at last. "I think that's it. A pretty haul, but your luck's run out. Get them to the cellar, lock them in, and bring us the key."

"Wait," the Duke said. "You, sir." He drew himself up, glaring at Jerry. "You abused the hospitality of my house, came here as a guest with evil intent, in defiance of any common decency. Have you anything to say?"

Jerry considered that a moment, then shrugged as best he could, given the hold on his arms. "If you like. You're a dullard, your wife is intolerable, and your son can't play billiards for toffee."

"*Out,*" Susan said ferociously. "Go on, lock them up." She waited until the Lilywhite Boys had been removed. "All right, we need to send for the police, but first let's get this lot sorted out and locked up again— *Stop.*" That was in response to a concerted move towards the heap of gems. Everyone recoiled as she spoke. Susan had that effect. "Excuse me, ladies and gentlemen, but I've been in this situation before and you'd be surprised how things get mixed up, mistaken, or broken. I'll hand it out." She looked around, causing any objection to wither unspoken, then carefully extracted a gleaming bracelet from the pile. "Diamond and sapphire in gold, whose is this?"

"Mine," Mrs. Ayres said, sounding shocked. "They robbed my room!"

"Indeed they did. Be sure it's yours, and check if it's damaged. Diamond ring, solitaire." That was claimed by Lady Maitland.

One of the footmen returned. "The cellar key, Miss Lazarus."

"Give it to Sir Paul for now," Susan said, without looking up. "Thieves are police business. Whose is the cameo brooch?"

Alec attempted to make himself unobtrusive, standing back with the other men, aware of their sideways glances. Mr. Ayres edged pointedly away from him. Mr. Pelham was watching the division of the jewels, intent.

"Looks like they got into the men's rooms as well. A gold signet ring, cabuchon emerald," Susan said.

There was a tiny pause, then the Duchess said, "Mine."

"It's a man's ring, ma'am."

"It's mine."

"It may be mine," the Duke put in.

"Your safe was untouched, sir," Susan said, so neutrally that she could never have been accused of calling him a liar.

The Duchess stiffened. "It was in my safe, because it is mine. It is a gift for Ilvar."

"Oh, I *see*. I beg your pardon, ma'am. Here you are." Susan held the ring out. The Duchess swept forward and plucked it from her palm, and Susan's other hand snapped up, closing around her wrist like a cuff.

"What—" The Duchess pulled back. Susan didn't let go.

"It was in your safe and you say it's yours. That's *extremely* interesting. Mr. Pelham?"

The supposed businessman came up. The Duchess's fist clenched tight around the ring. Susan's thumb flexed on her wrist; the Duchess gave a sudden gasp of pain and her hand opened. Susan plucked the ring from her palm and held it out, and Mr. Pelham took it.

"Yes," he said after a moment. "This is it."

"What do you mean— What is this? Release me at once!"

"Certainly. But if you hit me, Your Grace, I will hit you back, and I hit harder." Susan let her go. "Thank you, Mr. Clayton."

The Duchess's mouth fell open. "Wh—?"

Mr. Pelham stepped away, watching her. "No, I suppose you don't recognise me. I'm Oliver Clayton, Frank's brother. Then again, we haven't met since your wedding, have we? I was in India when he was killed, if you remember. And this is his signet ring, the one stolen from him when he was murdered. The one you were supposed to return to our family."

"It wasn't on his body when he was found, and it's been missing ever since," Susan added. "You testified you didn't know of his death until the police came to fetch you, madam. So how was it in your safe?"

"I don't know what you are talking about," the Duchess said savagely. Sir Paul made a tiny noise, and Mr. Pelham, or Clayton, turned to him.

"I've read the reports of when my brother was shot, Sir Paul. You said at the inquest that the discovery of my brother's signet ring would solve the question of his death. Do *you* know what I'm talking about?"

"This is most extraordinary," Sir Paul said. "Your Grace, you must realise that if this is indeed the ring in question—"

"It was a family heirloom," Clayton said. "We have pictures, descriptions. It belonged to the head of the family, it was not hers to keep, and it was taken from my brother's corpse when he was shot. I *will* have an answer."

"To that and a number of other questions," Susan said. "Including what happened on the night of the first Lady Ilvar's death." She swung to face the Duke. "Are you aware Lady Cara left a written testimony of what she witnessed on the night your first wife died?"

The Duke recoiled. "Spite," the Duchess said loudly. "This is nothing more than lies and malice."

"Spite?" Susan asked. "Really? We have Lady Cara's testimony, unchanged over twenty years. The account of the housemaid who asked about the stained pillowcase that went missing and was dismissed. You might remember her, Sir Paul? And I'm sure you recall the policeman who took her statement, and who was discouraged from asking about the so-convenient deaths of those two inconvenient spouses within six months." Sir Paul had gone white. Lady Maitland's mouth was set in a line that boded ill for someone.

"But it's all spite, you say," Susan went on. "Such a lot of spite, so consistently from so many unrelated people over so many years. What a dreadful and complicated conspiracy against you, unless of course it's simply the truth. You've had a good run, Your Graces, but it's coming to an end."

"Who *are* you?" the Duchess demanded. "This woman is a fraud. I engaged her as a private detective to prevent thefts. She is here on false pretences."

"I'm Susan Lazarus of Braglewicz and Lazarus Enquiries, just as I said, but you're quite right about the false pretences." Susan didn't sound apologetic. "I didn't come here for jewel thieves, even if I caught some. I came here to find out what happened twenty years ago."

"What happened?" Sir William asked on cue. All the spectators were caught, Alec realised. Susan was working the room superbly, restrained feeling humming through her normally flat tones and compelling everyone to hang on her words.

"It started with a death in the night," she said. "It's no secret the Duke was having an affair with Mrs. Clayton." Miss Hackett made an outraged noise. Susan turned, looked steadily at her, and turned back. "That's not a crime. And then Lady Ilvar was found dead for no clear reason. The Duke's doctor called it a seizure, and if a maid claimed she'd seen a stained pillowcase, well, she could be dismissed without ado, leaving the Duke free to marry again. But the woman he loved was still tied to her husband, and Frank Clayton dug his heels in, no matter the pressure put on him to petition for divorce, or the grounds you gave him. It must have been maddening." Susan cocked her head at the Duchess. "The man you wanted, a ducal coronet, and untold wealth, all within your grasp if only you could be freed from your marriage vows. But Clayton refused to seek a divorce, and he didn't give you reason to seek one on the basis of cruelty or adultery, so there wasn't a thing you could do about it. When I say he didn't give you reason, I mean legally," Susan added. "The law asks women to show black eyes and broken noses, as if beatings are the only cruelty, and everything else—the vicious words, the worse silences, the conjugal demands—is tolerable. You were tied to a man you loathed, because he hated you so much that he preferred to stay chained together in misery than to let you be rich, happy, and free."

The Duchess's face was a picture, not one Alec wanted to draw. There was raw shock, and old rage, and something twisting darkly underneath, like devils in a Hieronymus Bosch painting. The Duke's lips were white. The younger Clayton's jaw was set.

"So you killed him," Susan said. "You killed him because he was ruining your life, and you took his ring because it was a jewel. Even though it would place you at the scene of the crime, even though the way was clear for you to marry a duke and live in a castle, you still couldn't let go of it, because by rights, by any justice, by *marriage*, it was yours. You'd earned it."

"Yes," the Duchess said. "It *was* mine. As Clayton's wife—"

"It was a family heirloom, to be returned to us on his death," Clayton said. "You knew that."

"It became mine when I married him!"

Mr. Clayton drew in a breath. Susan said, over him, "You kept it. You were entitled to it, and you kept it. Now tell us how you got it."

The Duchess opened her mouth to answer, and paused, and the pause was fatal. Alec could feel the fascinated onlookers drawing themselves away as the silence stretched out. Miss Hackett's hand came up, covering her mouth. "It…was sent to me. Anonymously. In a letter."

"It was taken from your husband's corpse, and posted to you? Good heavens. Did you report that to the police?" Susan let the answering silence spool out, then shrugged. "Well, you're welcome to try that in court." The insinuating sympathy had vanished from her tone.

"No," the Duke said. "I won't, you may not—I will not have this. None of it. These, these insults— Sir Paul, I demand you take action at once." He pulled himself upright; Alec could see him gathering his dignity. "These slanderous accusations, this conspiracy—"

"You killed my mother!" It came out as a shout. Alec hadn't even meant to speak. "Cara saw you go into her room and heard Mother greet you. And you came out, and Mother was dead, and there was a wet, stained pillow on the bed. You killed her." He took a step forward. The Duke took a step back. "Cara saw you. She told me. We *know*."

"Not true. Lies. You always resented my marriage."

"No, you resented us. Was that guilt, Father? Because you knew what you had taken from us? Did you come to hate us because you'd wronged us?"

"I can't bear this," Mrs. Ayres said, quite suddenly. "I *can't*."

"Agreed," Lady Cooke said. "Sir Paul, I imagine you will be summoning the police to investigate, and I will gladly bear witness to this…conversation, but I should strongly prefer to leave this house today."

"The police, at once," Mr. Ayres agreed. "And we shall order the bags while we wait. Jewel thieves and murderers, my God."

"You dare not repeat that allegation," the Duchess said. Her lips were white.

Lady Cooke looked her up and down, dispassionately. "In fact, I do dare, and I shall. I would thank your Graces for your hospitality, but *really*. Come, William."

"I think I should assist Sir Paul," Sir William said. "But the ladies should undoubtedly retire. This is an unfit scene for women."

"Absolutely," Susan said. "I have a dossier for you, Sir Paul, and two witnesses that you will wish to interview. It's time to act. Time and past."

Her tone was implacable. The Chief Constable drew back his shoulders. "Your Graces will understand, I have no alternative. I will need to send several telegrams. I must also request that your Graces remain on the premises for the moment."

"In separate rooms," Susan added helpfully.

"You'll regret this," the Duchess snarled. "You'll all regret it."

The Duke didn't speak. His mouth worked, he put a shaking hand to his throat, and then he toppled like a tree.

"Father!" Alec yelped.

"Oh, God," Susan said with disgust. "Apparently we'll need a doctor too. If you want to help, Sir William, take Alec out of here, make him eat something, and keep him occupied. I've had quite enough melodrama."

Sir William took his mission seriously. He rang for sandwiches, brought by a maid who could barely contain her excitement, made Alec eat two, and then dragged him out on a long walk across the moorland. He didn't touch on the obvious subject except once, as they walked, to say, "What you said, about your father—"

"My sister's testimony. I believe her. There was only ever her word until now, and she was only a child, so nobody else listened. But she always swore it was true."

"Yes. I see. And the business of the ring?"

"He was shot, the ring was taken from his corpse and the Duchess has been hoarding it since," Alec said. "I don't know anything more, but that seems to me quite enough."

"Yes. My God," Sir William said. "My God. I don't know what to say. And, uh, what about Mr. Vane?"

"I have no idea. We struck up a friendship in a club a few months ago, and I found him very pleasant company. I had no idea that he was fooling me, or what he intended. None at all."

"What an extraordinary thing. To think the proof of a murder should be revealed by a thief. The Lord moves in mysterious ways."

"That he does," Alec said. "That he really does."

The Lord's ways seemed even more mysterious a few hours later, when they returned to the castle. Here they found a large number of police, the Duke in bed with a suspected stroke, the

Duchess being interviewed under caution, and a total absence of jewel thieves.

"Scarpered," Susan told Alec and Sir William as they stood in the hall. "We unlocked the cellar door and they were gone."

"But how?" Sir William demanded.

"If you mean, did someone let them out, Sir Paul Maitland had the cellar key in his pocket all the time, and I very much doubt he's their accomplice." Susan shrugged. "They got through the Bramah lock on that safe; I dare say they can pick anything. My mistake. I should have had them tied up. Or clubbed round the head."

"Do you think they've got away?" Alec asked. "That is, surely they can't have gone far yet?"

"On the contrary. It seems two men matching their descriptions took a train at Broughton an hour ago. The carriage has been going up and down the Castle Speight line non-stop, you understand, with doctors and police, and it appears our villains hitched a ride. They got on a train to Lancaster at Broughton, they'll have got on a different one there, and that's the last we'll see of them."

"Wait. What? They rode down in the private train?" Alec demanded. "And nobody said anything?"

"They hung on the outside, I think. The guard at Broughton did say they looked rather windswept."

"Good heavens," Sir William said. "Good Lord."

"That's one way to put it," Susan said grimly. "Before they left, they found time to nip upstairs and finish emptying Her Grace's safe."

"*What?*"

"I will have someone's hide for this. Ah, no, I won't though, because I've been sacked," she added. "Her Grace made rather a point of not wishing to employ me further, and even instructed that secretary fellow not to pay my firm, which means her jewels are officially none of my business."

"So you'll just...let the thieves go, then?" Alec said tentatively.

"I suppose I'll have to," Susan agreed, and strolled off.

George and Annabel arrived the next day, in response to Alec's urgent telegram. They had to come, and he had to face them, but it didn't make the prospect of the meeting any easier.

He let himself imagine telling them that all his apparent failings had been a noble deception in the service of justice, but had to reject the temptation. He couldn't risk sharing Susan's involvement in the burglary, for fear that might muddy the waters of any prosecution, and in truth he wasn't convinced George and Annabel would be happy about the catastrophic scandal he'd ignited, no matter their resentment of the Duke and Duchess. No; he'd chosen this path, keeping his brother and sister in the dark, and he'd stick to it. He would say only that Jerry had led him into gambling and bad ways, that he'd realised his terrible mistake on coming to Castle Speight, that he was sorry. It would have to do and, he told himself, his misbehaviour would be far from the greatest matter on anyone's mind. He still felt nauseous with the prospect of more rebuke to be endured and grovelling to be done as the great door opened and his siblings came in.

George handed his hat to a footman and looked to where Alec hovered nervously. "Alec. What the devil has been going on here?"

"Well," Alec began, and couldn't think what to say next. "Uh. It's all been rather awful."

"I'm damned sure it has," George said. "Come here, you idiot."

Alec, barely believing, found himself pulled into a rough hug. "Oaf," George muttered in his ear. "I'm sorry, Alec. I should have realised you weren't managing on your own."

"I'm sorry, too." Annabel's arms snaked round his waist from behind, and she rested her face against his shoulder. "It's been horrible for everyone. But we're going to stick together now, aren't we? We have to."

Alec had simultaneous urges to insist, *But it was all my fault!* and to object in strong terms to the idea he needed George's help. He bit both back. "Stick together," he agreed, and clamped his eyes shut against the overwhelming relief as he held his siblings tight.

That reconciliation gave Alec strength he sorely needed, because everything else was awful. The Duke lay, unspeaking, in bed. The doctors weren't sure if he had had some sort of stroke, or a nerve-storm; one of them called it a moral collapse. Between his unresponsive catatonia, the appalling accusations, and the undeniable evidence of the ring, the Duchess's authority had slithered through her fingers. She was interviewed by the police several times, and asked not to leave Castle Speight, and since that could only be done via a walk of many miles or with the assistance of the servants, she didn't leave.

It was not pleasant. She argued furiously with Miss Hackett, who nevertheless remained at the castle, bitter in her humiliation. The Duchess had several ghastly exchanges with Alec and his siblings, every threat sounding more hollow than the last, retreated to her rooms in a form of self-inflicted house arrest and raged impotently there, speaking to nobody but the Duke's lawyer, who looked grim. The maids took to leaving her tray outside her door rather than have food thrown at them.

The grand dinner had been cancelled, thanks to Merrow sending frantic telegrams. Reporters were gathering in Broughton, and coming in ones and twos up the steep hill. Alec fully expected the castle would soon be besieged.

"It's horrible," he told Susan, as she packed. "I keep thinking the Duchess is going to do something awful. Burn the place down out of spite, perhaps." He wished she wasn't leaving; he wished that

Jerry was here, or that he had any idea where Jerry was. "When is the Detective Inspector going to act?"

"Soon, I think. He's good, and he's right to be careful about this; the case will have to be watertight. I've given him everything I can." She snapped her case shut and sat on the bed. "I need to tell you something. About Crozier."

Alec felt an unpleasant twinge of dread. "What?"

"He volunteered."

That didn't make any sense. "Sorry? For what?"

Susan sighed. "There was always going to be a tricky part after I'd got into the Duchess's safe. One can't really go to the police and say, 'I found evidence of murder in the course of committing a burglary.' It might have fatally weakened the case against the Duchess, or left me open to a prosecution. Crozier had asked how I was intending to handle it that very morning, in fact. Well, when you and the Duchess started shouting at one another, I went up to the bedroom to see if Crozier had found the ring, which he had. I told him that things were about to fall apart quite spectacularly and that he'd better clear off. And Crozier—you have no idea how much this pains me—Crozier said, 'Wouldn't it be more effective if you caught me red-handed?'"

"It was his idea?" Alec said. "To be arrested?"

"Specifically, that I should catch them with their pockets full of loot, and play the whole thing out in public. It was something of a gamble, in that we could well have ended up with the Duchess denying everything and the Lilywhite Boys hauled off in handcuffs, but there you are, it worked. Crozier's got the devil's own nerve, I'll give him that."

"I can't believe Mr. Lane went along with it."

Susan scowled. "I dare say Crozier leant on him."

Alec shook his head. He'd assumed it had all been Susan's plan, that the Lilywhite Boys had followed orders. He hadn't expected this.

"You look shocked," Susan said. "As well you might, at the idea of an altruistic act by that pair. Well, there you are. Crozier volunteered for arrest to make our scheme work, and would have let himself and James in for some very serious trouble if they hadn't escaped. I thought you should know."

"Thank you," Alec said. "When you say *escaped*, though..." He raised a brow in his best imitation of Jerry.

"Are you implying I let them go?"

"You deliberately got me out of the way with a witness so nobody could say I was involved, and made sure everyone knew you didn't have the key. Did you pick Sir Paul's pocket for it?"

"I see you're getting the hang of this subterfuge business," Susan said. "I was planning to send them on their way as a gesture of goodwill, yes. But I didn't have to, because by the time I got back to the cellar, they'd let themselves out, sauntered upstairs, reopened the safe, and helped themselves to a very nice selection of the Duchess's jewels. Bastards," she added with feeling.

"But how? If it takes an hour to pick a Bramah lock—"

"Crozier's key device works by sliders, adjustable mechanisms to create a sort of skeleton key. I assume they stay adjusted, meaning that once he'd opened it the first time, he had a key to the safe. I didn't think of that at the time, so I didn't take it off him, and my guvnor's not going to let me live that down in a hurry. If you see Crozier again, you can tell him I want everything back."

"I'm sure it's covered by the amnesty. You did say *including this job*."

Susan narrowed her eyes. "Don't you split hairs with me. I told them they weren't allowed to steal anything."

"Yes, but those jewels belong to the Duchess," Alec pointed out. "There's no guarantee she'll be convicted, and even if she's sentenced to hang, she can still dispose of her possessions as she pleases. I'd rather Jerry and Lane had it all than see Miss Hackett inherit a fortune."

"Well, if you put it like that." Susan stood. "Anyway, that's it. Good luck, Alec. You've done Cara proud, and—oh, damn it. I hope your trust isn't misplaced."

Alec made a face. "I don't even know if I'll see him again."

"James Vane turns up like a bad penny, and they're two of a kind," Susan said. "I have every expectation of running into that pair again, sooner or later, pockets full of green-oh."

"Sorry?"

"The Lilywhite Boys. The song? 'Green Grow the Rushes-O'?"

"They did *not* take their name from a carol. Surely."

"Merry Christmas, one and all." Susan gave him a quick hug, hoisted her case, and left. Alec heard her singing down the corridor.

"Three, three, the rivals.

Two, two, the lily-white boys

Clothèd all in green-O,

One is one and all alone

And evermore shall be so."

A week after what everyone was now calling The Discovery, Sir Paul Maitland returned to Castle Speight. He took George aside and warned him that the Detective Inspector in charge of the case intended to charge the Duchess with the murder of her first husband. There was insufficient evidence to prosecute the Duke and in any case it was questionable if he would be fit to stand trial. He was eating and sitting up, if only in his dressing gown, but he had not spoken a word and didn't appear to hear much that was said.

"This is going to be awful," Annabel said as they sat together in the drawing room that evening, all the windows open against the residual heat of the day. "A murder trial. Our stepmother in the dock. Oh goodness. It has to be done, I know, but...awful. And what about Father? What will he do?"

Alec flopped back in his chair. "Lord knows. I think it will kill him if she hangs. There's his pride and the public humiliation, but it's more than that. He really does love her. I don't know if he'll be able to carry on without her."

"What happens if he can carry on *with* her?" Annabel asked. "Suppose she's found not guilty? Suppose she's released and they go on, visiting London, doing as they please?"

"I intend to talk to a solicitor about that," George said grimly. "If I have to sue the Ilvar estate and my father as unfit to manage it, I will. I've spent long enough living at the whims of that pair and it ends here. I'm reclaiming my birthright, and yours."

"George!" Annabel clapped her hands. "*Good.* Melissa will be so proud of you."

"Melissa deserves a great deal better than I have given her," George said. "You all do, and I'm going to make sure you have it."

"Not me," Alec said. "I mean, yes I deserve better, but I want to get it myself. I realised that over the last weeks. I'm going to keep drawing, I am going to work on my portraiture, and even if you do sue the estate and so on, that won't change my plans. I hope it doesn't bother either of you, but it's what I want to do."

"As you please. Goodness knows, it hardly matters if my brother is an illustrator, given my stepmother is a murderer."

"Quite," Annabel said. "I think we have all the family scandal we'll ever require."

"It'll go away," Alec assured them. "Lord Moreton became an earl because one of his predecessors was a bigamist and the next heir was murdered, and nobody holds that against them. If anyone looks askance at us for what the Duke and Duchess did, that just shows they're a person we can do without."

"Well said." George leaned forward to give Alec's knee a nudge. "By the way, talking of the Moretons…"

Oh God. Alec had a feeling he'd be unpicking the tangle he'd made for months. "Don't listen to the gossip. Penny's lovely but she's far too young to marry, as her mother has very firmly said, and I don't think it would be fair to bring anyone into the family under these circumstances. Which…what's your Henry going to think about all this, Annabel?"

"We'll find out," Annabel said. "If my fiancé wants a girl whose stepmother isn't being arrested for murder, that's up to him. It's not my fault, and I'd rather know now if he's not prepared to stick out a bit of trouble."

"Good for you," Alec said. "He's an idiot if he doesn't. And Melissa?"

George winced. "Melissa wrote to me to say that she feels she's now fulfilled the 'for worse' as well as 'for poorer' part of her vows and she'd rather like the 'for better' and 'for richer' to start soon. She's a wonderful woman," he added hastily. "I suppose you're right, Alec, and Father will stand by *her*?" George never used the Duchess's name or title if he could avoid it. "Presumably he'll be called as a witness?"

"I should think so," Alec said. "I was wondering, though, what if her lawyer tries to cast blame on him? To argue that she operated under his instruction? That's got more than one woman off the gallows before now."

"Oh my God," George said. "You don't seriously think so."

"That she'd sacrifice Father to save herself? I don't know. Maybe not. I'm not sure she'll be able to admit anything at all, in fact, for sheer pride. This will be torture for both of them. Prison, trial, shame, the newspapers, the crowds. I know they deserve it, but all the same, it must be agony. Frankly, I wouldn't be surprised if the humiliation kills her before the noose does." George's eyes widened, and Alec realised that he might, perhaps, be sounding a little too much like Jerry. "I'm sorry, but really, I don't know how either of them will bear it. They're people who break before they bend."

"You may be— What was that?" Annabel looked around.

"What?"

"I thought I heard something, in the hall. I heard a shuffling earlier and—you don't think there's something got in? Or someone listening?"

Alec went out, peering into the dark, shadowy hall. "Nobody there. For heaven's sake, George, put in electricity when it's yours."

"Electricity? Do you think I'm a grand hotel?" George demanded, and the conversation went on.

Alec was in the middle of a confused dream. Jerry and Templeton Lane were painting a picture of the Duchess on the outer walls of the castle, to be visible from the moors, but they were using chalk and the rain was washing the work away. Alec was trying to explain that they ought to be using oils when the Duchess herself arrived, saw the distorted, rain-smeared picture, and began screaming, screaming—

He woke fully, blinking, and the screaming was still there, a woman shrieking from some distance. He pulled on his dressing gown and ran down the corridor, nauseated and blinking at the abrupt awakening, colliding with George and a sleepy butler as they approached the corridor where the Duke and Duchess's state rooms lay.

He wasn't entirely surprised by what they found when the hysterical tweeny maid opened the door. The Duchess lay, eyes wide and staring, face livid, a stained pillow lying half off the bed next to her. The Duke was nowhere to be seen, and a frantic search was mounted, family and servants alike running through the castle, until a footman shouted from outside and they discovered his body in a crumpled heap. He had finished the Duchess as he had finished his first wife, and then he had gone to the window and stepped out.

# Chapter Fourteen

It was another three weeks before Alec was back in London. He hadn't been able to leave George or Annabel through the nightmare of those last days, the guilt and recriminations, Miss Hackett's wails, the barrage of journalists and police and questions, the financial issues. The Duke's will left everything unentailed to the Duchess, and made no mention of anyone else, such as old servants or his children. Since his wife had predeceased him, if only by minutes, that meant the entire estate went to George, although Miss Hackett, as the Duchess's sole heir, was heard to speculate that the Duchess might have survived long enough for the Duke to step out of the window before she breathed her last, and was said to be looking for an enterprising lawyer to argue as much. Alec left that to his brother to deal with. He'd done his part, and had no desire to do more.

Once he felt he could leave, he went back home to Mincing Lane. There Mrs. Barzowski was already on her second scrapbook of newspaper reports, and demanded he give a full account of everything that had taken place as interest on his forgotten back rent. She'd held a heap of post for him, and Alec took it upstairs to sort.

There were multiple offers of work or representation. He had an angry letter from the publisher of the fairy tales book demanding his uncompleted work, and a grovelling letter from the same source dated two days later, presumably once they'd seen the papers, offering him an extension for as long as he needed, and wondering if he'd care to double the number of illustrations. There was also an invitation from Lord and Lady Moreton to stay at Crowmarsh for as long as he needed, which left Alec in tears. The Moretons had been part of Susan's plot from the beginning; he wasn't even sure how they came into it, except that she seemed to treat them as family to be relied on. Alec had no real connection to them at all, and the kindness of the letter made him wish he did. Also thoughtful, though less unselfish, was a communication from Sir William Cooke, offering best wishes in his family's time of trouble, and delicately suggesting he would be most interested to see Alec's portrait work.

And that was everything of importance. Alec hadn't really expected anything more, or at least he'd told himself there would be nothing. There could be nothing. The Lilywhite Boys had left Castle Speight with approximately £44,000 worth of jewels, a feat that came second only to the rumours of the impending Murder in High Life case in the newspapers but was entirely knocked out of the public consciousness by the Duke's final acts. It nevertheless had the full attention of the police. Alec had quietly hidden all his pictures of Jerry and given a description that mostly hung on the facial hair; Susan, he rather thought, had done the same. Even so, the hue and cry was up. Jerry would probably be on the continent by now, if he had any sense.

He accepted the publisher's offer, but declined the Moretons', albeit with regret. He didn't want to leave London for a while, somehow. Not that he was waiting for anything, not that he wanted to be easily found if anyone were looking, but... Well. He had work to do.

About ten days later he went out to get luncheon at a Lyons' coffee house, and when he came to pay there was an envelope in his pocket. He fished it out—it was sealed but blank—turned it over, and waited to open it until he was back at his desk.

The message, typewritten, read simply *Victoria Park, Palm House, 4.*

Four what? Four pm today? Alec couldn't put any other interpretation on it. He had no idea how the envelope had come into his pocket—for all he knew it was some new advertising stunt—but it didn't matter. He had to see.

Victoria Park was in the East End, up towards Hackney. Alec knew it as a place where the poor went for their leisure and radical meetings were held, and dressed in one of his older suits accordingly. In fact, it proved to be a rather lovely, very sizeable space, lush green in the still-warm September weather, and the Palm House was a soaring confection of white-painted metal supports and glass, filled with tropical foliage. He was there twenty minutes early and it would, he suspected, be unpleasantly hot inside, so he retreated to a tree near the ornamental lake for shade and sat on the grass, to see what might happen.

Five minutes later someone sat down beside him. Alec didn't look round.

"Hello, there," Jerry said softly.

"Hello to you." There were ducks on the lake, splashing and quarrelling over bread thrown by a couple of urchins. "How have you been?"

"Lying low. You look marvellous. I wish I did."

Alec had to turn then. Jerry was clean-shaven, his hair considerably darker, and his eyebrows much less sharply shaped. He wore a rather vulgar waistcoat and a Paisley scarf of which the colours didn't quite go, and looked like a clerk with aspirations to poetry on his day off. The cumulative effect was spectacularly different; Alec wasn't sure he'd have recognised him in the street. "Good God."

"Yes, sorry about this." Jerry grinned ruefully, and was himself again with that smile. "You should see Temp. Who, I may add, is barely speaking to me. I must upset him more often, it's wonderfully peaceful."

"Susan told me what you did." Alec tugged some grass out of the ground, running it between his fingers. "Thank you."

"Not at all. I should say, I tried to take only newer stuff, but if any of it is your mother's, let me know."

"It's my brother's now. Really, you ought to give it all back."

"That is a school of thought."

Alec tossed the grass away. "I wasn't sure if I was going to see you again."

"I had my own doubts on that when I took a trip down from Castle Speight on the wrong side of a railway carriage," Jerry said, with feeling. "Are you all right, Alec? Financially, and so on? Is your brother doing the decent?"

"Yes, of course. He's giving us, Annabel and me, an allowance now and intends to make over a substantial sum once the whole situation has calmed down and he can take a look at the estate and what Father's done over the last years."

"And the situation in general?"

"Fine. Well. Annabel's fiancé wrote to her indicating that she ought to release him from his promise what with the trial coming up and all the scandal. The letter arrived the morning we found the bodies. Then, as soon as that had made the papers—no trial, George becoming Duke—he wrote to say that he'd thought again and naturally he would stand by her."

"Whoops. What's she going to do?"

"Wrote back releasing him and burned the second letter. He was an idiot anyway. Melissa and the boys are at Castle Speight with George. The Duchess's sister is making a fuss about the will, but nobody thinks it'll get anywhere."

"And how are you?"

"You mean, having set off the events that ended with my father killing his wife and himself?"

"Yes," Jerry said. "Having told lies, and orchestrated multiple levels of betrayals, and put yourself through untold shittiness, and got caught in the murderous selfishness of those two swine with those spectacular consequences, *and* plunged into a damn fool mess of a situation with a bloody stupid criminal…how are you?"

"Oh, you know. So-so."

Jerry grimaced, starting to speak. Alec held up a hand. "You can't expect me to have an answer. I don't know how I feel. I don't know how I'll feel about it tomorrow, or in ten years."

"If you could change anything, about any of it, would you?"

"The divorce laws, so none of it would ever have happened in the first place. Look, my father made his decisions, and so did the Duchess, and so did Mr. Clayton, even. Any of them could have done things differently, and all of them chose not to, and I'm sorry for them in much the way I'm sorry for that man under Waterloo Bridge. I wish none of it had happened, but everything I did was because of what other people did in the first place and I don't have to feel guilty that they eventually faced the consequences. Or, at least, I don't think I have to, and I'm trying not to."

"Fair enough." Jerry didn't offer anything further, no *It wasn't your fault.* Alec was glad of that. He didn't want reassurance or platitudes; he didn't need anyone's approval. This was up to him.

After a moment's silence Jerry leaned back, looking around in an entirely casual way. "I should probably say, I hope you understand that I couldn't get in touch before. I've been rather busy lying low, but also there was always the risk that you'd be suspected of collusion, and I am reluctant to incriminate you."

"You could have *not* robbed the Duchess if you didn't want to be pursued," Alec pointed out.

"Yes and no. Bear in mind, I had no way of knowing what was going on after we got locked up, including whether the Duchess would have the sense to say she'd never seen the ring in her life. I didn't know if any charges were likely to stick, and the Duke and Duchess had more than a few bones to pick with you, so I thought a bit of cash in hand would be useful in case you had to clear out."

"Forty-four thousand pounds' worth?"

"Oh, we wouldn't have got anything like if we'd had to flog it all in a hurry, not with the stones that hot and so many to sell. Probably no more than seven thousand, but that would still be a useful sum if we'd needed to make a sharp exit to the Continent, for example."

"You and Mr. Lane?"

"You and me. Or even just you, if you didn't want me around." Jerry shrugged a shoulder at whatever he saw in Alec's face. "Offering people choices is entirely pointless if they don't have the wherewithal to make those choices. If you had the readies and thus didn't need me, I thought you'd be in a better position to consider if you might want me."

"Wait. You *actually* stole those jewels for me? Really?"

"Yes," Jerry said. "I did. Implausible, I know, but if it helps convince you, I'll—God, how far have I fallen—I'll give them back."

"What would Mr. Lane say about that?"

"I can tell you exactly what he said because we've discussed it. It's scarcely flattering, though."

"What?" Alec said, with some foreboding.

Jerry plucked a daisy from the grass, rolling the stem between his fingers. "He says I've been no damn use since I met you, and that he doubts I'll be any damn use in the future unless I do something about you. He added, grudgingly, that the Duchess's jewels will be too risky for Stan to handle safely for years and Lazarus might well consider our fencing them somewhat provocative, so I can do as I please, except for a very nice opal bracelet which he says is the least he's owed for all the fucking about. I do hope you don't want that back, because I think I mentioned Templeton and opals."

"Yes, you did. Um, what 'something' is it that you intend to do about me?"

"That's up to you," Jerry said. "In an ideal world, you'd fall immediately into my arms and I'd take you to bed—I have a place five minutes away, safe as houses. However, that would be a world in which the last time we fucked went rather differently. In this world, I'd probably have to start by asking if you want to see me again at all, and if you're prepared to accept the risks involved. I will, needless to say, do my best to keep you safe and my head low, but still."

"And if I do want to see you again?"

Jerry opened his hands. "Then, I suppose, I'd remind you that I love you. Your kindness, your courage, the way you see the world, the way you see me. I want you to be happy. I'd like you to believe I love you, to know it so deeply you won't doubt it again, and I'd very much like thirty years or so to prove it to you. But it's your choice, all of it. And in the interests of full disclosure, I do need to stress that the police want me rather urgently."

"Yes, well, they're not the only ones," Alec said. "Five minutes away, did you say?"

Jerry's place proved to be a little two-up two-down house. It was clean, plainly furnished, apparently uninhabited. Alec didn't much care who it belonged to, or why. He simply followed Jerry upstairs, stepped into his arms, and met his mouth with a sense of desperate release as though every muscle in his body had been twanging tight for a month and then all relaxed at once. Jerry had his hands on Alec's face; Alec gripped his lean hips, the curve of his muscular arse, holding on for dear life. They kissed breathlessly, leaning into one another, Alec learning the feel of Jerry's mouth and chin without the expected prickle of beard, until Jerry pulled away a little to inhale, dropping his hands to Alec's waist. "God. Alec."

"I love you." Alec had thought he'd have to work up to it, but the words rushed out, carried on the flood of relief at being held again, and Jerry's expression made the rest easy. "Being with you—

it's like I was living in a pencil drawing, and you turned the world to oils. Colourful and rich. And far more complicated and difficult to manage, obviously, but that can't be helped. I love you and—" This was the hard part. He squared his shoulders. "I believe you love me. I do."

Jerry's fingers tensed convulsively. "I'm glad you believe it, because it happens to be true. I'd like to make the idea less of a struggle for you."

"I dare say I'll get used to it, given time. I'm not at all sure how we'll find the time, or how we go on from here at all, but you're awfully good at getting away with things. Do you think you can get away with us?"

Jerry's dark eyes were locked on his, as unguarded as Alec had ever seen. "Of course I can, you utter glory. I'll get away with anything you ask me to. I'd steal you the Crown Jewels if you were sufficiently vulgar to want them."

"The question was never whether I loved you," Alec whispered. "It was, *How brave am I?* or maybe *How afraid am I?* And it turns out I'm slightly braver than I am afraid when it comes to you. Tell me what I need to do so we can be together and neither of us gets arrested for anything, and I'll do it. Does thirty years still count as a long game?"

"The longest." Jerry slid his thumbs up Alec's neck. "Anything, Alec. Anything you need of me. If you have opinions about my profession, even—"

Alec shook his head. "I'm not going to ask you to mend your ways. I knew who you were all along, I've no right to demand you become someone else. Of course, if you want to reform, you should," he added hastily. "Don't let me put you off. But that's up to you. Don't rob my friends, please."

"Good God. Call yourself an upstanding member of the nobility?"

"I may have low moral standards," Alec acknowledged. "It runs in the family."

"And who better for a degenerate aristocrat than a professional criminal, when you think about it?" Jerry brushed a hand over his face, through his hair. "Talk about making a profit on a job. I stole you, and I'm keeping you."

Alec nodded breathlessly. Jerry smiled into his eyes. "With all due care and attention. And talking of such matters—"

"I never lied about what I want," Alec said over him. "I like you having the control. In here, I mean, or in a theatre box or under Waterloo Bridge; I don't want you ordering my food or any such. But between us."

"You want to be in my hands?"

"Yes. Please."

"Obedient to my orders, pliant to my will— For heaven's sake, Alec, it's no good saying you want me in control and then looking at me like that." Jerry's fingers slid down his spine. "God, I adore you. I have no idea how I'm supposed to maintain a façade of cool authority under these circumstances."

"Practice from a lifetime of dishonesty?"

"That will doubtless help." He took Alec's chin, tilting his head up. "This is ridiculous. I've been thinking about fucking you every night for a month. I planned to make up for that unspeakable last time inch by inch over your skin, to render you so helplessly mine you'd need reminding to breathe. And now you're here, and I want to do nothing but tell you how beautiful you are."

"You could do both."

"I probably could." Jerry's eyes narrowed in a familiar way that made Alec's skin tingle. "Or I could pull myself together—at your expense, needless to say. It may take some time. Do you have anywhere you need to be tonight?"

"No."

"Will you stay here?"

"Can I?" Alec asked. The thought was astonishing. "I mean, is it safe?"

"Entirely. Stay with me, sleep with me, in every sense. I'm Jeremy here, by the way, Jeremy Brant."

"Jeremy. Right."

"I do realise there are inconveniences to a lover whose name changes quite so frequently," Jerry said, with a hint of apology.

"Oh, well. I knew you were a Lilywhite Boy when I got into this."

"I really don't think it works as a singular. The point about the lily-white boys in the song is that there's two of them, no?" He reached for Alec's necktie, tugging it undone.

Alec tipped his head back to give access. "Two, two, the lily-white boys, clothèd all in green-O…"

"One is one and all alone," Jerry sang in a surprisingly deep baritone, fingers dancing down Alec's buttons. "And nevermore shall be so."

"It's 'ever more', isn't it?"

Jerry leaned forward, brushing a gentle kiss over Alec's lips. "Certainly not."

"Oh." Alec could feel himself going pink. "But you can't just change a Christmas carol to suit yourself."

"Suit *us*. And I can do any damn thing I please." Jerry tugged his shirt-tails free and winked at him. "Watch me."

A murdered man.

A stolen necklace.

An old flame in deep trouble.

Susan Lazarus returns in *Gilded Cage*, coming soon.

# Author's Note

Duncan Hamilton's book *Harry the Valet* is a fascinating account of a jewel thief in late Victorian England, and includes the story of the ghastly Duke and Duchess of Sutherland, who inspired the Ilvars. Yes, they were that bad.

*Sophia: Princess, Suffragette, Revolutionary* by Anita Anand is an excellent biography of Princess Sophia Duleep Singh and her family.

Susan Lazarus and Greta, Countess of Moreton first appear in my Sins of the Cities trilogy, set twenty years earlier. Justin Lazarus's story is told in *An Unnatural Vice*.

# Acknowledgements

My early readers were invaluable—May Peterson, Kris Ripper, and Moog Florin. Thank you all. As always, big love to my agent, Courtney Miller-Callihan, and to the KJ Charles Chat group whose enthusiastic baying for Victorian jewel thieves and Susan Lazarus, Lady Detective kept me going.

Massive thanks to Veronica Vega for editing, Vic Grey for the stunning cover art, and Lennan Adams for the design.

**For more Victorian shenanigans by KJ Charles, try the Sins of the Cities series**

London 1873. As one of the worst fogs of the nineteenth century closes in on the city, long-buried crimes are crawling into the light. Clem Talleyfer is an unassuming lodging-house keeper; Nathaniel Roy is a lawyer turned journalist who likes nothing more than a crusade; Mark Braglewicz is a private enquiry agent. And all three friends are about to find themselves dragged into an aristocratic family secret that turns deadly.

# **An Unseen Attraction** (Sins of the Cities #1)

Lodging-house keeper Clem Talleyfer prefers a quiet life. He's happy with his hobbies, his work—and especially with his lodger, taxidermist Rowley Green, who becomes a friend over long fireside evenings together. If only neat, precise, irresistible Mr. Green were interested in more than friendship.

Rowley just wants to be left alone—at least until he meets Clem, with his odd, charming ways and his glorious eyes. Two quiet men, lodging in the same house, coming to an understanding—it could be perfect. Then the brutally murdered corpse of another lodger is dumped on their doorstep and their peaceful life is shattered.

Now Clem and Rowley find themselves caught up in a mystery, threatened on all sides by violent men, with a deadly London fog closing in on them. If they're to see their way through, the pair must learn to share their secrets—and their hearts.

*"both an intriguing and engrossing story and a tender romance between two well-drawn protagonists whose unique personality traits inform their emotional and sexual relationships."—All About Romance*

*"A plot that's unabashed pulp, made poignant by its effects on the two bruised souls at its center."—Publishers Weekly starred review*

*"I never thought taxidermy could be this sexy."—Aliette de Bodard*

# **An Unnatural Vice** (Sins of the Cities #2)

Crusading journalist Nathaniel Roy is determined to expose spiritualists who exploit the grief of bereaved and vulnerable people. First on his list is the so-called Seer of London, Justin Lazarus. Nathaniel expects him to be a cheap, heartless fraud. He doesn't expect to meet a man with a sinful smile and the eyes of a fallen angel—or that a shameless swindler will spark his desires for the first time in years.

Justin feels no remorse for the lies he spins during his séances. His gullible clients bore him, but hostile, disbelieving, utterly irresistible Nathaniel is a fascinating challenge. And as their battle of wills and wits heats up, Justin can't stop thinking about the man who's determined to ruin him.

But Justin and Nathaniel are linked by more than their fast-growing obsession with one another. They are both caught up in an aristocratic family's secrets, and Justin holds information that could be lethal. As killers, fanatics, and fog close in, Nathaniel is the only man Justin can trust—and, perhaps, the only man he could love.

*"A great story that's excellently written and researched; characters who are well-drawn and appealing; a book that stimulates intellectually as well as emotionally… An Unnatural Vice has it all and is easily one of the best books I've read so far this year."—Romantic Historical Reviews*

*"fierce and frantic enemies-to-lovers romance … a powerful and fascinating conflict."—Romantic Times, Top Pick*

# **An Unsuitable Heir** (Sins of the Cities #3)

On the trail of an aristocrat's secret son, enquiry agent Mark Braglewicz finds his quarry in a music hall, performing as a trapeze artist with his twin sister. Graceful, beautiful, elusive, and strong, Pen Starling is like nobody Mark's ever met—and everything he's ever wanted. But the long-haired acrobat has an earldom and a fortune to claim.

Pen doesn't want to live as any sort of man, least of all a nobleman. The thought of being wealthy, titled, and always in the public eye is horrifying. He likes his life now—his days on the trapeze, his nights with Mark. And he won't be pushed into taking a title that would destroy his soul.

But there's a killer stalking London's foggy streets, and more lives than just Pen's are at risk. Mark decides he must force the reluctant heir from music hall to manor house, to save Pen's neck. Betrayed by the one man he thought he could trust, Pen never wants to see his lover again. But when the killer comes after him, Pen must find a way to forgive—or he might not live long enough for Mark to make amends.

*"I love the way KJ Charles has incorporated the elements of Victorian popular fiction into her plotlines; the writing is sublime"—All About Romance*

*"With a lively cast and a tangled, entertainingly pulpy plot, Charles delivers a sensitive, powerful romance full of humor, humanity, and suspense."—Publishers Weekly starred review*

# About the Author

KJ Charles is a RITA®-nominated writer and freelance editor. She lives in London with her husband, two kids, an out-of-control garden, and a cat with murder management issues.

KJ writes mostly historical romance, mostly queer, sometimes with fantasy or horror in there. She is represented by Courtney Miller-Callihan at Handspun Literary.

For all the KJC news and occasional freebies, get my (infrequent) newsletter at kjcharleswriter.com/newsletter.

Find me on Twitter @kj_charles

Pick up free reads on my website at kjcharleswriter.com

Join my Facebook group, KJ Charles Chat, for book conversation, sneak peeks, and exclusive treats.

www.ingramcontent.com/pod-product-compliance
Lightning Source LLC
Chambersburg PA
CBHW070319190726
48291CB00014B/2289